The assassin who moved like a ghost waited patiently...

The assassin, the ghost lady, scared and fascinated Cloud Singer, but the woman kept herself to herself, letting none of the tribe get close. Finally, crouching on his haunches beside the glowing laptop screen, Rock Streaming gazed at the others, waiting for everyone's reactions. "Well?" he asked.

"A weapon that exists on a higher plane of consciousness is one that can be activated on a higher plane of consciousness, as well." The assassin spoke from the shadows of the cave, her soft voice carrying eerily through the enclosed space.

"The assassin is right," Bad Father said in his rumbling-thunder voice. "With this and the Dreamslicer, we could establish the new baronies and carve the world up for the original tribe."

"But how would we take it?" Rabbit in the Moon asked.

"By force," Neverwalk chirped, slapping a fist into his open palm.

Other titles in this series:

James Axler
Outlanders®

DEATH CRY

A GOLD EAGLE BOOK FROM
WORLDWIDE®

TORONTO • NEW YORK • LONDON
AMSTERDAM • PARIS • SYDNEY • HAMBURG
STOCKHOLM • ATHENS • TOKYO • MILAN
MADRID • WARSAW • BUDAPEST • AUCKLAND

First edition November 2008

ISBN-13: 978-0-373-63860-4
ISBN-10:   0-373-63860-4

DEATH CRY

Copyright © 2008 by Worldwide Library.

Special thanks to Rik Hoskin for his contribution to this work.

Printed in U.S.A.

Even when still, your mind is not still; even when hurried, your mind is not hurried. The mind is not dragged by the body, the body is not dragged by the mind. Pay attention to the mind, not the body. Let there be neither insufficiency nor excess in your mind. Even if superficially weakhearted, be inwardly stronghearted, and do not let others see into your mind.

—Miyamoto Musashi (1584–1645),
The Book of Five Rings

The Road to Outlands—
From Secret Government Files to the Future

Almost two hundred years after the global holocaust, Kane, a former Magistrate of Cobaltville, often thought the world had been lucky to survive at all after a nuclear device detonated in the Russian embassy in Washington, D.C. The aftermath—forever known as skydark—reshaped continents and turned civilization into ashes.

Nearly depopulated, America became the Deathlands—poisoned by radiation, home to chaos and mutated life forms. Feudal rule reappeared in the form of baronies, while remote outposts clung to a brutish existence.

What eventually helped shape this wasteland were the redoubts, the secret preholocaust military installations with stores of weapons, and the home of gateways, the locational matter-transfer facilities. Some of the redoubts hid clues that had once fed wild theories of government cover-ups and alien visitations.

Rearmed from redoubt stockpiles, the barons consolidated their power and reclaimed technology for the villes. Their power, supported by some invisible authority, extended beyond their fortified walls to what was now called the Outlands. It was here that the rootstock of humanity survived, living with hellzones and chemical storms, hounded by Magistrates.

In the villes, rigid laws were enforced—to atone for the sins of the past and prepare the way for a better future. That was the barons' public credo and their right-to-rule.

Kane, along with friend and fellow Magistrate Grant, had upheld that claim until a fateful Outlands expedition. A displaced piece of technology…a question to a keeper of the archives…a vague clue about alien masters—and their world shifted radically. Suddenly, Brigid Baptiste, the archivist, faced summary execution, and Grant a quick termination. For

Kane there was forgiveness if he pledged his unquestioning allegiance to Baron Cobalt and his unknown masters and abandoned his friends.

But that allegiance would make him support a mysterious and alien power and deny loyalty and friends. Then what else was there?

Kane had been brought up solely to serve the ville. Brigid's only link with her family was her mother's red-gold hair, green eyes and supple form. Grant's clues to his lineage were his ebony skin and powerful physique. But Domi, she of the white hair, was an Outlander pressed into sexual servitude in Cobaltville. She at least knew her roots and was a reminder to the exiles that the outcasts belonged in the human family.

Parents, friends, community—the very rootedness of humanity was denied. With no continuity, there was no forward momentum to the future. And that was the crux— when Kane began to wonder if there *was* a future.

For Kane, it wouldn't do. So the only way was out— way, way out.

After their escape, they found shelter at the forgotten Cerberus redoubt headed by Lakesh, a scientist, Cobaltville's head archivist, and secret opponent of the barons.

With their past turned into a lie, their future threatened, only one thing was left to give meaning to the outcasts. The hunger for freedom, the will to resist the hostile influences. And perhaps, by opposing, end them.

Chapter 1

It was snowing in North Dakota, though it wasn't particularly cold. Wrapped in a light jacket over his shadow suit, Kane hunkered down beneath the snow-laden branches of a fir tree, watching two guards patrol outside the mine entrance. Kane was a tall man, built like a wolf, all muscle piled at the upper half of his body while his arms and legs were long and rangy.

He took shallow breaths, ignoring the fog that formed as he expelled them, trusting the tree cover to hide his breath as well as it hid him. He wasn't cold. In fact, the jacket was worn more for camouflage and the convenience of extra pockets while on mission. The tight-fitting one-piece shadow suit he wore beneath served as an artificially controlled environment, regulating his body temperature. It also possessed other useful properties, most crucially acting as armor in the event of an attack. Despite this, the suit allowed for remarkable freedom of movement.

Kane turned to look behind him, sensing as much as hearing the approach of his partner. Grant, an ex-Magistrate like Kane, held his massive body low against the fluttering snow as he jogged toward Kane's hiding place. He was a huge man, all of his bulk muscle without an inch of fat. His skin was like polished ebony, and a drooping gunslinger's mustache brushed his top lip. Like Kane, Grant wore a white jacket over his shadow suit, camouflaged for the snow-covered landscape, with a white beanie hat pulled low over his head.

They hadn't expected to need camouflage. When Lakesh had outlined the mission back at the Cerberus redoubt, he had made no mention of other parties being interested in the acquisition. Straight in and out, don't let the delicate structure collapse on you as you pass through.

The delicate structure in question was a long-buried Air Force base, predating the nukecaust, in a town that had once been called Grand Forks. Close to the old Canadian border, from a time when country borders meant something, rumor had it that the base had been used as a backup data-storage facility. Now all that remained was a pile of rubble that served as firewood for the local roamers. But Mohandas Lakesh Singh, the nominal head of the Cerberus exiles, had recently stumbled upon evidence that suggested some useful data may have been stored at the Grand Forks base, data that might not have survived in other forms. A quick look-see and they'd be out, or so Lakesh had said to Kane's three-strong survey crew.

Grant's deep, rumbling voice cut the silence, despite his speaking in a low whisper. "It's the same all over," he told Kane. "Guards everywhere. Not many, but plenty enough if they want to make trouble for us."

Kane continued to watch the pair of guards patrolling the minelike entrance that led into the old underground network of the abandoned Air Force base. "That's what I suspected," he answered quietly. "You see any other ways in?"

"Not me," Grant growled. "Looks like the millennialists have provided the best and only entryway to our buried treasure."

The millennialists that Grant referred to—or, more properly, members of the Millennial Consortium—were treasure hunters with a solid organizational structure and plenty of backup for their field ops. They dealt in prenukecaust matériel, mostly military ordnance, which they would either sell to the highest bidder or use for their own political ends—quite often both at once. If the millennialists could get someone else to do their dirty work, and pay for the pleasure in the process, so much the better. Kane and Grant had come to blows with the Millennial Consortium a few times, both in America and elsewhere across the globe. Despite claiming noble aims, most who belonged to the Millennial Consortium were opportunistic pirates, bottom-feeders of the worst sort as far as Kane was concerned. Their bold agenda listed a desire to restore civilization to the country, but there was no doubt in Kane's mind that they'd sell him their own grandmothers.

Three Scorpinauts, the preferred land vehicles of the millennialists, were parked close to the squared-off entrance. The low-slung, boxlike vehicles moved on eight heavily tracked wheels and were sturdily armored. They sported numerous rocket pods and weapons ports, and .50-caliber, swivel-mounted machine guns stuck out from two armatures at the front of the vehicles like a pair of foreclaws. The ten-foot-long snout of a 40 mm cannon protruded from the rear on a huge, swiveling arm, docking in a resting position at the back of the vehicles, resembling a scorpion's stinger-tipped tail.

Seeing three of them there meant one thing: it was a lightly manned rather than a priority operation.

Kane noticed the misting puff of disturbed snow off to the right, at the edge of his sight, and he turned to see the third member of his crew—Brigid Baptiste—making determined headway through the thick carpet of white as she came to join them. A striking woman, Brigid had hidden her vibrant red-gold hair beneath a white scarf, leaving her pale face clear. Her high forehead pointed to intellect, while her full lips suggested a passionate side to her personality. Wrapped in a white jacket with a sable collar similar to those worn by her colleagues, hair masked and the cold draining the color from her face and lips, Brigid's bright emerald eyes and thin, ginger eyebrows were a little flash of color in the pale surroundings. She shook her head as she crouched with Kane and Grant beneath the low-hanging branches.

"No good?" Grant asked, his voice low.

"No back door." Brigid shrugged.

Kane continued to watch the entrance to the underground structure. The roughly built square tunnel was boxed with wooden struts and rusty, paint-flecked metal poles. "Guess we're going in the front, then," he told his companions.

"No way, Kane," Grant spit. "I'll always back your play, but look at them. Walking in there would be suicide, plain and simple."

Brigid nodded her agreement. "The entrance is too

well guarded, Kane. We can't just sneak past them. And there are too many to just start blasting people, even if that was a reasonable option." She narrowed her eyes in frustration. "Face it, the scavengers have won this round. Maybe we'll be able to buy the tech from them sometime later on."

The trace of a thin smile crossed Kane's lips as he turned to look at his partners. "O, ye of little faith," he chided. "You're always telling us how we need to use our guns less and diplomacy more, Baptiste."

"I don't see what…" Brigid began, but Kane was already unclipping something from the built-in belt of his jacket.

Kane stepped out of the tree cover and walked down the slight slope toward the mine entrance, holding aloft the small gunmetal canister with his thumb pushed tightly against its circular top.

"Everybody relax," Kane shouted to the confused guards as they raised their rifles toward him. "This here is what's known as a dead man's switch. You all know what that means, right?"

The two guards nodded and tentatively lowered their blasters, still clutching them in readiness. Their outfits were patched together, not uniforms as such but uniform in their raggedness. Both had heavy fur hats pulled low to their brows, and their hands were wrapped in dirty gloves or bundled in rags.

"Now, me and my friends here have some business inside," Kane continued. "We don't plan to be long and we don't intend to take much, but if we don't get our way, then you, me and this whole underground shaft thing you have going on is about to meet the glorious maker and sing hallelujah."

Brigid looked annoyed as she followed Grant out from beneath the tree. "This is what he calls diplomacy?" she whispered from the side of her mouth as she moved alongside Grant.

One corner of Grant's wide mouth lifted in the barest hint of amusement. "If I'm not mistaken, he's threatening them with a flask of water," he whispered back.

As he spoke, Grant tensed the tendons in his right wrist and his Sin Eater sidearm was thrust into his hand from beneath his right sleeve.

The Sin Eater was the official sidearm of the Magistrate Division, and both Grant and Kane had kept them when they had fled from Cobaltville. The Sin Eater was an automatic handblaster, less than fourteen inches in length at full extension, firing 9 mm rounds. The whole unit folded in on itself to be stored in a bulky holster just above the user's wrist. The holsters reacted to a specific flinching of the wrist tendons, powering the pistol automatically into the user's hand. If the index finger was crooked at the time, the handblaster would begin firing automatically. The trigger had no guard.

As Mags, Grant and Kane were schooled in the use of numerous different weapons, but both of them still felt especially comfortable with the Sin Eater in hand. It was an old friend, a natural weight to their movements.

Just now, Kane's own Sin Eater was still sheathed in its wrist holster beneath the white sleeve of his coat. He paced forward, holding the flask aloft and keeping the attention of the two guards as they wondered whether to leave their posts. "I want you all to step away from the entrance there," Kane advised them, his voice steady.

Grant leveled his Sin Eater meaningfully at the guards, holding it for a second first on the one to the left, then tracking swiftly across and pointing it at the other guard before returning to the first once more. "Guns in the snow, gentlemen," he warned.

"Maniacs," Brigid muttered as she stepped over to Kane's other side and revealed her own pistol—a black TP-9 handgun.

"How many are inside?" Kane asked, addressing the left-hand guard as he placed his rifle flat in the snow.

"Um…" The guard's eyes lost focus for a moment as he began a quick count in his head.

"Come on, son," Grant urged, "quickly now."

"Eight," the other guard piped up, the unsteady voice of a young man muffled by the scarf he wore over his nose and mouth.

"You got a way to speak to them?" Kane asked. The hand holding the gunmetal canister was stretched out steadily before him, a little above head height.

"Shoutin'," the young man replied. "Just shoutin'."

"No radios? No comm devices?" Kane queried.

"Only in the tanks," the young man explained, looking across to the parked Scorpinauts, "to communicate with home. Nothing for here."

This rang true to Kane and his team. The Millennial Consortium was not renowned for its lavish treatment of staff. Its operations were executed at minimal expense to generate maximum profits.

Kane strode toward the open, box-shaped entrance.

Low-ceilinged, the tunnel dipped into a shallow slope, burrowing under the wrecked firewood and open foundations that had once formed buildings above. Kane could see a few paces into the tunnel, after which its contents were lost in darkness.

"Me and my buddies here are going to go in," Kane explained to the guards as he tried to penetrate the darkness with his gaze. "You're going to wait here, and you're not going to do anything stupid. If you are under any illusions about how a dead man's switch works, and you decide to be a chancer with your popguns, let me assure you that we will all be having the remainder of this discussion in the afterlife. Am I clear?"

The guards both nodded, their eyes wide in fear, but Kane didn't bother turning to them. He was busy scanning the gloom of the tunnel and listening for any hint of approaching reinforcements.

"Now," Kane continued as he led the way into the tunnel, "if nobody does anything stupid, nobody will get hurt and we'll be out of your hair before you know it."

Grant held back as Brigid followed Kane into the dark tunnel, covering the two guards with his Sin Eater.

"Sit tight, boys," Grant told them. "We won't be here long." With that, Grant ducked his head and jogged the few steps it took for him to catch up to his colleagues.

Brigid looked from Grant to Kane, a sour look on her face. "This is insane, you realize," she whispered.

Still holding the flask aloft, Kane glanced at her. "We're in and nobody's been hurt so far," he replied in a low voice. "Score one for diplomacy, I think."

Grant sniggered for a moment at that, before Brigid pierced him with her emerald glare.

"The pair of you seem to have mistaken diplomacy for insanity," she snarled.

Grant held his hands up in the universal gesture of surrender, despite the automatic pistol in his right hand. "Whoa there," he muttered. "This is strictly Kane's insanity. I just follow the leader."

Brigid's green eyes were narrowed slits and she bit back a curse at the huge, dark-skinned man before turning to address Kane once more. "So you plan to bluff your way inside, and then what?"

Even in the semidarkness, a mischievous twinkle seemed to play in Kane's eyes, just for a second. "I'll insist they all leave or I'll set off the bomb."

"What bomb?" Brigid snapped. "You're holding a flask."

"They don't need to know that," Kane said.

Grant agreed. "I'd say it's preferable if they don't know it," he muttered.

"Scared by the loco bomber," Kane continued, "they all wait outside a safe distance and we get the place to ourselves. You find what you need, then we head back to Lakesh and Cerberus."

Brigid reached a hand up and fidgeted with the white scarf that covered her hair as she let loose a frustrated sigh. "Brilliant. And what, pray tell, is your plan for getting out again? You know, with maybe fifteen armed and now very much antagonized millennialists waiting for us at the end of a bottleneck."

Kane's smile was bright in the darkness. "This used

to be a military base, right, Baptiste? We'll use their mat-trans. Simple. And yet, genius."

The mat-trans chamber was found in many of the prenukecaust military bases, and offered a quick way to move from one to the other by the almost instantaneous transfer of particles. Having been originally constructed as a military installation, the Cerberus redoubt, the headquarters of Kane's field team, had a mat-trans chamber. However, they had traveled to Grand Forks via two Manta flyers, which acted as both transatmospheric and subspace aircraft. It would be a simple matter, Kane reasoned, to collect the hidden Mantas once the heat had died down.

The Cerberus exiles had a variety of ways to transport people, the Manta aircraft and the mat-trans network were just two. In the past few years they had come to rely increasingly on another form of teleportation called the interphaser, which exploited naturally occurring centers of energy both around the world and on the Moon and other planets. The interphaser was ideal for traveling between known locations but, like the mat-trans, could be dangerous when gating into the unknown. There were other limitations on the interphaser, as well, but for the right mission it was ideal.

Keeping pace with Kane, Brigid eyed him for a few moments before she spoke. "Nothing can go wrong with this, can it?"

"Not unless he drinks the bomb by mistake." Grant grinned.

Kane led the way along the ill-lit tunnel, assuming the role of point man. Taking point was an unconscious habit for Kane, dating back to his days as a Magistrate. He exhibited an uncanny knack for sniffing out danger, a sixth sense in some respect, though it was really an incredible combination of the natural five he possessed, honed to an acute sharpness. Walking point, his eyes darting right and left, his hearing seeking changes in sound at an almost infinitesimal level, Kane felt electric, tuned in to his surroundings at a near Zenlike level. Walking point in the danger zone, Kane felt alive.

They met another pair of guards as they worked their way down the incline into the underground base, and each time they played the same bluff, with Kane insisting that anyone who disagreed with his proposal would end up picking his entrails off the tunnel walls.

By the time they reached the concrete exterior of the base itself, even Brigid was feeling quietly confident.

At the end of the shaft, a huge circular hole had been bored through the thick concrete wall of the old military base, taller than Grant and wide enough for two people abreast. Kane and Grant led the way into the interior, finding it lit by a string of dim, flickering lights that had been attached to vicious-looking hooks rammed into the ceiling. The lights hummed as they flickered, and the whole system had to be running off a generator of some kind, installed specially for the Millennial Consortium operation. Large gaps between the flickering lights left sections of the corridor in complete darkness.

"No expense spared," Grant said wryly, pointing to the humming lights with the barrel of his Sin Eater.

The first thing Brigid noticed as she stepped into the underground lair was the stench of stale air. Slushy, muddy prints could be seen on the tiles beneath her feet, and there was a little mound of pale-colored powder where the hole had been drilled through the wall. She checked behind her, peering into the dark shaft they had just walked through to make sure no one had followed them.

"Know where we're going?" Kane asked her as she tried to get her bearings. Brigid had an eidetic memory, more commonly known as a photographic memory, and she'd studied maps of the Grand Forks base before leaving for the mission.

"Computer core's a little down this way," she said after a moment's thought, pointing to the left corridor. "Twenty paces, maybe."

As the three of them marched down the corridor, they could hear the sounds of voices and hammering coming from farther ahead. As they got closer, Brigid indicated a set of double doors to one side, and Kane locked eyes with Grant, putting a finger to the side of his nose for a moment, before they led the way inside. The gesture was a private code between the two ex-Mags, an old tradition to do with luck and long odds.

"Hello, gentlemen," Kane announced as he entered the computer room, his hand holding the gunmetal flask prominently out before him.

Inside it was gloomy, with smoke damage on the walls. Three guards spun to face the intruders, reaching for their sidearms. Two other men were in the room, and they looked up from their work at the stripped-down computer banks.

"I'd like to introduce you to my friend," Kane said,

"the dead man's switch. Some of you look like scientific types so I'll put this in terms you're all familiar with—get out of here or I will blow us all up. Any questions?"

One of the guards pointed his Calico M-960 subgun at Kane and growled between gritted teeth, "What's to stop me offing you right now?"

The other people in the room looked at the guard a moment, horror on their faces, and a heated argument erupted between the millennialists.

Kane stood utterly amazed as the various players before him argued about the practicality of shooting a man holding a dead man's switch. After a few seconds he put two fingers from his empty left hand in his mouth and made a piercing whistle to get everyone's attention.

"Look," he told his audience when they had all turned to him, "we don't have time to argue about this. Make your decision now—either get out or stay here and get blown up. Don't complicate the very simple set of options I'm giving you."

One of the whitecoats, a bespectacled man with thin blond hair, spoke up. "This is highly unusual. Our section leader would be terribly upset if we were to just leave this operation."

Grant took a step forward and grabbed the blond scientist by his collar, ramming the nose of his Sin Eater in the man's terrified face. "My man here is holding a bomb. We don't give a crap how upset your boss is going to be."

Grant tossed the man aside, and the scientist stumbled backward, tripping over his own feet and crashing into a wall between two of the armed guards.

The other scientist, a man with a round face and the

black hair and gold skin of an Asian, spoke up, addressing his colleagues. "There are only three of them—how much can they take? This isn't worth getting blown up over."

Kane nodded. "Smart man. You all get out of here now, and we won't shoot you in the back or anything like that—you have my word on that much."

Warily, the guards and scientists made their way from the room. Grant followed them, the Sin Eater poised in his hand, and instructed them to continue through the tunnel until they were outside the facility. Grant watched them leave, walking down the corridor with heavy heads and muttering desperately as they left.

Inside the computer room, Kane was clipping the flask to his belt. "You know," he said with a laugh when he saw Brigid's scowl, "I could get used to this diplomacy thing."

"You were lucky," she told him as she stepped toward one of the computer terminals and started tapping at the keyboard. "They've got juice going to the computers at least," she added after a moment.

Grant reentered and Kane gave him instructions. "I need you to find us that mat-trans," he told his colleague. "I want to be out of here in ten minutes."

"Ten?" Brigid echoed, shock in her voice. "Kane, that's impossible. I can't get into this network in ten—"

"This bluff won't last long, Baptiste," Kane explained, and she noted that his humor had abruptly faded. "Ten minutes is the absolute maximum we have here, you understand?"

She nodded and went back to work on the keyboard, pulling a pair of small, square-framed spectacles from her inside pocket and propping them on her nose as the screen before her came to life.

Grant stepped back to the double doors, turning back to address Brigid. "I saw a map on the wall a ways back. Do you remember roughly where this mat-trans is, Brigid?"

Brigid didn't look up as scrolling figures rushed across the screen before her. "Not sure," she said. "I don't remember seeing one in the part of the map I looked at."

Kane nodded toward the corridor. "Get to the map and look for anything that says 'transport.' The mat-trans gateway won't be far."

Grant put a finger to his brow in salute before ducking through the door and jogging back down the corridor to the wall map.

"You realize that this won't work," Brigid breathed after a few moments.

"How's that?" Kane asked, annoyed.

"This is a two-hundred-year-old computer running off a generator. Whatever's inside is encrypted up the wazoo, and I don't know what it is I'm looking for anyway," she explained in an even tone.

Kane sighed. "And you didn't think this was worth mentioning beforehand?"

Brigid pierced him with a frosty stare, anger bristling in her tone. "I thought we'd have maybe an afternoon here, do a recce, come back at a later date once we had decided what it was we were looking at. You're the one who got all gung ho and decided to threaten armed people with a bomb unless you got your own damn way."

Kane looked annoyed, his voice defensive. "Hey, it's called improvisation, Baptiste."

OUTSIDE THE COMPUTER ROOM, Grant made his way back
along the corridor to the place where he had seen the map.
A large color-coded illustration, the map sat behind hard,
transparent plastic to one side of a T-junction corridor that
disappeared farther into the disused military base.

Leaning close as the overhead light flickered and
hummed, Grant swept grime from the plastic covering
with the edge of his free hand before wiping the hand on
his pant leg. The map showed five different-colored
sections that formed a bulging rectangular shape. The
key to the right-hand side of the map gave a broad term
for what each section represented, green for research,
orange for personnel and so on.

Grant looked swiftly over the map and located the
computer room he had just come from. Then he carefully
ran his finger along the key to the side, reading the names
of all the different divisions and subdivisions. He was
halfway down the list when he heard footsteps off to his
right, coming from the same direction as the entry from
the mine shaft. He turned to his right, automatically lifting
the Sin Eater and pointing it into the darkness of the
dusty, ill-lit corridor.

If I can't see them then they're probably having just
as much trouble seeing me, Grant realized, holding the
pistol steady as he took a step away from the wall and
crouched to make a smaller target. At two hundred fifty
pounds of solid muscle, it wasn't easy for the big man to
make an appreciably smaller target.

Grant thought back to the discussion with the millennialist guards outside. They'd said there were eight people
down there, and with the two they'd found in the shaft

plus the five in the computer room, Grant realized that they were still one man short. "Guy chose the wrong time to take a leak," Grant murmured as he darted lightly forward along the corridor, his movements quiet and economical.

As he moved forward, holding the Sin Eater before him with his left hand steadying his grip, Grant spotted movement in the dark. Someone was approaching, walking along the corridor toward him. Grant was suddenly very conscious that, despite the poor lighting, he was still dressed in white jacket and hat for the snow. He sank into a crouch, holding the pistol steady as he dropped out of the stranger's potential eye line.

Silhouetted against the flickering light for an instant was a tall, bulky figure reaching for a rifle that was slung from a shoulder strap across his chest. "Who's there?" the newcomer asked, his voice deep but cracking with fear. "I can see you're there."

A tiny glint of light reflected from the muzzle of the rifle as it swung toward him, and Grant leaped forward, powering himself at the man in a driving rush of coiled muscles. In two steps, Grant was upon the gunman, his arms wide as he gripped the man's shoulders, toppling the gunman backward onto the hard floor. The long barrel of the gunman's rifle spit a half-dozen shots as the man's finger twitched on the trigger, their report loud in the enclosed area of the corridor, but Grant was already inside the firing arc, his heavy body crushing the man beneath it. With a loud crack, the gunman's head smacked into the floor tiles, splitting one across its center.

Grant pulled back his right hand, ready to shoot the

guard with his pistol, but the man was already unconscious. Breathing heavily through his clenched teeth,
Grant watched as a trickle of blood seeped across the
cracked tile from the back of the gunman's head. Grant
got up and stepped away from the unconscious gunman,
holstering his Sin Eater and kicking aside the man's
rifle.

"Mouse, meet cat," Grant muttered as he turned from
the fallen guard and headed back down the corridor to
look at the map.

INSIDE THE COMPUTER ROOM, Brigid's fingers were frantically racing across the keyboard as a stream of digits
raced across the screen.

"I'm into the basic coding," she told Kane without
looking up, "but the whole thing is encrypted. Whatever's
in here is either very important or it's the diary of a very
paranoid teenager."

Kane looked at her, brushing concrete dust from his
short, dark hair. "Thinking of anyone in particular,
Baptiste?"

"What?" she asked as her fingers sped across the keys.
Then she looked up, seeing the sly grin on her colleague's
face. "Well, don't look at me. Do you think I ever had
time to keep a diary when we were in Cobaltville?"

Kane shrugged, laughing to himself as she went back
to work on the computer code. As he did so, they both
heard shots coming from a little way down the corridor,
and Kane took two swift steps across the room to the
closed double doors, the Sin Eater appearing in his hand.

There had been six shots, fired rapidly as if from an

automatic. No further noise followed, and Kane risked opening one of the double doors, pushing his back against it as he raised the pistol in his hands.

"Grant?" he called tentatively. "Grant? You okay?"

Grant's deep, rumbling voice echoed back along the corridor. "Just fine. Rodent problem, but I dealt with it."

Kane stepped back into the room, his pistol returning to his sleeve as he walked across to stand behind Brigid.

She didn't look up as she spoke. "I don't feel safe here, Kane."

"We'll be out of here in a few minutes," he told her.

Just then, Grant came running through the double doors, clutching his Sin Eater. "We have got a problem," he announced, a scowl across his dark brow.

"What now?" Brigid asked in exasperation.

"Unless I am very much mistaken," Grant told them, "there is no mat-trans in this facility."

Kane and Brigid looked at Grant, their eyes wide as they took in his statement.

"No back door, people," Grant reiterated, shaking his head.

Brigid shook her head, as well, as she continued working the keys of the computer terminal. "Worst plan ever," she growled without looking up at Kane.

Chapter 2

Kane was pacing the computer room like a caged tiger, head low as he tried to think through the situation. He had assumed that this installation would have a mat-trans, but there had been no guarantee of that. "There's got to be a way out," he assured the others. "A back door. Something."

Brigid watched him over the rims of her glasses as she sat at the computer terminal. "This place has been buried for two hundred years, remember?" she told him. "Any back doors that might have existed are long since sealed. Essentially, we're sitting in an archaeological dig."

"Then we go out the same way we got here," Kane decided. "We use the shaft."

"We *get* the shaft, you mean," Grant rumbled. "You heard what Brigid said when we came in. That route is a bottleneck with fifteen, maybe twenty armed millennialists just waiting to take a pop at us."

Kane reached for the gunmetal flask that hung from his belt. "So we'll use the same trick, the dead man's switch." He smiled. "They won't shoot me while I'm holding the dead man's switch."

Grant shook his head. "Oh, yes, they will." Kane shot a questioning look at the huge ex-Magistrate, and Grant began counting off points on the fingers of his free hand. "One, they know exactly where we're coming from this time. Two, they've had time to think about it. Three, they've had time to set up sharpshooters."

"Four," Brigid chipped in, a sour smile on her face, "they'll most likely shoot your arm off at the elbow."

"What makes you so sure?" Kane asked, his tone abrupt as angry frustration bubbled to the surface.

"'Cause that's what you'd do," Grant told him, locking his gaze with Kane's fierce stare.

After a moment, Kane looked away, shaking his head heavily. "Yeah, you're right," he admitted.

Stepping over to the double doors, Grant pushed his way through and glanced warily down the corridor, waving the Sin Eater in a slow arc before him. As the lights flickered, he made out the slumped form of the gunman he had disarmed, still lying unconscious close to the rabbit-hole exit. "I don't think we have a whole lot of time, either," Grant told the others as he came back through the doors. "I met a hostile outside. He's out for the count, right now, but…" He shrugged, leaving the sentence hanging.

Turning from Grant, Kane addressed Brigid. "How's the computer hack going, Baptiste?"

"Slowly," she admitted. "Even with a ville full of luck, it could take all day to stumble on a lead that takes me anywhere. Plus, Lakesh didn't really know what we were looking for. It's like secret Santa—you hope it's something good but you have no idea what it's going to be till the wrapping's off."

Kane tilted his head as he assessed the black metallic

base of the computer terminal. "Then we'll take the whole unit with us," he decided. "Can't weigh more than twenty, thirty pounds. Shut it down, and let's get the thing unhooked."

Brigid flashed him a withering look. "Do you know anything about how computers work, Kane? This is a delicate piece of equipment and it's attached to—"

Kane held up a warning finger. "Stow it," he said firmly. "It's survived the nukecaust and two hundred years of dust. We'll take what we can and get out of here alive."

Brigid looked plaintively to Grant, and the huge ex-Mag returned her look.

"Wrap it up, people," Kane said, raising his voice as he walked across the room to the double doors. "We're moving out in two minutes. Grant, you carry the computer." With that, Kane disappeared through the doors, Sin Eater in hand, to scout the corridor for opposition.

Once Kane had left, Brigid muttered to herself as she powered down the computer terminal. "He's actually gone insane," she stated.

Grant crouched beneath the computer desk and began unplugging connections, including the jury-rigged power that the millennialists had attached to get it running in the first place. "Insane or not," he told Brigid, "would you trust your life in anyone else's hands?"

Brigid didn't even need to think about it. A dozen images jockeyed for position in her mind's eye, situations where Kane had covered her back, taken care of her and saved her life. A hundred further instances were rushing through her head as she helped Grant unwire the base of the computer. Photographic memory could be a double-edged sword when you wanted to be mad at someone, she decided.

"Any idea how we're getting out of here?" she asked as they discarded leads and Grant pulled the blocky computer from the desk.

"None at all," he told her, smiling broadly, "but I'm not worried. Kane'll do something. He always does."

Brigid grabbed the TP-9 pistol from where she had placed it beside her on the desk, and she and Grant walked briskly across the room to the double doors and out into the corridor.

Kane was waiting for them just by the door, the gunmetal flask back in his hand. Grant took one look at the flask and shook his head. "That'll never work," he warned his friend as the lights flickered above them.

Kane started off toward the hole in the wall at a fast trot, trusting the others to keep up. "Oh, I've added a little something-something this time," he said, grinning maliciously as he stepped over the unconscious gunman on the floor and headed for the large gap in the wall that led into the boxed tunnel.

Grant was right behind him, hefting the computer under his left arm. The black, metal-covered unit stretched from beneath his armpit right down to the curled tips of his gripping fingers, and he was forced to keep his arm straight to carry it. They had left the monitor and keyboard behind, knowing they could substitute these items when they reached their headquarters at the Cerberus redoubt. "This thing is going to throw my aim off," Grant advised the others. "I can keep you covered, but I don't think I can do much pinpoint work."

"Won't be necessary," Kane assured him, still clutching the flask. "Baptiste and I will handle things, won't we?"

Brigid sight-checked the chamber of her TP-9 before answering. "Can't wait," she said grimly.

With that, the three-person reconnaissance team began to jog along the shaft, making good speed without exhausting themselves as they worked their way up the muddy incline.

They didn't meet anyone along the shaft, but as they turned a slight corner close to the exit, they suddenly found themselves assaulted by a volley of bullets. Kane urged his companions backward, and the Cerberus trio waited just around the corner as a stream of bullets peppered the wall across from them.

"Told you," Grant said quietly as the stream of bullets slapped the wall.

Taking point, Kane edged forward to the turn in the shaft, answering Grant without looking back. "They'll get bored in a minute."

Kane drew his right arm back and stepped two paces forward before tossing the gunmetal flask ahead of him like a baseball pitcher. The flask hurtled through the air toward the entrance to the mine shaft. Still tucked behind the curve in the shaft, Brigid and Grant heard the astonished cries of Millennial Consortium guards as they saw the projectile fly toward them.

Kane ducked behind cover as a stream of steel-jacketed bullets poured into the shaft. "Look away," he instructed Brigid and Grant. "Close your eyes and look away!"

All three of them turned to face the underground lair that they had just come from. A second later an almighty noise assaulted their ears, and even from behind lidded eyes they could see the bright flash of an explosion.

Moments later, Grant and Brigid were chasing after Kane as he led the way, Sin Eater in hand, up the last part of the shaft and into the open air.

"What the hell did you just do?" Grant asked, incredulous.

Kane snapped off a shot from his pistol, and the bullet swept the legs out from under a millennialist guardsman who was rubbing at his eyes, his own pistol forgotten in his limp hand. "I stuffed the flask with flash-bangs," Kane explained as he darted out of the entrance and continued running, head low, across the snow-carpeted ground.

Once outside, they could see that the millennialists had arranged themselves in a crescent shape across the open entrance in a determined bid to trap the Cerberus exiles inside the shaft and, presumably, contain the expected explosion when the dead man's switch was detonated.

Brigid loosed three shots from her TP-9, catching two of the dazzled millennialists in the chest and clipping the gun hand of a third. A few paces ahead of her, Kane was firing 9 mm bursts from his Sin Eater, mostly as warning shots rather than aiming at specific targets. The way he saw it, they were pretty much home free with the opposition blinded by the flash-bangs; it didn't warrant unnecessary deaths now.

The flash-bang was a little explosive charge that

provided exactly what its name implied: a big flash and a loud bang. Kane and Grant carried various different types of the little capsules, some able to generate copious amounts of smoke or a foul stench upon breaking, and they used them for distraction in favor of actually hurting an enemy. The bright glare of the flash-bangs could temporarily blind an unsuspecting opponent and make his or her ears sing, but it wouldn't leave any permanent damage.

Grant didn't want to think about how many of the little explosive spheres Kane had packed into the flask, but he could see that it had dazzled the millennialists into submission. "Vintage Kane," he muttered as he chased across the snow after his colleagues, his rolling gait compensating for the weight of the computer unit.

The snow was falling heavier than when they'd entered the shaft, thick flurries obscuring their sight as they rushed up the low hill and past the fir tree that Kane had used for cover. Kane took point with Brigid and Grant a few paces behind. As they ran, their boots leaving heavy tracks in the deepening snow, they heard the familiar report of a gunshot, and a bullet zinged past Grant's ear.

"What the—" Grant yelled as he spun back to look over his shoulder.

The gunman he had encountered inside the underground lair had awakened and was running after them out of the square shaft entrance. Grant threw himself at the ground, using his right shoulder to cushion his fall as he saw the gunman sight and fire again.

A spray of bullets zipped past over Grant's head as he sank into the soft snow, still clutching the computer base unit to his side. "A little help here, guys?" Grant called as he clambered up the hill amid a further hail of bullets.

Kane and Brigid stopped running, spinning on their heels and sighting the gunman outside the boxy entrance. Their guns blazed in unison as bullets flew over their heads, and suddenly the gunman's head snapped back in a spray of crimson.

Kane leaned forward to give Grant a hand up. As he pulled the big man back to his feet, a movement caught Kane's eye. He looked up, over Grant's head, and spotted the large black object moving between the ridges of snow like a prowling panther. It was a Scorpinaut, one of the tanklike vehicles that the Millennial Consortium employed for field operations, and it was heading their way.

"Troops," Kane began, "we've got bigger problems." He pointed a little to the left of the minelike entrance, and Grant and Brigid looked where he indicated. Suddenly, the dark shape came into view between two mounds of snow, weaving around a copse as it headed up the slope toward them.

"Must have been looking the other way when you set off the flash-bangs," Grant speculated. "Got any ideas?"

Kane's mind raced as he calculated the various factors that were now in play. "The Mantas are about a click away. We could get there in under five minutes without that computer slowing you down."

Brigid gasped and looked at Kane with pleading eyes. "No, we can't leave it behind after everything we just went through to get it."

"Nobody's leaving anything behind, Baptiste," Kane told her. "Just need to find a way to give Grant a head start. You guys go on, and I'll catch you up as soon as I'm able."

Just then, the amplified voice of a well-spoken woman split the air, and they realized that it was coming from a speaker unit set on the hull of the Scorpinaut. "Attention, runners," the woman's voice said, "you have stolen properties that belong to the Millennial Consortium by right of salvage. Please cease and desist your current actions and return the property immediately, or we will be forced to reclaim by any means necessary. We urge you to swiftly comply."

Grant started trekking up the slope, shifting the computer beneath his arm as he did so, struggling to secure a firmer grip.

Brigid turned to join Grant, the TP-9 still in her hand, then she stopped and turned back to their team leader. "What are you going to do?" she asked.

Kane shook his head, watching the Scorpinaut navigate up the slope. "Play chicken with five tons of heavily armed wag, by the look of it," he told her, shrugging out of the white jacket he had worn for camouflage. Then he was off, a dark shadow against the white snow, running back down the slope toward the approaching Scorpinaut, the Sin Eater held in his upraised hand.

Kane half ran, half jumped down the snow-covered incline, his legs and arms pumping as he made his way toward a group of low trees off to the right of the approaching vehicle. He saw the foreclaws of the unit whirr in readiness, and then they were spitting fire in his direction as a stream of bullets began cutting through the air. Kane leaped and weaved, always moving, giving the crew of the Scorpinaut the least possible chance of getting a bead on him.

Bullets clipped the ground at his feet, ricocheting off trees and rocks all around him, cutting lethal tracks through the snow as they sought their target.

Still running, Kane held the Sin Eater across his body and reeled off a quick burst of gunfire. The 9 mm bullets zipped through the air in the direction of the Scorpinaut before slapping harmlessly on the armor plate at the front of the vehicle in a shower of sparks. Kane kept running to his right, checking over his left shoulder to make sure the vehicle was still following. Wearing the black shadow suit, he wouldn't be hard to spot, and having taken a few shots at the Scorpinaut, he figured the crew would be just about mad enough to forget about his colleagues until they had finished with him.

Over to the right, at roughly the same height on the snowy bank as he now found himself, Kane saw a pair of trees. Their trunks were thin and their branches loaded with snow like cotton wool. Head down, he forced himself to run faster, kicking his legs high to get clear of the snow that threatened to pull him over or slow him. He aimed his body toward the trees, a plan forming in his mind.

At that moment, a loud crack split the air and a 40 mm shell hurtled over Kane's head, slamming into the snow-bank twenty feet above him and exploding with an almighty crash. Kane felt the shock wave of the explosion as it slammed into the right side of his abdomen, and dislodged snow tumbled past him as it slid down the slope.

Kane looked back over his left shoulder and saw that

the Scorpinaut crew had brought the tail cannon into the fray. The flexible cannon arm was doubled back to shoot over the main body of the vehicle, launching its massive shells in his direction. While the crew could not get the swivel arm low enough to hit its target, if enough snow was dislodged or one of those trees cut down so that it knocked Kane off his feet, then he was done for. He whipped his head back and pushed his body harder, limbs pumping, determined to keep ahead of the approaching vehicle.

Bullets riddled the ground as the Scorpinaut's fore-claws spit lead at the running figure. Kane skipped to one side, his breath coming heavily now, the cold air burning his nostrils and throat. He was almost at the trees, and the Scorpinaut was just behind him. In fact, it was so close that suddenly he found himself inside the foreclaws' arc of fire and he realized, horrified, that the millennialists would be just as happy to mow him down.

The snowfall was turning into a blizzard now, every-thing becoming white on white, so heavy that Kane could barely see two body lengths ahead as he ran. He glanced behind him once more, the dark shadow of the approach-ing Scorpinaut an ominous presence just a few feet away, its grinding engine loud in his ears. He heard the drums of the machine guns in the foreclaws spin as they reloaded and prepared to shoot once again, and he looked ahead once again to see the two thin trees just feet away. As the machine guns began blasting, Kane threw himself for-ward, diving between the tree trunks and hurtling face-first into the cushion of the thick snow, bullets racing overhead. There was a sudden, resounding crash, and

Kane felt the jarring impact as the Scorpinaut slammed into the thin tree trunks in its way. They were thin but Kane had judged that they had to be hardy, growing there in the harsh wilds of North Dakota.

Still lying on the ground, Kane looked behind him and saw that the Scorpinaut was tangled between the sturdy trunks, its foreclaws still spitting leaden death into the air. It had become wedged at an angle, its claws tilted and pointing into the sky at thirty degrees; good now only for shooting birds, there was no way that the crew would be able to target anything on ground level. Kane heard the angry spluttering of shifting gears as the driver attempted to reverse or move forward, desperately trying to disentangle the vehicle from the trap he had driven into at full speed.

Kane smiled, his breath clouding before him as he watched the millennialists struggling to free their vehicle. Then he pulled himself up, brushing snow from his shadow suit and rolling his shoulders to loosen them after the hard landing. Kane holstered his Sin Eater and made his way back up the hill at a fast jog and continued in the direction of the Mantas.

The snowstorm was so heavy that Kane almost ran straight past where the Mantas were stowed close to a clump of trees. Kane had assumed he would recognize the formation of the trees, but by the time he got there they had been covered with thick snow, blending into the white landscape.

As he jogged by, Kane spied a flash of sunset-red and recognized it for Brigid Baptiste's brightly colored hair. She was brushing snow from her hair and face when he approached, the white scarf now draped loosely over her shoulders.

"What kept you?" she asked, favoring Kane with a knowing smile.

"A little—" Kane thought for a moment "—horticulturalism."

Brigid tilted her head querulously. "Were you picking flowers again?"

"More…rearranging trees," Kane replied evasively, displaying a knowing smile of his own.

Grant appeared from inside one of the Manta craft as he slid down the subtle curve of its bronze-hued wing. Two of the strange aircraft were parked in the clearing by the trees. They had the general shape and configuration of seagoing manta rays. Flattened wedges with graceful wings curved out from their bodies to a span of twenty yards, with a body length of close to fifteen yards and a slight elongated hump in the center as the only evidence of the cockpit location. Curious geometric designs covered almost the entire exterior surface of each craft, with elaborate cuneiform markings, swirling glyphs and cup-and-spiral symbols all over. The Mantas were propelled by two different kinds of engine—a ramjet and solid-fuel pulse detonation air spikes.

"Computer's all packed," Grant told both of them. "You about ready to move out?"

Kane looked at the heavy snow falling all about them. "I think we've pretty much outstayed our welcome," he decided. He knew that they wouldn't be able to navigate in this horrendous weather by sight alone, but the remarkable transatmospheric vehicles had a dizzying array of onboard sensors that would alert them to any danger long before they eyeballed it.

Brigid leaped into the Manta behind Kane, in the same spot that Grant had secured the computer in his own vehicle. Then, moving together, the two craft took to the skies and blasted away from Grand Forks, heading back to the Cerberus redoubt far to the west.

Chapter 3

When a weary-looking Kane, Grant and Brigid entered the ops center of the Cerberus redoubt, Dr. Mohandas Lakesh Singh rose from his swivel chair and rushed across the large room to greet them enthusiastically. Called Lakesh by those who knew him, the doctor appeared to be a man of perhaps fifty years of age. He was a distinguished man who held himself upright, with an aquiline nose and refined mouth, dusky skin and sleek black hair showing the first hints of white at the temples. However, Lakesh was older than he appeared—much older. He had been a physicist and cyberneticist for the U.S. military before the nukecaust back in 2001, and had spent much of his life in cryogenic suspension.

The ops room was large with a vast Mercator relief map of the world spanning one wall, forming a panorama over the wide door through which the field team entered. The map included more than a hundred tiny lights, each illustrating a point where a known, operational mat-trans unit was located. A plethora of colored lines linked them in a representation of the Cerberus network, the central concern of the redoubt when it had been built over two hundred years before. Strictly speaking, Cerberus was a nickname for the headquarters.

Like all of the military redoubts, this one had been named for a phonetic letter of the alphabet, as used in radio communications. Somewhere in the long-forgotten computer logs and paper files stored deep within the three-story complex, Cerberus was still Redoubt Bravo, a facility dedicated to monitoring the use of the miraculous mat-trans network. But lost somewhere in the mists of time, a young soldier had painted a vibrant illustration of a vicious two-headed hound guarding the doors to the redoubt, like Cerberus at the gates of the underworld. The soldier was long since forgotten, but his bold version of the hellhound lived on as a lucky charm and a mascot to the sixty-plus residents of the complex.

The redoubt was located high in the Bitterroot Range in Montana, where it had remained forgotten or ignored in the two centuries since the nukecaust. In the years since that nuclear devastation, a strange mythology had grown up around the mountains, with their dark, foreboding forests and seemingly bottomless ravines. The wilderness area surrounding the redoubt was virtually unpopulated. The nearest settlement was to be found in the flatlands some miles away, consisting of a small band of Indians, Sioux and Cheyenne, led by a shaman named Sky Dog.

Tucked beneath camouflage netting, hidden away within the rocky clefts of the mountains, concealed uplinks chattered continuously with two orbiting satellites that provided much of the empirical data for Lakesh and his team. Maintaining and expanding access to the satellites had taken long hours of intense trial-and-error work by many of the top scientists on hand at the base.

Now, Lakesh and his team could draw on live feeds from an orbiting Vela-class reconnaissance satellite and the Keyhole Comsat. Despite delays associated with satellite communication, this arrangement allowed access to data surveying the surface of the planet, as well as the ability to communicate with field teams.

The high-ceilinged ops room was indirectly lit to better allow the computer operators to see their screens without suffering glare or obtrusive reflections. Two aisles of computer terminals stretched across the room, although a number of these currently stood unused. The control center was the brain of the redoubt, and Lakesh ensured that it was continuously manned. Right now, there were eight other people sitting at workstations dotted around the room, a mixture of long-term Cerberus staffers and several from the more recent influx of personnel that the base had acquired from a cryogenic-stasis squad found in the Manitius Moon Base.

"It is good to see you in such rude health," Lakesh announced as he greeted his friends. Almost immediately, his eyes zeroed in on the black, metal-encased unit that Grant carried beneath one arm, and a confused frown furrowed his brow. "Over the comm, you said you were bringing the important files you had located."

Weary, his muscles aching from his frantic dash across the freezing snow not an hour earlier, Kane's explanation came out as an emotionless growl. "And that's exactly what we've done."

Grant walked over to a free workstation and flipped the computer base from under his arm as though it didn't have any weight to it at all. Gently he placed the computer on the desk and gestured to it theatrically. "One computer full of important files."

Lakesh leaned forward, one hand reaching up to rest under his chin. Then he tilted his head, looking at the scarred computer from several angles before finally muttering, "Highly irregular." He turned back to his trusted field team, noticing for the first time how exhausted the three of them appeared. "This is highly irregular," Lakesh said again, more loudly this time as he addressed his colleagues, "but doubtless it is of incalculable value." There was the trace of a lilting Indian accent to Lakesh's speech, adding an almost musical tone to his words.

Brigid nodded. "Oh, it is," she assured him. "I skimmed over the bulk of the files before we left the Grand Forks base. I can't tell you what's on there, but it's encrypted to an almost implausible degree. It's got to be some important material."

Lakesh smiled, admiring the battered processor once more. "It certainly sounds promising," he agreed. "Perhaps all of you would care to take a few hours for yourselves while I make a start on accessing these files."

Grant didn't need telling twice; he was already through the door and into the corridor without so much as a goodbye. Kane offered a halfhearted wave as he dashed out of the room after his partner, while Brigid Baptiste remained behind.

"What do you think it contains?" Brigid asked. "And more importantly, do you really think we can still access it? I told Kane that this was an insane way of looking at the files, but he wouldn't hear of it."

"Oftentimes there is an admirable directness to Kane's

actions, I find," Lakesh told her as he reached across the desk and pulled out several cables from the powered-down computer terminal located there.

Brigid smiled. For all of the apparent friction between herself and Kane, they were a good fit when push came to shove. Grant had reminded her earlier of the number of times that Kane had stepped in and put himself at risk to protect her and ensure that she reached her objective. She had done the same for him, of course—they were partners in peril. But there was more to it than that, a mystical bond that the two of them didn't speak of often. They were *anam-charas,* soul friends, bonded throughout history to accompany each other as they faced whatever destiny threw at them.

Brigid unzipped her sable-collared jacket and pulled out the spectacles she had tucked safely in the inside pocket during the rushed exit from the underground base in North Dakota. "What can I do to help?" she asked, reaching past Lakesh to unplug the keyboard from the unused computer terminal.

He turned to watch her as she began searching for the right port at the back of the black box to insert the keyboard jack. He admired her utter focus and unwavering determination, feeling at that moment that he could watch her work forever. He stopped himself, blinking and remembering the task at hand. "Why don't you take a few minutes to wash up and get yourself a change of clothes, Brigid?" he told her. "I can handle this and I'm sure that the joint expertise in this room can likely pull me free if I get tangled in any loose wires."

Smiling, Lakesh gestured the breadth of the room, and

Brigid looked up. Among the operatives at the terminals in the vast control center she could see Brewster Philboyd, an inspired astrophysicist of some renown, Dr. Mariah Falk, a caring woman and expert in the field of geology, and Donald Bry, the communications specialist who had helped get the satellites online. Lakesh was right. Between them, she realized, these people could probably fashion a working computer from scratch given enough pieces.

Brigid glanced at her reflection in the glass screen of the dead computer monitor before her, seeing her disheveled hair where it had been freed from the scarf, the mud-spattered white coat and scarf she still wore about her shoulders, and she realized that Lakesh had nothing but her own health at heart. "Yes, siree, I'll take that advice," she said breezily, plucking the glasses from her nose and turning to the exit doors of the ops center. "But you promise you'll call me the second you find anything, okay?" she called back as she stepped toward the door.

KANE HURRIED TO CATCH UP with Grant as he left the ops center. The redoubt's main corridor was a twenty-foot-wide tunnel carved through the mountain rock, with curving ribs of metal and girders supporting its high roof.

"What's the hurry, hero?" Kane asked, keeping his tone light despite the creeping exhaustion he felt washing over him now that he was out of the field. "You hardly said a word on the flight back here—something on your mind?"

Grant held up his left arm, fist clenched and his wrist chron close to Kane's face. "I promised I'd cook for

Shizuka tonight," he grumbled, "and didn't expect to be out in the field most of the afternoon."

Tilting his head, Kane looked at the wrist chron and noted that it was almost six o'clock. "So?" he asked. "Cooking is just cooking, it won't take that long."

"Sure." Grant nodded. "Cooking will take no time at all. It's not the cooking that I'm worrying about." He brushed a hand over his chops and beneath his chin, feeling the first, spiky itch of forming stubble as it met with his fingers. "Shower, shave, clean clothes—gotta look my best."

Before he could stop himself, Kane blurted out a loud guffaw. "Man, when did you two become such an old married couple? Listen to you!"

"Old married nothing," Grant replied. "What are we doing all this for, Kane—what are we fighting this crazy-ass war for—if not for people like Shizuka?" He held Kane's gaze for a moment before turning and heading to his private quarters.

Kane remained standing in the corridor, stunned and feeling suddenly very alone. The war. Sometimes he forgot about the war. When he was in point-man mode, when it was all instinct, all action and do-or-die, he just went with the flow, didn't think too much about where it was all leading. But Grant was right. They were in the middle of a war, a war that had raged on the planet Earth for more than five thousand years.

An alien race called the Annunaki had arrived on Earth in an effort to prevent their own stagnation. They had toyed with the primitive creatures that they had found there, shaping them to their own ends, for their own amusements. And when the toys had begun to lose their luster, the Annunaki had unleashed a great flood to wash away the remnants of this childlike race called humanity and begin anew. New forms of terrestrial subjugation emerged, and humankind was once again exploited by the alien master race.

Nobody really knew how long the Annunaki had shaped world events, and no one really understood why an all-powerful race would take so much time over what were, to them, little more than insects. And yet, the Annunaki had set events in motion to build up the Earth only to have the great civilizations destroy each other in another cataclysm, this time seemingly of their own making. Where water had failed the first time, fire took its place.

The planned nuclear holocaust had served a simple purpose, akin to leaving a field fallow so that the crops could be better harvested in the next cycle. The small percentage of the population that survived that fateful day in 2001 reverted to a state of savagery that ensured only the very strongest survived.

Two hundred years after that first nuclear strike, the Annunaki had reappeared as the overlords, reborn in new bodies formed from the chrysalis state of a mysterious ruling elite called the barons. As far as Kane could understand it, the whole trick had been pulled through a computer download; an organic computer on a starship called *Tiamat* found orbiting Earth, utilizing vastly superior technology to regenerate the godlike Annunaki pantheon. But for all intents and purposes, it was just another file download, a saved memory opened and accessed once more.

And working with Brigid and Lakesh had taught Kane that one file download meant that you could do another.

And another and another and another. *Tiamat* had taken a crippling hit during a recent squabble between different factions of the alien Annunaki, and their tight grip on the affairs of Earth seemed to be relenting, but Kane suspected—as did all of the Cerberus exiles—that the chances were good that a backup file of Annunaki personalities was just waiting to be downloaded. The threat had abated temporarily, but the war was far from over.

Grant was right. He had Shizuka, the beautiful leader of a society of samurai warriors called the Tigers of Heaven who inhabited Thunder Isle in the Pacific. She was a noble warrior, every bit as brave and formidable as Grant.

And who did Kane have? Who was his fight for?

"The hell with it," the ex-Mag muttered, turning toward his own quarters to take a hot shower to loosen the kinks in his muscles. He didn't need to hang a face or a name on the person he was saving. He was there to save humanity, there to save himself and others like him. It wasn't a war; it was basic survival.

As LAKESH ATTACHED a new keyboard to the recovered computer in the ops center, communications expert Donald Bry, sitting several seats across from him, thought he saw a quick flash of code whip across the monitor at his workstation.

A round-shouldered man of small stature, Bry wore a constant expression of consternation, no matter his mood, beneath the curly mop of unruly, copper-colored hair. Bry was a long-serving and trusted member of the Cerberus crew, acting as Lakesh's lieutenant and apprentice in all things technological.

Bry leaned forward in his seat, peering at his computer monitor, waiting for whatever it was to reappear. His monitor was linked to the Keyhole communications satellite, allowing Cerberus to remain in touch with field operatives and to pass information to them as required.

As he watched the surveillance image with thermal overlay taking up the main window on-screen, he urged whatever it was that had flashed up to reappear. When nothing happened, he began typing frantically at the keyboard, then slid his chair a few feet along the desk to review the past forty seconds at a separate monitor to his left.

Nothing appeared to be out of the ordinary. No code. No flash. Nothing.

Turning back to the live feed, Donald Bry leaned forward once again and ran his index finger across the lower right-hand side of the screen, where he had thought he had seen the code flash for a fraction of a second.

Farrell leaned over from a nearby desk, a quizzical look on his face. "Everything okay, Donald?" he asked.

Bry looked up, feeling awkward and suddenly stupid. "I thought I saw something for a moment," he told the other operator, "but it was nothing. Just tired, I guess. Been looking at the old boob tube too long."

Bry accepted when Farrell offered to cover communications monitoring for a while, and he got up to stretch his muscles and get out of the room for a few minutes, assuring his colleague he would be back shortly.

As Bry passed him, Lakesh was hooking a new monitor to the recovered computer. "Be sure you save some of the action for me," Bry instructed Lakesh with forced geniality before exiting the ops center into the vanadium-steel corridor.

Outside the quiet hum of the operations center, Bry stood and rubbed a hand over his eyes. "What did I see?" he asked himself quietly, trying to remember. Whatever it was, if it had been anything at all, had flashed across the screen so quickly that it had to have been there for no more than a nanosecond, utterly subliminal. If it had been anything at all, he reminded himself.

Chapter 4

On the plateau outside the heavy accordion-style doors to the Cerberus redoubt, two figures were sparring. A rough circle had been etched in the dirt around them, stretching to a diameter of roughly twenty feet. The early-morning sun was rising over the mountain, casting long shadows across the ground as the two combatants paced the edge of the marked area as they prepared to battle.

The two figures could not have been more different.

To one side of the circle stood Grant, the dark-skinned, heavily muscled ex-Mag dressed in loose-fitting combat trousers and a dark-colored vest. His outfit was finished by a pair of scuffed, black leather boots, a souvenir of his Magistrate days.

Across the circle, her bare feet crossing each other as she walked around the edge of the temporary arena, her eyes never leaving those of her opponent, was Domi. Lithe and thin, Domi was an albino, her skin chalk-white and her short-cropped hair the cream color of bone. She wore an olive-drab ensemble made up of an abbreviated halter top that barely covered her tiny, pert breasts and a pair of shorts, rolled up high in the leg. The most startling aspect of Domi's appearance, however, were her ruby-red eyes. The young woman weighed little more than a third of her opponent, yet showed no fear as she prepared to do combat with the bigger man.

"First outside the circle, toss or misstep," she told him, "either counts as a loss."

"I know the rules, Domi." Grant smiled tightly. "Give it your best shot so I can toss your sorry ass out of here and get to the cafeteria in time to catch the decent breakfast chef."

Domi's pale lips parted in a frightening, feral smile. "In your dreams, Grant." She laughed. "I'm saving my best shot for someone *good.*"

With that, Grant loosed a cry of offended rage and charged toward her, his boots kicking up dirt as he closed the space between them. Domi watched calmly, balancing lightly on the balls of her feet as this relentless juggernaut of a man hurtled toward her, his head down like a charging rhinoceros.

She timed the leap perfectly, her hand whipping out to scuff momentarily across Grant's left shoulder where he held it low to the ground. Suddenly she was flipping into the air, her feet at the highest apex as she pivoted off the ex-Mag's body. As silent and graceful as a ballerina, Domi landed behind Grant, pulling her body into itself.

With Domi out of his way, Grant saw the edge of the circle in the dirt just three steps ahead of him and he rolled his body and slapped his right hand hard on the ground to bring himself to a bone-jarring halt. He slipped for a moment, his hand drifting perilously close to the circle's edge, and managed to stop just short of the line.

As Grant righted himself, lifting his huge frame from

where he had slid, he heard Domi bark out a single laugh. "Ha! You're getting sloppy, old Mag man," she told him.

Crouched low to the ground, Grant turned to look at the thin-framed young woman, his lips curling back in a snarl. She was clearly enjoying this rare chance to show off to one of her peers, but Grant was beginning to wonder how he had been talked into this morning sparring match.

Domi, like Grant, Kane and Brigid, had once been a denizen of Cobaltville, though her position as sex slave had been far less salubrious than that of the Magistrates and the librarian. But circumstance had thrown them all together, a little unit that made up the solid core of the Cerberus exiles together with Lakesh as their mission controller. These days, Domi was sleeping with mission control, but that was a different story altogether.

As a child of the Outlands, she was naturally a loner, used to relying on her own wits and often abrupt around others, making them feel uncomfortable. But now and then she missed true company, that inherent human need for social contact, and Grant and Kane had always shown nothing but respect for her despite her background.

Grant looked to where Domi stood in the center of the circle and he noticed Kane was now standing a little way back from the circle's edge, over by the large doors to the redoubt. His eyes flicked to Domi once more, just standing there, waiting for his attack. Fine, he decided, you want an attack? You'll get one.

Grant was a massive engine of muscle as he drove forward, swinging punches left and right as he closed in on Domi. She weaved back, ducking low, and swung her right leg out in a sweeping arc, attempting to trip the bigger man. The front of her calf slapped into the top of Grant's heavy boot and just stopped, like hitting a solid metal bar.

Domi yelped in surprise, pulling her leg back and rolling her body out of the way of Grant's pile-driver punches. Suddenly she was standing again, a blur of motion as she darted her outstretched hands at him, holding them flat, like blades.

Grant put up a rock-solid arm to halt her attack, blocking each blow between wrist and elbow as her hands flitted toward his face. He sensed the opening in her attack before he saw it, an old Magistrate instinct, and his right leg kicked out as he pivoted at the torso, dropping low to ensure that his foot made solid contact.

Grant's kick slammed Domi just beside the breast-bone, and she staggered backward, the wind knocked out of her. She looked down as she drew a calming breath, and saw that she was just one footstep away from the edge of the circle that she had marked out before Grant arrived.

"Not laughing so much now, huh?" Grant goaded as he centered himself and walked warily toward her.

"Don't worry," she said, smiling, "I'm still laughing on the inside."

Grant stopped in his tracks, just outside of the range where Domi might reach him, and a wide smile broke out on his face. "And just what is that supposed to mean?"

Domi thought for a moment and shrugged. "I don't know. It just seemed the thing to say."

Kane's voice drifted over to them from the doors to the redoubt. "Blah-blah-blah," he said, heckling. "Are you kids going to talk or are you going to fight? I came here to see blood, people," he added, ensuring that they knew he was kidding by his tone.

Grant gave him a sneer before turning back to his tiny opponent. "You want to finish this?"

She nodded. "Ready when you are."

Kane had stepped over to the edge of the circle, a little behind where Domi was trapped. He punched a fist into his hand and began counting them in. "This is it, people," he announced, "Beauty versus the Beast. My money's on Beauty there, but don't take offense—I've known him a lot longer than I have you, Domi."

"Har-har," she responded, not looking back, taking a step closer to Grant. In a flash, Domi had spun her body, swinging first her left leg and then her right in Grant's direction, repeating the action as he skipped back to avoid her kicks. Grant slapped her legs away from his face as he continued backward.

Grant timed Domi's movements in his head, and suddenly his arm shot out and he grabbed her right ankle as it swung toward his face. Not expecting the move, Domi overbalanced and tumbled to the hard-packed ground, her momentum pulling Grant over with her.

Together, the pair of fighters slammed into the dirt, with Grant spinning to avoid crushing Domi's birdlike frame beneath his massive build.

"You okay?" he asked her after a moment, letting go of her ankle.

Lying prone on the ground, Domi peered over her shoulder down the length of her body at Grant's concerned expression. His vest was darker now, she saw, where sweat had pooled between his pectoral muscles. "Yeah, I'm fine," she told him. "Thanks."

Grant eased himself off the ground and stood over her, offering her one of his huge hands to help her up.

"Aren't you going to finish me off?" she asked, confused.

Grant shook his head, pointing to the ground at his feet. "I stepped outside the circle when I rolled."

Domi took his hand, a sour expression crossing her features. "Yeah, but you did that to avoid hurting me."

Grant shrugged. "Still counts," he assured her. "Besides, breakfast is becoming a nagging priority just now. Tough to fight on an empty stomach."

Domi brushed herself down and watched Grant return to the redoubt and disappear into the darkness of the tunnel mouth. After a few moments, she turned to Kane, still standing at the side of the circle. "Did you want to see me?" she asked him.

Kane shook his head. "Nah, I just came out here to get some peace and quiet. Didn't realize that fight club was in session this morning."

Domi smiled shyly, the barest hint of color rouging her pure white cheeks. "You wanna fight?" she asked Kane after a moment.

Kane looked out over the plateau, watching as wispy cotton-candy clouds drifted slowly over the distant sky, before he reached for the top of his shirt and began unbuttoning it. "What the hell, why not," he told her, tossing his shirt to one side. "But no pulling hair, okay?"

"I won't if you won't," Domi promised him as she walked across to the far side of the dirt circle.

As he stepped into the circle and dropped his body into

a fighter's stance, Kane felt the nagging doubts of the past few days ebb away. It felt good to be alive.

BRIGID WAS BESIDE Lakesh in the ops center while Brewster Philboyd sat before them, tapping at the keyboard Lakesh had attached to the recovered computer. They had spent three days trying to decode the encrypted information, and every false lead had sapped just a little of their enthusiasm for the task.

The question remained: what was stored on the hard drive and would it be worth this effort? Lakesh had one answer, and Brigid consoled herself that his was the wisest way to look at the problem. "It doesn't matter what's in the files," he had assured her. "This is a scientific investigation to find out the truth—that there *is* something in the files." In their ceaseless quest to find out what that something was, Brigid wasn't entirely sure that any of them had gotten enough sleep.

An astrophysicist, Brewster Philboyd was in his midforties and wore black-rimmed glasses above his acnescarred cheeks. His pale blond hair was swept back from a receding hairline, and his lanky six-foot frame towered above many of the other scientists in the redoubt. Philboyd had joined the Cerberus team along with a number of other exiles from Manitius more than a year before, and had proved to be a valuable addition to the staff. He was the first to admit that he wasn't a fighter, but Philboyd was as determined as a dog with a bone when a scientific or engineering problem crossed his path. He had stepped in to help with the Grand Forks database when he overheard the exasperated cries coming from Brigid and Lakesh on the second day of attempting to probe its files.

"This stuff was really important two hundred years ago," Brigid said, "but for pity's sake, couldn't they have put a time-sensitive release on the damn coding?"

"There's every possibility that it's just as important today," Lakesh said, chastising her lightly before turning back to the streams of code that whizzed across the screen, seeming to blur into one continuous, green glowing mass after three solid days of watching them flash before his eyes.

"Well," Philboyd chipped in, "we know that the code is alphanumeric and that it uses uniform block placement to disguise any natural patterns that might be there. Maybe if we drop some of the letters and transpose others…"

"And stand on our heads and rub our stomachs," Brigid added.

Philboyd scratched at his head absently. "That might help, too," he admitted.

Lakesh took them both in with a kindly look. "We'll break it, my friends," he assured them calmly. "Just let's all take things logically, one step at a time.

"And the first step," he added firmly, standing up and feeling the twinge in his joints where he had been hunched over the computer terminal too long, "is to make everyone a cup of tea so we can all retain our sense of focus."

A few minutes later, as the three of them sat nursing mugs of tea, Cerberus's resident communications expert, Donald Bry, left his post as the day shift began and came across the room to join them.

"I've worked up a quick program that you can use to

reverse selected batches of the coded sequence," he explained, brandishing a shiny CD with the words *Reverse decoder* scrawled across it in permanent marker.

Lakesh reached across and took the CD, thanking Bry as he did so. "We've thought of reversing every other sequence, but it didn't generate any definite patterns," he told the communications man, "but this will open up more options, I'm certain."

Bry nodded. "All we can do is try, right?" he told them, trying to buoy their spirits.

Her hands clasped around the warm mug of tea, Brigid nodded. "Thanks, Donald," she said, feeling the cold ache of tiredness creeping over her and clutching the mug tighter to stave it off.

Lakesh stepped across to a free terminal and began running Bry's program from the CD, while Brewster Philboyd transferred a copy of the recovered hard drive across for him to work with.

Bry stood behind Lakesh as he began typing instructions out at the keyboard. "Maybe if you reversed every third or fourth or, I dunno, tenth part of the string," Bry suggested.

Lakesh's brilliant mind was already several steps ahead. "I'm adding something to your program," he told Bry. "A little randomizer so that we can test different parts of the coding in different ways. That should save us quite some time, assuming this provides a key to open the files."

Still sitting beside Philboyd, Brigid felt Lakesh's words wash over her as her eyelids began to get heavier. The steady rhythm of clicking computer keys had an oddly calming effect as she closed her eyes and began thinking, for no particular reason, about a game she used to play in her childhood that involved chasing boys to kiss them, much to their disgust. Eyes closed and her breathing deep and regular, Brigid smiled at the memory.

THE CAVE WAS ALMOST entirely dark, the only light source coming from the faint glow of a computer screen. Five men had come there to confer, away from prying eyes.

"Somebody has tapped into the Keyhole orbital comsat," Rock Streaming explained to the others as they stood together in a tight circle. Rock Streaming was a tall man in his early twenties, with long black hair tied in a ponytail and light brown skin the color of milky coffee. He had a wide forehead and a wide, flat nose beneath dark, intelligent eyes. He wore boots and combat pants with a long, tan-colored duster worn open across his bare chest. Tribal tattoos could be seen beneath it, dotted across his wide chest, swirls and black flames surrounded by curlicues.

The other men in the cave bore the signs of similar ethnicity, with café-au-lait skin, dark hair and flat noses, and the younger ones had harsh, bold tattoos striping the sectors of bare skin that they displayed.

One of the older men nodded sagely. His face displayed a tangled beard, as dark as his messy hair, and he was dressed in a simple loincloth, leaving the rest of him, including his feet, bare. A strange-looking cuplike object was tucked into his waistband, connected to a long section of twine. "Have you secured the feed?" he asked, his voice a low mutter.

Rock Streaming nodded, flexing his fingers for a moment like a prestidigitator warming up for his act.

"They don't know we're there, Good Father, I guarantee it."

The older man nodded once more, his eyes distant as he considered the implications of the young man's statement. "Where is the link?" he asked after a moment. "Where is it that you are monitoring?"

The long tails of the duster coat whipped behind him as Rock Streaming strode across the cavern to the quietly humming laptop. He crouched, displaying uncanny balance as he dropped to rest on pointed toes, and tapped at the keyboard for several seconds. "The old United States," he replied as a satellite image appeared to one side of the main display on the terminal. As Rock Streaming worked the keys, labels flashed up on-screen, identifying different parts of the image. "A place called Bitterroot in the area known as Montana by the old mapmakers."

Another of the men spoke then, addressing his question to Rock Streaming. Like Good Father, this man was older than the other three, with a clumpy beard and flecks of gray appearing in his tangled hair. He wore a waistcoat over his chest and rounded belly, with grubby shorts, and had also left his feet bare. His gray eyes held a quality of tremendous age that seemed somehow out of place in a human being. "And you are sure that they have no inkling that you are monitoring them?" he asked, his voice the low rumble of a distant storm. "You are *sure?*" he emphasized.

Rock Streaming nodded, looking up from his crouching position before the glowing laptop screen. "These Americans have no idea that I'm watching them, Bad Father," he said with certainty.

One of the tattooed young men spoke up, his tone re-

spectful to the older tribesmen but still proud of his contemporary. "They say that to be hacked by Rock Streaming is to be caressed by a secret lover, Bad Father," he
assured the old man in the vest. "The system cries out for
more but refuses to speak of the tryst to its operators."

Bad Father nodded, his lips pressed together in a thin
line. "Let me know of any developments," he instructed
Rock Streaming. Then he turned away in unison with
Good Father, and the pair headed toward the tunnel that
led out of the cave.

Still crouching at the glowing laptop monitor, Rock
Streaming turned to his two remaining colleagues and
nodded once in silent acknowledgment. In the linear, subjective world, the time was coming.

Chapter 5

The breakthrough finally came two days later, when geologist Mariah Falk recognized a sequence of digits tucked away in the streams of coded information as an old-fashioned grid reference. As soon as she pointed it out, Lakesh slapped his forehead for being so stupid as to not notice it before.

"But where is this coordinate referencing?" he asked her as they sat together in the cafeteria that sometimes doubled as a meeting hall for the Cerberus personnel.

Brigid sat with them, prodding a fork through a yellow swirl of scrambled eggs on her plate. "Let me see," she suggested, looking at the deciphered location code on Lakesh's printout.

Mariah, a large woman who, while not especially attractive, had an ingratiating smile and an amazingly resilient personality, closed her eyes tightly as she tried to work out the reference numbers. Her arms moved before her, gesturing up and to her right for a few moments before she opened her eyes and spoke. "Northwest Russia somewhere, I think. I'd need to see a map to get you any closer than that, though," she admitted.

"Great," Brigid muttered disconsolately, "more snow."

Lakesh was already standing, and he took in a hearty

breath as he looked at his companions. "If Mariah is right, we can use this system to decrypt the contents of the computer and find out what it is we've been looking at for the past five days."

It took another half day to write the decryption software and run the program through the files they had found, and even then parts of it appeared to be horribly vague or incomplete. But it turned out that Mariah's observation was a Rosetta stone, giving them the key. After a few tweaks, a refined version of the decryption was applied and a wealth of military reports opened up to Lakesh and his team.

A lot of the files were nothing more than personnel records and requisition forms, but several items held interest. Brigid took it upon herself to investigate one sequence further, putting in long hours to piece together all of its scattered parts.

Lakesh called Kane, Grant and Brigid together for an informal meeting in the empty cafeteria the next evening, and he sat beside Brigid, facing the two ex-Mags. Brigid had worked throughout the past thirty hours, transcribing important details from the files and piecing the information together with her own formidable knowledge. What she had come up with had been quite astonishing, Lakesh agreed, assuming that it was accurate.

"The main files on the recovered computer dealt with information from one of the U.S. spy networks," Lakesh explained as Grant poured everyone water from a large jug in the center of the table. "From what we can divine, this network was a crucial player in the days leading up to the Cold War, when the U.S. was focused on the growing threat of Russian military might. They kept files on a variety of military projects that were being researched behind the iron curtain, some of more questionable value than others."

"Watching folks through gaps in the drapes." Kane smiled. "Nice work if you can get it."

"Now, the vast majority of this information is bitty and of very limited use over two hundred years after it was amassed," Lakesh continued, "but we've found one item of exceptional interest. Brigid has been concentrating on going through and deciphering all of its related notes."

Lakesh turned to Brigid and she picked up the explanation after stifling a tired yawn. "According to the U.S. report, it seems that the Russians had developed a project dubbed Chernobog. Chernobog is the name of a Slavic god known as 'the bringer of calamities.'"

"Sounds like a honey," Grant chirped.

"Now, the mythology behind the name isn't important," Brigid continued, "but the threat that it implies may very well be. From what the intelligence network could piece together, Project Chernobog was set up as a subsection of the Cheka Agency. The Cheka was the government division that ultimately became the KGB, a lethal secret police force at the beck and call of, at the point of its inception, Lenin. In 1920, with the First World War just behind them and growing alarm at the potentially disruptive influence of outside forces on their then nascent communism, the Russian Communist Party set things in motion to create a weapon so powerful that it could eradicate all forms of life from a specified area." She drew a long breath before continuing. "Furthermore, this weapon was apparently proposed as a fail-safe not for the 'evil' outside forces of America and Western Europe, but for something conceived as a far more insidious and dangerous threat—the Archons." She stopped, her emerald eyes skewering each of the three people sitting at the table. "Aliens," she said finally.

"Kind of stands to reason," Kane admitted after a moment's thought. "Our boys are spying on them and they're spying on us. They see the U.S. government getting pally with the Roswell day-trippers and they start to think, 'Hey, maybe we need one of those ultimate-weapon-type things just in case.'"

"The Roswell visitation was in 1947," Brigid told Kane, "over twenty years after Project Chernobog was initiated."

"Well," Kane responded, "the point is there has been a lot of alien activity over the years, and we've seen more than our share of evidence the visitors had their fingers in the U.S. government pie for a long time. If I was building up a society that stood opposed to that government, I'd make damn sure I could take out their benevolent, technologically advanced friends."

Brigid nodded, conceding his point. "Now, and I must emphasize this, what we're looking at here are spy reports. Which is to say, the veracity of this information is suspect, and it is almost certain that all of the facts are not present. Furthermore, given the general climate of the espionage divisions on both sides, it's a given that any report will put the worst possible spin on a situation concerning the enemy."

Grant poured himself another glass of water and gestured the jug around to see if anyone else wanted more. "So lay it on the line for us, Brigid," he said. "What are we actually looking at?"

"At face value?" she asked, and Grant and Kane encouraged her to continue. "There's a redoubt tucked away in Georgia, Russia, that's the storage facility for a weapon so powerful that it could destroy the Annunaki once and for all."

There was a sharp intake of breath from all parties around the table at that point, and everyone looked relieved, then increasingly uncomfortable.

"So," Kane suggested, drawing a route with his finger over the shiny plastic table, "let's say we mosey on over to Georgia and pick up this Chernobog device—"

Brigid stopped him. "The division is called Chernobog, a kind of statement of intent when they set it up, I guess. The weapon... Well, the best translation I can come up with is 'the Call of Death. Death Cry.'"

Kane nodded. "So, we get ourselves this Death Cry and then what? The Annunaki have been a thorn in our sides for a long time, using it against them would send a message and potentially...potentially what?" he asked.

"Kill every last one of them," Lakesh said solemnly.

"Assuming the information is correct and that the weapon was ever actually constructed," Brigid added. "This is information from the people watchers, remember?"

Kane looked at Grant and, after a moment, both men smiled gravely.

"This is too good an opportunity to pass up," Kane stated firmly.

"Seconded," Grant added.

Lakesh and Brigid were nodding, too. "That's what we thought when we first deciphered the report," Lakesh admitted. "But there is another question."

"Yeah," Kane said, "and we all know what it is. Even if we obtain this Death Cry, do we dare pull the trigger?"

Grant rubbed his jowls thoughtfully, brushing down the edges of his mustache. "The Annunaki have pushed humanity around for at least five millennia," he told everyone. "If there's the slightest chance of getting rid of their lizard faces once and for all, we have to take it."

"Yeah," Kane agreed, "that's pretty much the way I see it, too."

Brigid looked at the notepad that rested before her, its pages full of notations in her tidy, precise hand, before looking back at Kane and Grant. "If only we'd had this thing when they first revealed themselves," she said quietly.

Kane reached across the table and placed his hand over hers, looking her in the eye. "Yeah," he said quietly, the single word holding the weight of meaning that all four adventurers felt at that moment, survivors in a seemingly unending battle against an almighty evil.

Grant clapped his hands loudly, breaking the somber mood with his wide smile. "Well, kids," he announced, "looks like we're going to Georgia for the holidays!"

THE FIRST RAYS of sunlight streamed over the horizon, turning the bronze-hued metal hulls of the twin Manta aircraft into twinkling, golden stars as they cut through the skies over the Pacific.

Kane and Grant took piloting duties in their respective vehicles, and once again Brigid took the passenger seat behind Kane. He sat before her, wearing a helmet that enclosed his whole head, forged from the same strange, bronze-hued metal as the Mantas themselves. Within the helmet, a heads-up display fed Kane vast streams of detailed information concerning wind speed, air pressure and a dozen other factors that might affect the pilot's decisions. But for the purposes of this trip, dusting the clouds as they flew west, the Mantas would pretty much fly themselves. Which suited Kane and Grant just fine, well acquainted as they were with the concept of point and shoot from their previous lives as Magistrates.

The Cerberus field teams had been to Russia before, had encountered their local equivalent known as District Twelve. But for the purposes of this mission, Lakesh had agreed that keeping a low profile was for the best. If this Death Cry superweapon turned out to be a dud, bogus surveillance information or a theoretical project that never got off the drawing board, Kane's team could potentially look very foolish to their Russian contemporaries. And, by contrast, if this Death Cry really did exist, there was no question that District Twelve would stake a claim on it, despite the actual discovery work being the province of the Cerberus people.

"We'll take the Mantas in low," Kane had proposed before they set off, "fly in via China and sweep up toward the location so we don't spend too much time in Russian airspace. Chances are good they won't spot us, and they'd expect us to come at them via the Atlantic route anyhow."

Now, having passed his eyes across the various readouts to make sure that things remained steady, Kane tilted his head back and spoke with Brigid. "Any idea what this place is like?" he asked.

Brigid had been checking through the notes she had made the day before, refamiliarizing herself with everything she had uncovered. She glanced up at Kane, at the strange bronze helmet propped atop his neck, and watched as rain-heavy black clouds zipped past through the exterior view port. "The coordinates place the redoubt in the Caucasus Mountains, about seventy clicks from the Black Sea," she replied. "A temperate area, the closest big settlement on the old maps would be Pyatigorsk, but satellite pictures show that's long since gone."

"Huh," Kane grunted. "Probably bombed back to the Stone Age like most everything else during the nukecaust."

"The state of Georgia was about as far west as you could go in the old Soviet Union," Brigid continued. "It was actually one of the last states to be incorporated into the Union of Soviet Socialist Republics, remaining a semi-independent satellite district for the first twenty years of rule by the Communist Party."

"That's pretty strange," Kane said thoughtfully. "Constructing a doomsday device outside your borders."

Brigid shook her head, even though she knew that Kane couldn't turn to see her while he wore the bulky helmet. "Not that unusual really," she explained. "There are political benefits to keeping the really nasty stuff out of your own country, especially in a climate of worldwide hostility. The U.S.A. and other countries used similar tactics, storing nuclear missiles and the like in territories that were sympathetic to their political ideology rather than inside their own borders. Makes it less easy to get caught, and if you do, your government can simply deny all knowledge."

"Ah," Kane responded. "You're talking that diplomacy speak again, Baptiste."

Kane scanned the heads-up displays for half a minute before continuing. "It's funny," he told his flight companion, "I never gave much thought to the location of the Cerberus redoubt up to now. It's kind of interesting that the military brass stuck the crucial development arm of their mat-trans system close to the border between the U.S. and Canada. Guess they didn't want it too close to Washington, just in case something went askew."

"Yup," Brigid agreed, "there was certainly a time when the mat-trans was new—and potentially unstable—technology. Lakesh could tell you more about how things were in those days."

"I'm sure he could." Kane nodded. "So right now we've left one out-of-the-way mountain installation to go visit another."

"That's about the size of it," she confirmed. "You were hoping for something else?"

Kane sighed. "Just once," he told her, "I'd like to get a nice mission in the sun somewhere. You know, grab a few rays, maybe a spot of surfing, some fishing, build a sand castle."

"The last time we tried that, I wound up a hostage for pirates in the Florida Keys," she reminded him.

"Yeah, but at least you got to work on your tan," Kane grumbled.

At that moment, the Commtact units that were attached behind the ears of Kane and Brigid clicked and Grant's voice could be distinctly heard by both as though he were there in the cockpit with them. The Commtacts were top-of-the-line communication devices that had been found in Redoubt Yankee years before. They featured sensor circuitry incorporating an analog-to-digital voice encoder that was subcutaneously embedded in the mastoid bone. Once the pintels made contact, transmissions were picked up by the auditory canals, and dermal sensors transmitted the electronic signals directly through the skull. Theoretically, a deaf wearer would still be able to hear normally, in a fashion, using the Commtact.

"Just coming up on the East China Sea now," Grant said. "We're at about the halfway point."

"Let's just fly steady," Kane responded, "keep it nice and smooth."

"That's a roger," Grant acknowledged before signing out.

The Mantas dipped below the clouds for a moment, and Brigid took in a sharp intake of breath as she saw the huge landmass that encompassed Asia and Europe stretching out before them. They were on their way.

Chapter 6

It was a little after midday local time when they arrived in Georgia. Kane and Grant took several passes over the mountainous area in the Mantas over a period of fourteen minutes. The Mantas split formation and separately took several swift runs across the Caucasus Mountains, surveying the general territory and ensuring nothing untoward was waiting close by to surprise them.

While they didn't expect to run into any particular problems, Brigid reminded them that the local authorities might not take too kindly to their rummaging through their military sites for plunder.

"We're not plundering," Kane grunted, "just…finding."

"How do you figure that?" Brigid asked as their Manta cut through the air for another pass at the location in question.

"You can only plunder stuff if it belongs to someone else," Kane told her through the bulbous flight helmet. "Way I see it, anyone with any real claim to this Death Cry device is long since in the grave. No one's seen fit to go look for it for two hundred years, right?"

Brigid shook her head, even though she knew that Kane could not see her. "Well, we don't know that," she admitted, "but it's a pretty out-of-the-way location and redoubts tend to be well protected against casual intruders, so there's every chance—"

"You see?" Kane cut her off, triumph in his tone. "Like I said—just finding."

Brigid chose to defer to Kane's judgment for now, but she knew that if District Twelve or another Russian agency got wind of their presence there, there would be a lot of explaining to do.

Once Grant had made his sixth pass, this time beneath the cloud cover and at what amounted to a slow crawl for his Manta craft, he confirmed that the area was definitely uninhabited.

"Think we can go in?" Kane asked over the Commtact, his own Manta hidden in a high bank of wispy, white clouds.

Grant's even tone came back to Kane after a moment. "Now's as good a time as any."

The Cerberus field team had located evidence of a military installation nestled between two of the snow-capped mountain peaks and decided that this was likely the installation that they sought. A tiny concrete building, perfectly square and little more impressive than a tool shed, stood guard at the end of a small paved road. From the air, the short road curled around into the shape of a hangman's noose, a turning circle for vehicles. The rusting remains of a military transport lurched to one side of the road, its canvas roof cover long since lost. Other than the black strip, there seemed little to distinguish the area from anywhere else in the mountain range, but Brigid confirmed that this area tallied with the coordinates listed in the decrypted surveillance files.

Kane deployed the Manta's various scanning capabilities, but the data that came back was inconclusive. "Could be there's an underground bunker there," he told Brigid, "but it sure ain't anything special." He ticked off the basic scanning checklist for her. "No reactors, no indication of any power source, no personnel showing on thermal—no one alive, at least. No significant metallic content, nothing out of the ordinary for the mountain range in general.

"I'm no expert," he continued, "but I think the best we're going to find is an air-raid shelter."

"How big?" Brigid wondered.

She heard Kane suck air through his teeth in thought. "That," he told her, "is something that would require landing and maybe getting the shovels out."

Shortly thereafter, Grant brought his Manta in for a fast vertical landing, bringing the craft down swiftly and smoothly to park beside the short strip of blacktop. Kane followed two minutes after, descending rapidly from high cloud cover once he was certain that no one was coming to investigate Grant's appearance.

Grant waited across from the landing area that he and Kane had chosen, crouched within a small patch of scrub grass, clutching a Copperhead close-assault subgun, scanning the area with alert eyes and ears. The Copperhead subgun was almost two feet in length but looked like a toy in Grant's huge hands. The grip and trigger of the gun were placed in front of the breech in the bullpup design, allowing the gun to be used single-handed, and an optical, image-intensified scope coupled with a laser autotargeter were mounted on top of the frame. The Cop-

perhead possessed a 700-round-per-minute rate of fire
and was equipped with an extended magazine holding
thirty-five 4.85 mm steel-jacketed rounds. Besides the Sin
Eater, the Copperhead was Grant's favored field weapon,
thanks to ease of use and the sheer level of destruction it
could create in short measure.

Grant wore his favorite long black coat over his
shadow suit, and remained as alert as a hawk while his
colleagues exited their aircraft. There was no one about.
No one, nothing. Just a few insects crawling across the
rough terrain beside the narrow ribbon of roadway, two
lost honeybees flitting around in the crisp air of the higher
altitude.

Up close, the short stretch of road looked worn and
beaten. It had been more than two hundred years since
the strip of tarmac was last resurfaced, and the elements
had taken their punishing, relentless toll. The tarmac had
split into little islands of hard, black scabs, with weeds
and grasses attacking it from beneath and pushing their
way through to the surface.

The square building at the end of the road had not fared
much better, its gray paint cracked and evidence of animal
burrowing and gnawing here and there. Beside the building stood the remains of a manually operated barrier; a
long pole painted red and white, long since fallen from
its rusted hinge, lay hidden in the vegetation that threatened to consume the road.

Brigid slid down the graceful wing of the Manta, and
Kane followed a moment later, a small satchel of equipment hanging over his shoulder and the Sin Eater gripped
tightly in his right hand. Brigid wore a washed-out denim

jacket over her shadow suit, tan-colored boots with chunky heels and had left her red-gold hair flowing freely. Kane had added a light, khaki-colored jacket over his own shadow suit, again a concession to camouflage and a need for extra pockets. The right sleeve of the jacket had been roughly torn, creating a wider armhole at the wrist so as to easily eject Kane's Sin Eater from its bulky holster.

Kane steadied his right wrist as he scanned the area with the Sin Eater in sharp, birdlike twitches of movement. "Everything clear?" he asked in a loud voice.

"All clear," Grant pronounced from his hiding place.

Kane eyeballed the area again, with Brigid providing backup with her unholstered TP-9, before announcing, "Stand down." As he drew his steadying left hand away, he reholstered the Sin Eater.

Grant stood up, dusting off his coat as he approached Kane and Brigid, the Copperhead grasped loosely in one hand. "No one around," he told them. "Not even any signs that anyone was ever around. This place has probably been deserted for a hundred years."

"Let's hope it's more," Brigid said, the TP-9 still cradled in her hands. "Two hundred years is a long time for a place like this to be left completely alone."

"Happens, though," Grant told her reassuringly. It was pretty much what had happened to the Cerberus redoubt.

Still alert, Kane led the way down the broken, lumpy tarmac toward the concrete building. "What do you reckon that is?"

"Figure it for a sentry post," Grant told him. "See the

barricade there?" He pointed to the red-and-white striped bar nestled in the leafy green overgrowth.

"Let's take a look-see," Kane instructed, and the three of them spread out, warily approaching the dilapidated building from separate sides.

The concrete installation had a handful of slit windows, long horizontal lines like the windows of observation buildings found in bomb-testing sites, and a heavy slab of door offset to the left of the wall faced away from the road, right next to the stump that had once held the manually operated barrier. Kane stepped lightly toward the door, feeling a little ridiculous, and rapped his knuckles firmly against it. "Open up," he shouted. "Come out with your hands up."

Kane stepped away and to the side of the door, close enough to pounce on anyone should they come through, while Grant and Brigid had taken positions covering the door with their blasters. Kane did a slow count to ten in his head before calling the same instructions again, this time without rapping on the door. After another slow ten count he gave Grant a silent instruction with his hand, and the big ex-Mag took a step toward the solid door.

"If anyone's behind this door," Grant warned loudly, "they had better get themselves a long way back." With that, he reeled off a quick burst with the Copperhead, driving 4.85 mm slugs in a horizontal streak across the door from handle to hinge.

As empty shell casings clattered around Grant's booted feet, he took another step closer to the door, and Kane swung around to join him. "Empty," Kane mouthed, indicating the little building, and Grant nodded.

Kane stepped to the door and tried both the knob and pushing the butt of his hand against the solid slab of steel, but it resisted. "It's either locked or jammed," he told the others.

"Want me to use my key?" Grant asked, pushing the nose of the Copperhead against the doorknob.

"If you would," Kane stated, stepping aside and holding his empty right hand ready, index finger crooked, pointing at the door. If anyone appeared, his Sin Eater would be in his hand, firing rounds, in less time than it took to think it. Magistrate training had made this an instinctive reaction in both himself and Grant, to the point that it was a muscle memory more than a conscious thought.

There was a loud blast and sparks flew from the door handle as bullets from Grant's Copperhead obliterated the old lock. A moment later, Grant had stepped forward and booted the door open with a swift kick, with Brigid covering from over his shoulder with the TP-9.

Inside, the main area appeared empty, but they could see a second door near the back of the boxlike room, pushed closed.

Brigid darted forward to check the inner door, Grant and Kane just behind her. She pushed open the second door to reveal a tiny sink and porcelain chemical toilet.

They closed the door and stepped back into the larger area, looking around the starkly painted room. The walls were an unimaginative, soul-destroying shade of gray, and there were what looked like four television monitors in the room. The Cerberus field team flitted around the room quickly, confirming that none of the screens showed anything, and they tried flicking switches to see if any of them would power up but were rewarded with nothing but lifeless glass. One of the screens had been shattered, but there were no clues as to what had done this or why, and too long a period had passed to assume human intervention was responsible. Light fixtures and other paraphernalia had fallen from the walls and ceiling over time, and anything could have knocked into the screen.

Brigid walked across to a circular monitor that lay at a forty-five-degree angle to the desktop, tapping her finger against the glass. "Radar," she declared. "This place was used as a monitoring facility of some kind."

"Maybe to see what was coming," Grant suggested. "Make sure no one was sneaking up."

"Fair assumption," Brigid confirmed.

Kane looked around the tiny room, the light inside minimal from the slit windows and open door. "Anyone see anything that looks like a superweapon?"

"Gonna have to go with no," Grant admitted.

"Trapdoors, hidden exits, mat-trans?" Kane asked, scanning the little hut.

"Nothing," Grant and Brigid said in unison, checking around and under the desks and tapping at the walls, listening to the echoes their knuckles made.

"Well, this is a blowout, then," Kane stated.

Brigid shook her head. "A sentry post in the middle of nowhere, tucked away in a mountain range, with a strip of roadway beside it," she said thoughtfully. "We can safely assume that the road stretched on down the mountains once upon a time, meaning the Russian army was bringing something up here."

"But where?" Kane shrugged.

"Let's check out the road," Brigid told him, leading the way through the door and back outside.

The party of three scoured the length of tarmac that stretched from the fallen barricade to the turning circle, less than a hundred yards in all. There was some evidence of where the road had once reached down into the valley between the mountains, but it was mostly a dirt track and Brigid postulated that it had perhaps always been thus, keeping the location secret.

The old Soviet transport truck remained parked to one side of the turning circle, listing at an angle where it had slipped from the road. The rusty truck was flecked with olive-drab paint, all that remained of its original sheen, and there were a few ragged tatters where a canvas cover had once been stretched over the flatbed on metal arches, high enough to allow a man of Grant's height to sit or kneel comfortably within and even stand with a stoop if need be. The vehicle's tires had rotted away.

Kane hopped up into the high cab and peered inside, opening the glove box and reaching in. He came out with a handful of maps showing the local region, a road map of the Eastern states of the USSR and a Russian-language copy of *The Communist Manifesto* by Marx and Engels. Whoever had left the truck there had taken the keys with them, which struck Brigid—seeing the state of the vehicle now—as a tragically human thing to do. The truck had probably been abandoned sometime around the end of civilization, but whoever had left it had been wary of letting anyone steal government property, just the same.

As they scouted around the broken flecks of the

turning circle, Grant called to the others to come join him. "See this," he told them, tapping his toe against a metal grate, almost entirely hidden beneath the tangle of vines and shrubbery that was encroaching on the road. The grate clanged with the sound of his boot, rattling in place. "Some kind of vent or something, you reckon?"

"I reckon," Kane agreed, crouching on his haunches to examine the metallic grate. He pulled up some of the plants and brushed them aside along with straggly strands of yellow grass, uncovering one section of what appeared to be a wide circle of metal with thick, rusty bars crossing from north to south.

When they realized the size of the thing, Grant and Brigid got down on hands and knees and began feeling for the edges of the massive circular grate. When they had finished, the grate stood revealed as a perfect circle approximately twelve feet across. It reminded Brigid of pictures she had seen of old storm drain outlets, only this was lying flat.

"You were right, Kane," she announced, giving him a bright smile, "it is an air-raid shelter."

Kane grunted, stepping away from the grate and looking out at the impressive mountainous vista that surrounded them. The far-off call of a bird that Kane didn't recognize came echoing across the peaks. "Kane to home base," he said quietly, unconsciously pushing his hand up to his ear, beside where the Commtact attached to his mastoid bone.

There was a brief period of silence, then Donald Bry's voice came clearly over the Commtact. "What news, Kane?"

"Site appears deserted," Kane stated. "Evidence of underground operation discovered. Am now investigating. Over."

Kane waited patiently, looking across to the grate embedded in the ground. They were half a world away from the Cerberus ops center, and there was an appreciable delay in satellite communications, he knew, but the pause took almost a full minute before Donald Bry's voice returned. It was evident that Bry had been discussing the situation with the rest of the team there, probably awaiting advice from Lakesh before he responded to Kane's sitrep. "Go inside, Kane," Bry advised, "but take care. Over."

"Always do," Kane responded. "Over and out." With that he broke contact and strolled back to where they remained examining the grate and brushing green tendrils away from its surface. "Reckon we're going in," he told them.

Grant nodded. "This thing's held together well," he told Kane, shoving his heel against the grate, "but it's mostly rust keeping it in place now. We could probably cut straight through the bars, or some well-placed C-4 would blow it clean away."

"Let's cut," Kane decided, "keep the noise down." He reached into the satchel and produced a pair of long-handled bolt cutters with telescoping arms for ease of storage. The Mantas were stealth craft, and Kane knew that their negligible engine noise would not have carried far. An explosion, however, would reverberate throughout the whole mountain range and could draw unwanted attention.

Brigid stood beside Kane as he got to work, while Grant ran back to his Manta to grab some equipment from the storage locker below the cockpit. "There's probably a door around here somewhere," Brigid hypothesized.

"Probably is," Kane agreed, continuing with the brutal work of cutting through the thick bars.

"These people didn't get into their air-raid shelter using the ventilation system, did they?" she continued.

"Don't think they did," he confirmed, gritting his teeth as he forced the pincers closed on the first rusty bar and sheared through.

"You think maybe we should just look for that, then?" she prodded. "It would be a little easier."

Kane looked at her, tongue working over dry lips. "That could take days to find, and I'd sooner just get inside," he told her. "It's too quiet around here, and I don't like being out in the open. Feel like a field mouse waiting for an owl."

Without thinking, Brigid glanced to the sky at Kane's words. "Fair point," she agreed.

Grant returned with a xenon flashlight and a bunch of rappel lines for cave exploring. He switched on the flashlight and pointed its brilliant beam through the bars covering the grate, revealing a sludge-carpeted floor about fifteen feet below. "First step'll get you," he warned everyone in his rumbling voice. Then he began attaching one of the rappel lines to his belt, silently volunteering to be first into the hole below.

Kane continued working at the rusted bars.

Eighteen minutes later they were out of the ventilation

shaft and into the main complex that had been hidden below the mountain. None of the team was especially surprised to find the redoubt there. Indeed, its location mirrored that of the Cerberus complex hidden in the Bitterroot Mountains in Montana. Mountain hideaways were clearly the worldwide military location of choice.

This one was surprisingly small, however. There was a total of twelve rooms, including shared sleeping quarters and a large room that had doubled as mess hall and lecture theater.

They had had to bash their way through a second, much smaller grate to get into the underground complex. The grate had been plugged up with sludge and dust and heaven knew what else. When they removed the grate, a stream of fresh air poured into the tiny complex for the first time in years, and the place would have a nasty smell about it until it fully aired.

The Cerberus warriors wore dark-lensed glasses. The electrochemical polymer of the lenses gathered all available light to give them a limited form of night vision, allowing them to sweep through the complex without relying solely on Grant's flashlight. The lenses also allowed them to check rooms without using light and hence alerting anyone who may possibly still be present.

There was no need. The complex was entirely empty. The single corridor and dozen rooms were scattered with the skeletal remains of long-dead people, soldiers and scientists, their identities forgotten, along with the frail bones of dead birds that had found their way through gaps in the grating years before, but nothing living remained.

Finally they made their way to an unassuming office

that Kane had quickly scanned on the first run through the complex, and the ex-Mags took places at two seats that were arranged before a wide desk located before the far wall while Brigid perched on a corner of the desk itself, facing them.

Grant pushed the dark glasses from his nose, leaving them propped in his cropped, dark hair before advising the others that he was going to switch the xenon beam on again. The others copied him, removing their lenses so that the powerful light wouldn't dazzle them and, after blinking back the abrupt change in light for a moment, looked around the room.

It was a small box, three times as big as the desk but with a line of metal filing cabinets across one wall. The walls were painted an austere shade of dusty white, either dusty from time or from a conscious decision to suck any life or character from the environment. In strange contrast, a Persian rug lay across the floor of the room, the only concession to color other than the washed-out gold of the beech-wood desk and a single metal sign that hung from the wall behind it. The metal sign was a gold color, and crafted into the shape of a shield with a screw-handled, thick-bladed sword drawn down its center like a pendulum. A five-pronged star with the familiar hammer-and-sickle symbol was placed atop the sword, and a molded red ribbon across the lower third of the shield, beneath the star, showed two words in bold gold lettering.

Brigid translated the words that ran across the red ribbon: "Cheka-KGB."

Chapter 7

"At least we're in the right place," Grant began after a long moment's silence.

Kane nodded as he rose from his chair and stepped closer to examine the shield emblem. He reached forward, rocking the shield on its hook. It was fashioned from brass, heavy and a little more than a foot in height from sword tip to hilt, perhaps ten inches at its widest point on the carved red ribbon. "Nice," he muttered.

"It's a fair assumption," Brigid said, her voice seeming too loud in the still room, "that this is the Project Chernobog HQ. All the indicators brought us here, so there's no reason to suspect otherwise."

"Which means," Grant stated, "this Death Cry thing is somewhere around here."

Brigid looked sternly from Grant to Kane. "If it was ever constructed," she reminded them.

Kane stepped back from the brass shield and addressed the others. "Order of priorities. One, find the exit—not the vent, the actual door that these people would have used. I want to find out if it's usable and make sure it's secure. Two, thorough search of the whole bunker to find this superweapon if it's here. Nothing leaped out at me on first scout through the rooms, but that doesn't mean anything. Hidden rooms, safes, could be there's another sublevel below us. We check every option, however slim. Three, Baptiste—I know you're itching to take a rummage through these old files…"

Brigid nodded. "They should provide more information on whatever was being conducted here, and probably give indicators on the status and final location of the Death Cry."

Grant smiled. "Oh, you can take the librarian out of the library…" he teased.

"Yeah, yeah." Brigid waved him away. "This paperwork could be the most crucial find in here, remember."

Kane flipped the dark lenses back over his eyes and walked across to the door with Grant beside him. "Leave the light for her to work by," he told his partner, "while you and I nose around a little." He produced two microlights from his satchel, handing one to Grant. These were smaller than Grant's xenon flashlight, just a little thicker than a pen, but they provided enough light for detailed examination work.

Grant pushed his own glasses back onto the bridge of his nose and followed Kane out of the claustrophobic, poky, underground office.

The twelve rooms of the underground complex were arranged on either side of a single long corridor. The corridor was narrow, just wide enough to allow for Grant and Kane to walk side by side with its ceiling mere inches above Grant's head. The majority of the rooms were small boxes with rudimentary ventilation units visible in their far walls. At the farthest end were two larger rooms, one on each side of the corridor. One was the canteen and the other a communal sleeping quarters crammed with a dozen bunk beds. The bunk beds contained a number of skeletons, many of them still fully clothed in Red Army uniforms.

One room toward the lower end of the complex was jammed to the ceiling with an old gas-burning generator. Once upon a time, this had provided all the heat and power that the little underground facility required, but when Kane searched around the room with his microlight he found that there was no fuel left to run the generator. They would have to continue working in darkness, relying on the electrochemical polymer lenses and whatever lights they carried with them.

The long corridor included several breaks where a small flight of three or four stairs led down, and Kane had the feeling that the whole complex was built at a subtle incline. The larger rooms of the canteen and sleeping quarters were at the lowest part of the small bunker complex; hence they were deeper into the mountain.

Grant examined the rooms flaring off at the opposite end of the corridor, reasoning that higher ground was the most likely location for the entry door. He found the door, but it had been bricked up as though someone inside was scared of someone or something getting through. He showed it to Kane and they concluded that it was too impractical to remove the bricks and that they would continue to use the large ventilation shaft to enter and exit the redoubt.

"Besides which," Grant added, "this is about as damn secure as we could make it short of planting mines." The bricked-up door itself was wide and the room had an especially high ceiling, just big enough to house a single army transport truck.

The large ventilation shaft that they had used to enter the bunker ran parallel to and slightly above the main corridor. Kane realized that the floor of the ventilation shaft had been built at an angle, allowing a steady flow of air into the complex but guiding rainwater away. It was a simple and elegant solution to the problem of continuously providing air to an underground facility, requiring no moving parts or any great complexity of construction.

The remainder of the cramped, low-ceilinged rooms appeared to have been dedicated to research in various forms. There were several testing areas, including a small rifle range and a modest armory, but nothing to suggest the mysterious Death Cry weapon.

"Nothing of value," Kane concluded when they finished checking the bunks for a third time. "No hidden doors, no false walls, no trapdoors."

"You think it's a bust?" Grant rumbled sourly.

Kane shook his head, absently running a dirt-smeared hand through his hair. "Baptiste has had three hours with the files," he said. "She should have stumbled on something by now."

When they returned to the office with the Cheka-KGB shield on the wall, they found Brigid sitting at the desk amid stacks of card-covered files. She had tied Grant's high-power xenon beam to the light fixture in the center of the ceiling where its incandescence served to illuminate the whole of the small office. There was no computer in the room, Kane realized when he reentered, and he hadn't seen one in the whole complex, which implied that the Soviets there were used to doing things the old-fashioned way. Having been party to more than one computer-hacking project in his time, Kane could readily appreciate the higher level of security protocol that would be observed by this seemingly laborious way of storing information. If you wanted a copy of a file, you sat down and made one.

"Sit down, make yourselves at home," Brigid said, briefly peering at them over the rims of her reading glasses.

Grant and Kane both looked at the two free chairs that faced the desk, now piled high with brown envelopes and cardboard folders, before turning back to Brigid. "Can we touch anything?" Grant asked tentatively.

Brigid looked up again from the paperwork that she had buried her nose in. "No, don't touch any of the files. There's an order to this stuff, and I need to keep it just so."

Kane looked down at the faded Persian rug, a mandala pattern, blue-and-gold thread interweaved with specks of green and red, and lowered himself down to sit cross-legged. Grant picked up his Copperhead close-assault subgun and took up a post by the door, leaning on the frame and examining the Copperhead's breech to make sure it was free of debris.

"So," Kane began after a moment, "what have you found so far?"

Brigid didn't bother looking up from her reading, and Kane saw the familiar hammer and sickle along with another representation of the Cheka shield stamped across the front of document she was immersed in. "You first," she said.

"Skeletons and dust," Kane told her. "That about sums it up. And the original exit's been sealed with bricks. Short of using explosives, we couldn't shift them if we wanted to."

"Handy," Brigid offered with a sarcastic edge to her voice. She put the file she was reading to one side, flattening out the page she was on with the heel of her hand before addressing Kane and Grant. "There's a lot of information here alluding to the Chernobog Project, but nothing very concrete about what they were actually developing."

"No Death Cry?" Grant asked.

"Not even a whimper." Brigid shrugged. "That doesn't mean it's not here, though. The Chekists were obsessive bureaucrats. Sure, they'd make you parade around your village naked in subzero temperatures if they thought you were a counterrevolutionary, but they made sure that they had a form filled in and filed in triplicate regarding the whole incident, including your time of death."

"That must have been very reassuring," Kane grunted.

"My point is," Brigid continued, "there's a lot of information here about how many staples and rubber-tipped pencils the Cheka required for this facility. And I mean *a lot.* I'm wading through that as quickly as I can, but without a computer version of these files I've got to do it manually and that means at least skimming every file here."

"Sucks to speak Russian." Kane grinned, rising from the floor. "We'll leave you to it."

"Not so fast," Brigid called as Kane stepped toward the door. She quickly wrote down two words on a piece of paper and copied it a second time, handing one sheet to Grant and the other to Kane. "These are the Russian words for 'weapon' and the word I translated as 'Death Cry.' You big, strong men of action are going to grab a pile of folders each and start scanning every single document for these words. If you see them mentioned in a file, I want you to put it to one side—" she gestured to an empty space on the floor by the wall "—where I can then go through them more fully to see what you've found."

Kane made a telephone sign with his outstretched thumb and pinkie finger and smiled. "I need to check in with Lakesh first, but I'm sure Grant will be only too pleased to brush up on his Russian. Isn't that right, *tovarishch?*"

Grant growled something under his breath as Kane stepped past him through the open door. Looking behind him as he left the little office, Kane saw that, despite his protest, Grant was already taking instructions from Brigid about which stack of files to start work on.

Ambling along the narrow, low-ceilinged corridor, Kane called the Cerberus ops center over the Commtact but received no response. "Kane to Cerberus," he called again, running a finger lightly across the Commtact to make sure that the pintels were connected.

After an excruciatingly long ten seconds, Donald Bry's

voice came through Kane's skull. "…just barely," it began before fading out.

Kane immediately realized that there was a problem with reception there in the underground redoubt. He began to jog along the corridor, repeating his hail and waiting a few seconds for any sign of response. He reached the room with the large ventilation shaft that had given the field team access to the complex.

"Grant, Baptiste, can you hear me?" he asked as he clambered into the shaft.

"…ceiving you," Grant's voice replied over the Commtact.

"Communications problem," Kane explained. "I repeat—communications problem," he said slowly while he made his way along the slippery air shaft. "I'm heading to the surface to speak to Cerberus."

Grant's voice came over the Commtact a moment later, and Kane noticed that the rich bass of his friend's voice sounded distorted, as though it was being electronically filtered. "You're breaking up a little, but nothing we can't cope with. Take it easy, over."

"You, too," Kane said, jogging back to stand beneath the overhead, circular gap where they had cut through the grate. They had left a rappel cord hanging from the gap, anchored above with a climber's pick pushed into the soil. Kane tested its strength before weaving the thin rope through his hands. "I'm heading to the surface now, Cerberus. Are you receiving me?"

Donald Bry's voice came back to Kane once more, still broken and patchy.

Kane scrambled up the rope the fifteen feet to the surface.

IT WAS AFTER MIDNIGHT in the Cerberus redoubt. Lakesh tried to look reassuring as Donald Bry, along with several others in the ops room, turned to him, concerned expressions on their faces. They had all heard Kane's first message, breaking apart as it came over the speakers almost six minutes ago, and the level of anxiety was growing as further messages continued to be of erratic quality.

"Do you think they're okay?" Domi piped up from where she was sitting beside a stripped-down computer hard drive that Brewster Philboyd kept assuring Lakesh he was working at.

Lakesh held up a placating hand as a number of other voices began asking the same thing. "Now, now, everyone," he said loudly, "let's not worry ourselves over nothing." He pointed to a computer screen that displayed a map of Georgia, along with a delayed-image satellite feed showing the Caucasus Mountains. Three green blips regularly blinked on the map and on a separate overlay on the delayed feed, showing precisely where the members of the field team were. The subcutaneous transponders could also provide the Cerberus nerve center with a constant stream of information about an individual's health and well-being, including heart rate, blood pressure and brain-wave activity.

"Something in the mountain range or within the bunker that they are exploring is interfering with the communications, nothing more," Lakesh firmly assured everyone, his voice calm. "Let's everyone just sit down and wait for Kane to contact us properly."

Kane's familiar voice came over the communications array again. "Kane to Cerberus, do you read? Over."

"Loud and clear," Donald Bry said, relief in his voice. "What's the situation, Kane?"

"Everything normal," Kane explained after a short delay for the satellite to relay the message halfway around the world. "Looks like the bunker's screwing with our comms but I'm hearing you fine out here, so I think we're just going to have to maintain an involuntary radio silence for a little while and I'll check in every two hours."

Lakesh gave Bry the thumbs-up and Bry relayed the message to Kane. "What's the current state of play?" Bry added.

There was another pause while the signal caught up with Kane and relayed his response. "We've found an old Cheka base but no weapons as yet. Baptiste is sifting through the evidence we've found here—a load of old typed files, not computer. She seems to think this could be the place. Over."

"The location is certainly correct," Lakesh stated clearly in his mellifluous voice. "I suppose it's a question of whether any weapon was ever built." He looked at the computer screen showing the signals from the transponders and idly brought up Kane's biometric feed as he spoke to his friend. "Over," he added after a moment, realizing that he had left the communication—and Kane—hanging. The Cerberus personnel did not always adhere to the old protocol of radio communications, but in a situation such as this one, which involved extended satellite delays to the feed, it became necessary simply because of the impossibility of reacting to the other party's statements in real time.

"Fingers crossed, Lakesh," Kane replied cheerily. "I'm

going back down below. One of us will speak to you again in a couple of hours. I'm still receiving bits of your messages while I'm down there so, if anything urgent comes up, keep trying until one of us responds. Might not be able to make a lot of sense of what you're saying, but at least we'll know you're saying it. Over and out."

"Good hunting," Bry responded automatically. "Over and out."

WHEN KANE RETURNED to the office with the Cheka shield on the wall, he found Brigid poring studiously over the pages of a thick report while Grant sat at her elbow, watching.

Grant looked up at Kane's approach and a wide smile crossed his features. "Brigid thinks she's found something," he told Kane.

"That's great," he replied. "Something in this rabbit warren is messing with our communications. We're going to have to go topside every time we need to contact Cerberus.

"Good news, however, is very welcome," Kane added after a moment, giving Brigid the floor.

Brigid peered at him, showing him the report. Kane could see the now familiar Cheka shield printed in black on the top of the title page. The rest seemed to be a page of writing, but on closer inspection it contained a lot of letters that Kane was not familiar with; unsurprisingly, it was written in Russian.

"This here," Brigid explained, "purports to be the case notes of one Dr. Anastas Djugashvili on research into something that is referred to simply as Device One at this stage. These date from 1922, which means that the KGB would likely have taken over Project Chernobog that same year. I guess from the stamp on the front and from the old-style shield on the wall here, the Chernobog people were pretty attached to the old Cheka setup, though, almost like time stood still for them."

Grant and Kane both looked at each other and shook their heads. "Let's not have any more Operation Chronos–type stuff," Grant grumbled, referring to the prenukecaust U.S. government investigation of time travel, something that had plagued the Outlanders before now.

"I don't think it's anything like that," Brigid reassured them, "more that these people got very involved in their research. Of course, that was probably the sensible thing to do with these brutal government spooks watching your every move."

She paused and flicked through a few pages of the report. It seemed to be endless reams of tightly spaced type with only the occasional line break or underlined section to break the monotony. "According to Djugash-vili," Brigid continued, "Device One was a proposed weapon to use in combat against 'supraterrestrial elements considered disruptive to the Soviet way of life.'"

"Space aliens," Kane translated, and Brigid nodded.

"I've read only a little way into this report," Brigid explained, "and it's not what I was expecting."

"What were you expecting?" Grant asked Brigid, and Kane encouraged her to continue.

"The same thing you were," Brigid told him. "The same thing we all were, even Lakesh. A nuclear device.

Or a gene bomb. Or, I dunno, some kind of big—" She stopped, trying to think of the right words.

"A death ray?" Kane suggested.

"Yeah," Brigid agreed. "But this isn't about that. Dr. Djugashvili and his team weren't concerned so much with what the weapon was, only how they would store it."

"What if the weapon was developed somewhere else?" Kane pondered.

"That's possible," Brigid agreed, but she didn't sound convinced. "But that's not really what I'm getting at. Let me find the part I was reading a moment ago," she told them, flicking through pages of the report before stopping about a quarter of the way through the file and running her finger over the words she found there. "It says, translating quickly here, that the problem with the supraterrestrial threat is that these creatures have displayed increased mental capacities. To create Device One in any established locale would potentially be to give the item directly over to their top thinkers…top brains. I don't quite know what this means here. What Djugashvili seems to be saying is that there's no location within Russia that would be safe to hide such a weapon."

"So we've come a long way to pick up a report?" Kane asked.

"No," Brigid insisted, "there's more to it than that. This is an examination of where you hide something from someone with ESP. How do you hide a weapon from someone who can read your mind?"

Chapter 8

It was early morning in Montana, just after dawn, and Mohandas Lakesh Singh sat by himself in the cafeteria, idly tapping a pen against the notebook before him, upon which was written a single problem in his own hand. Eight or nine other people were scattered about the cafeteria, sitting in groups or alone, readying themselves for the day or just coming off a long night shift. Lakesh himself had been up the whole night, presiding over operations in the ops center and absorbing the reports that were coming in from Georgia.

Kane's third report, received almost an hour ago, continued to address the dilemma of how to hide an item from a mind reader. The top sheet of Lakesh's pad showed a simple diagram of two stick figures along with a box. One stick man stood beside the box, upon which was written "Device One." Though drawn simply, the other stick man was clearly shorter and had a bulbous head with large, beadlike eyes—Lakesh had automatically drawn the classic "gray" alien design to represent a mind reader. Several arrows had been sketched and crossed through on the illustration, and a number of notes had been written along the side in Lakesh's precise hand, several of which had also been scored through. Across the top of the single sheet of paper Lakesh had written the following: "Q: How do you hide Device One from mind reader?"

He continued to tap the top of his pen against the notepad as he reread the question and took a sip of the cooling mug of tea that sat before him beside a plate of toast and fruit preserves.

Further sections of Djugashvili's report had referred to Device Two, although no details had been given. Brigid reported her impression that Device One had stalled at the planning stage, but concluded that details of this had to exist only in a separate file. Grant and Kane were, by Kane's own account, working their way through the mountain of paperwork as best they could to speed the discovery process.

As he sat there, the rich vapors of the steeping tea swirling in his nostrils, Lakesh became aware of a presence before him. He looked up and saw that Clem Bryant, one of the Manitius Moon Base refugees, was standing at the side of the table and looking at the sketch on Lakesh's notebook.

"Good morning, Mr. Bryant," Lakesh said, offering a friendly smile as he caught the man's attention.

"Good morning, Dr. Singh," Bryant said amiably, turning his attention away from the notepad to address the Cerberus leader. Bryant was a quiet, intelligent man in his late thirties. He had dark hair swept back from a high forehead, a trimmed goatee and intelligent blue eyes. His discipline was oceanography, and he had been part of the scientific brain trust that had been placed in cryogenic suspension before the nukecaust. However, upon arriving at Cerberus, Bryant had shown little interest in ocean studies, preferring to devote his time to helping in the cafeteria.

However, Clem Bryant was still very much a scientist. In his quieter moments, he could often be found working on a logic problem that he had found in an old book or newspaper, a mathematical question, a chess puzzle or a crossword. He was, in short, an obsessive thinker.

"Do you mind if I ask what it is you are working on, Dr. Singh?" Bryant asked in his sure, refined voice.

"Not at all," Lakesh said, standing to offer Bryant a seat. "Why don't you join me while things here are quiet. I'd very much value your opinion, Clem."

Clem Bryant insisted on fetching more tea for Lakesh, as well as a cup for himself, before he took a seat at the table.

"What we have here is a real logic problem," Lakesh explained. "The question that's been posed is how do you hide an item when your opponent is a mind reader?"

"Hmm," Clem Bryant said, "quite the conundrum. It seems to me that the question is flawed."

Lakesh looked at the ex-oceanographer, a frown creasing his brow. "How so?" he asked.

"It's a lateral thinking problem. The question is not *how* do you hide something from a mind reader, but rather *where*."

"Do go on," Lakesh encouraged, trying to follow the man's stream of logic.

"One has to assume," Bryant stated, "that any mind reader worth his salt would be able to extract the information from one's mind automatically. Thus the hiding place itself could never be kept secret."

"What about brainwashing?" Lakesh proposed. "Such techniques have been used by various government agencies across the globe before the nukecaust."

"Erasing the location from an individual's mind," Bryant pondered, taking a thoughtful sip from his tea. "It's conceivable, of course, but it would rather seem to defeat the purpose of the exercise. Rather like a squirrel who can't find the nuts he's buried for the winter." He laughed. "Besides which, brainwashing can be broken under hypnosis. Even if the subject himself isn't aware of it, the information generally still exists somewhere in the human mind. Memory is a very tricky thing. And if one's opponent can read minds, well…" Bryant concluded, holding his hands open to suggest that anything was possible.

"Which leads us back to the question of how you hide your item from a mind reader," Lakesh prompted after a moment's consideration.

"*Where* you hide the item," Bryant amended once more. "The how is a false lead, Doctor, a blind alley of semantics."

"Okay," Lakesh asked, grinning as the man opposite him warmed to the subject, "where, then?"

"You hide the item in the same place you hide the cookie jar from a child," Bryant said, smiling, "on a higher shelf. *Quod erat demonstrandum.*"

"So," Lakesh said with a smile, "if our mind reader is five feet tall we need to find a shelf that's—"

"Seven feet high," Bryant supplied.

"Which means," Lakesh continued, "we need to find a location that, hypothetically, our aliens couldn't reach."

"Aliens, Dr. Singh?" Bryant asked, raising an eyebrow.

"Theoretical aliens, in this case," Lakesh supplied. "This problem concerns a Soviet project revolving around the design and storage of a weapon for use against potential alien interference."

"You need to find somewhere that aliens can't reach even if they know it's there."

"Which would be where?" Lakesh wondered.

Clem Bryant ran his thumb and index finger thoughtfully over his beard as Lakesh thanked him and made his way back to the ops center.

THEY CALLED IT the Dreaming, and it was a place that their ancestors had been mapping from time beyond reckoning.

Rabbit in the Moon could hear the subtle droning of the outside world as he scouted the dark shadows of the Dreaming, stalking his prey. Good Father was spinning his bull roarer, generating the noise that granted full access to this place while still conscious. It was not lucid dreaming; it was exploring the dreamworld while thoroughly awake. Less than one hundred years earlier, such an exploration had been impossible.

They were original men, the originals, what the invaders had called Aborigines when they had arrived more than four hundred years before. The original men had always had a profound comprehension of time. The Dreamtime was the real world, the place where all of the connections were clear, where the fragile web that made up the world could be observed most clearly. And then there was subjective time, that strange sufferance that those awake had to endure and navigate, whose order became jumbled by its own linearity and the waker's often naive, sometimes selfish interpretations.

The nukecaust had done little to change the original men, but it had opened up the old sacred sites where the invaders had constructed their military bases, their temples to war.

It was in one of these temples, so the story went, that Good Father and Bad Father had found the item they had named the Dreamslicer, back when they were young men. It had taken some exploration, and one story told how Good Father had needed to walk with a stick for a long time after the trials. It was true that he still walked with a limp if you watched him closely, but they had discovered ways to use the Dreamslicer to their benefit, ways that allowed for full exploration of the Dreaming. Of course, the tribal elders had not been Good Father and Bad Father then; those names had come later, after the scope of their discovery had been realized.

Rabbit in the Moon spun suddenly as something brushed past him, and he turned to see Cloud Singer leaping across the great, flat expanse of the Dreaming, spinning through the air as she drilled her left fist toward his jaw. He ducked at the last second, watching as she flew past him, shock flashing across her features.

As she passed, Rabbit in the Moon's hand whipped up, snagging her trail of long, black hair. He twisted the hand, yanking Cloud Singer's head back, and both of them howled with rage and pain.

Suddenly they were back in Realworld, the small campfire burning atop the high cliff beneath the night stars, their tribe watching as the battle continued. The sound of the bull roarer—a cuplike object on the end of a long length of cord—droned through the air as Good Father spun it high over his head in a continuing circle. So long as it droned, Rabbit in the Moon knew, they could slip back into the Dreaming and fight across both levels of consciousness at the same time.

Rabbit in the Moon pulled hard on the handful of hair he had snagged in the Dreaming, yanking Cloud Singer down to the ground, her face scant inches from the spitting logs of the fire. "Yield," he instructed her. "Yield or I'll burn your face."

He felt her stiffen in his grip as he pushed her face closer to the flames. Suddenly there was that telltale feeling as she seemed to spin, like a leaf in the wind, and then she was gone, rolling back into the Dreaming, leaving Rabbit in the Moon toppling forward with nothing but the few strands of her black hair that he managed to hold on to.

He blinked, willing himself back into the Dreaming himself, feeling the fluttering at the back of his skull as the implant fired him across the breach. She was waiting for him, and he leaped out of the way as she fired a vicious snap-kick at his face. She followed with another kick, this one aimed at his groin, missed and clipped his leg, and he felt the pain lance through him like winter night.

Rabbit in the Moon leaped high, looking for the stars of the night sky above them, snagging one in his hand and throwing it back down to Earth. It screamed as it hurtled through the air, expanding into a colossal thing of burning brightness, shattering into shards as it met the ground.

Rabbit in the Moon landed, keeping his center of gravity low, and looked around as the remnants of the star burned out. Cloud Singer was nowhere to be seen; the falling star had clearly missed her. He looked at his hand then, checking to see the ugly burn of puckered skin where he had touched the star, willing it back to smoothness before the wound took hold in Realworld.

He ran across the desolate, open plain of the Dreaming, leaving the sound of the bull roarer behind him before he stepped into Realworld once more. The tribespeople were still there, poised around the campfire, waiting for the next move of the combatants. Cloud Singer was there, too, standing beside the fire, scanning the area for his reappearance. He ran across the cliff toward her, head down, fists pumping, the ends of his headband fluttering in the wind.

She laughed as she saw him approach, and he noted that Rock Streaming had come to join the other spectators, freed from his work at the computer terminal in the cave. Rock Streaming had been working solidly for eight days, tracing the satellite links across the heavens and the Earth below. His appearance there tonight indicated progress in his endeavors.

Then Cloud Singer was upon him once more, her legs snapping high as she drove rapid kicks in his direction. She was dressed in long, loose shorts with a strip of white material over her breasts, leaving her tattoos proudly on show. Her bare feet scuffed across the sand atop the cliff, kicking it at his eyes as he backed away toward the cliff edge.

Rabbit in the Moon took two hard kicks to the chest, grunting in pain, and Cloud Singer laughed, a brisk single note of triumph, as she launched a roundhouse punch at his face. Suddenly Rabbit in the Moon dropped, and Cloud Singer's punch swung long, missing his head and toppling her toward the sheer drop of the cliff. Lying beneath her, Rabbit in the Moon kicked out, sweeping her feet from under her and dropping her next to him. With a brutal punch, he snapped her head into the ground and she cried out in pain. "Yield," he told her again as he held her face in the dirt.

Slowly, reluctantly, a whimper came from Cloud Singer and her head nodded where he held it on the ground. Rabbit in the Moon looked over his shoulder to where Good Father and Bad Father stood, awaiting their final judgment. They both nodded once, in turn, before he released his opponent.

Good Father's bull roarer stopped spinning. All around, the tribe applauded and came over to congratulate Rabbit in the Moon as he walked across to the far side of the campfire.

With the exhibition match over, he made a beeline to Rock Streaming. "What news, brother?" he asked in a quiet, conspiratorial voice.

Rock Streaming kept his voice low as he spoke, restrained fury in his eyes. "They have found something in a place called Georgia, Russia," he told Rabbit in the Moon. "Something we would want."

Rabbit in the Moon looked at his colleague, encouraging him to say more.

"A weapon," Rock Streaming said under his breath. "Gather the elders," he added before turning away and returning to the cave beneath the cliffs.

"THIS IS CRAZY," Kane grumbled as he tossed another file on the growing stack beside the door of the Cheka-KGB office. "How do you find something that isn't there?"

"You need to get more Zen in your life," Grant admonished him.

"You listen to Shizuka too much," Kane retorted. "Look, guys, there is no secret weapon. No Death Cry. It's all a big joke. Spies playing tricks on other spies, cloak-and-dagger bullshit to fool the enemy."

Brigid looked up from the report that she was working through, the third that she had found with references to Devices One and Two, along with a single reference to a Device Four. "We need to be absolutely certain, Kane," she told him in a calm voice.

"I am certain," he blurted. "There's nowhere in this complex for the damn Russkies to have hidden this thing, and no amount of reading their reports is going to change that. Fact."

"Facts are tricky things," Brigid told him.

"And what's that supposed to mean?" Kane asked, anger rising in his voice.

"It means I think I'm onto something," she replied, "but I'm not quite sure what it is. Listen to this." She began reading from the report she was holding: "'With the use of ESP mapping Dr. Krylova has located a region dubbed Krylograd by her staff. Krylograd would seemingly contain enough empty space to contain Device Two, based on current projected size estimate.'" Brigid looked up from the report, the trace of a smile on her lips.

"Well, that was real pretty, but what does it mean?" Grant asked her.

"I think, if they made this device, whatever number it is, then they may have hidden it where no one was likely to stumble upon it—on a different level of human consciousness."

"Which is exactly what Lakesh was suggesting, I guess," Kane said, "when he spoke about the idea of the high shelf. If what you say is true, then the Archons or whoever would have difficulty locating or accessing such a region, right?"

Brigid nodded. "Presumably," she agreed. "But how are we supposed to find a room hidden in the human consciousness?"

Grant let out a low whistle and the others turned to him hopefully. "Well, don't look at me," he told them.

Chapter 9

Kane exhaled a long breath that he hadn't realized he had been holding.

"Yeah," Grant agreed with a chuckle, "it's kinda like that, isn't it?"

"Well, Baptiste," Kane asked, "you want to add anything else?"

Brigid's eyes flicked over the report in her hand for a moment before she placed it on the desk before her and addressed Kane and Grant. "It sounds incredible, but the idea that the Soviets were exploring different levels of consciousness isn't so outlandish as it first appears. There's plenty of evidence to suggest that the Russian military was well advanced in the exploration of psychic phenomena with an eye to application."

"But," Kane said, shaking his head, "hiding weapons in the human brain?"

"Not the human brain," Brigid explained. "This is about hiding something in a higher level of human consciousness. Bear in mind that, as a rule, the average human uses ten percent of his or her brain capacity at any one time, twelve at most. Things like entering trances and meditation are about accessing faculties that one was previously unaware of. Where does the mind go when you enter a coma, for instance?"

"I see what you mean," Grant commented. "If this meditation part of the brain is actually a physical area, then in theory you could hide whatever the hell you wanted in there. Right?"

"I think so," Brigid said, glancing over the report again.

Kane looked at them both before he spoke. "So we all meditate, pick up the Death Cry, come back to Earth. Job done."

"Not as easy as that, Kane," Brigid explained. "You don't just 'meditate' and find this place."

"Assuming it exists," Grant added quietly.

"You would need to know what you were meditating on, how to get there, where to look," Brigid told them. "You need to meditate on the right wavelength, if you see what I mean. Otherwise you're looking for needles in haystacks."

"You're talking about a key," Kane declared after a moment's thought. "A key to open the right door. Only this time the door's in your head."

"Theoretically, it's in everyone's head if only they knew how to get there," Brigid said, nodding.

Kane smiled grimly. "Keys I understand," he told Brigid. "So we look for this key and…what would it look like?"

Brigid shrugged. "How would I know?"

"It doesn't say anything in the report?" Kane urged.

"Nothing yet, but it could be in here." She gestured around at the numerous piles of paperwork that littered the room. "It could be in any of these files. Or in none of them."

"We keep on looking, then," Kane said firmly.

He checked his wrist chron and saw that it was almost

time to make his report. "One of us should contact Cerberus again," he told his colleagues.

"I'll do it," Brigid volunteered. "I'd like to bring Lakesh up to speed and I'd appreciate his advice on how we go about finding this key, as you called it. Besides which, I could do with some fresh air. Been cooped up in here for too long."

"Sure have," Grant grumbled. It had been six hours since he had been outside the facility. "Can't imagine what it was like for the poor bastards who worked here day in, day out."

Kane encouraged Brigid, pointing his thumb at the open door to the office. "Okay, people, let's keep moving. The sooner we get back to work the sooner we can go home."

BRIGID STOOD ABOVE THE underground bunker, looking up at the clear night sky as she spoke to Lakesh over the Commtact.

"It sounds incredible, Brigid," Lakesh enthused. "I dearly wish I could be there with you. Over."

"Well, all we've found so far are some dusty old files and a load of skeletons," she told him. "Over."

Lakesh's voice was almost childlike with wonder. "But a superweapon hidden inside a higher level of human consciousness. That's a truly radical concept. When Clem Bryant proposed the idea of the high shelf for the cookie jar, I certainly didn't think it would be anything quite so…ethereal." Lakesh was speaking so quickly that he was tripping over his words, desperate as he was to get all the information across. "Please, Brigid, do report in as soon as you find anything else. This is fascinating, quite fascinating.

"Have there been any other developments?" he added a few moments later. "Over."

"Nothing to speak of," Brigid replied. "We're out here, all alone in the mountains." She looked around her. "It's actually quite beautiful. The sky's a glorious indigo with moonlight sprinkling over the mountains. Be a nice place for a vacation. Over."

"We can talk about vacations when you get back," Lakesh chastised her in a friendly manner after the usual pause. "Take care of yourselves. Over and out."

"Over and out," she repeated with a nod. It really was beautiful out there, Brigid thought as she made her way back into the bunker. The croaks and chirrups of nocturnal animals could be heard faintly, along with the occasional barking of a wolf from far off. It felt so empty, only the little sentry station, the abandoned military truck and the Mantas, sitting low to the ground, giving any indication that anyone might be about. In the moonlight, it was easy to pretend that those things weren't there, that Brigid Baptiste was alone in the world.

"COULD SUCH A WEAPON really exist?" Cloud Singer asked timidly once she was certain that the communication broadcast had ended.

Bad Father shot a piercing glare at her. "Foolish girl," he muttered. "Sixteen years of age and half as wise."

She bowed her head, feeling ashamed as the other tribespeople in the cave looked at her. Besides Bad Father and herself, five other people were in the room. Good Father stood beside Bad Father, the bull roarer now tucked back inside the waistband of his loincloth. Rabbit in the Moon stood at his shoulder, his bare chest showing displays of tribal tattoos, combat pants slung low around his waist. Standing next to Rabbit in the Moon was the youngest member of the crew, the fifteen-year-old man-child currently known as Neverwalk but still waiting for confirmation of his adult title from Good Father. To the back of the cave, the assassin who moved like a ghost waited patiently, listening to the discussion but distancing herself from it. The assassin scared and fascinated Cloud Singer, but the woman kept to herself, letting none of the tribe get close. Finally, crouching on his haunches beside the glowing laptop screen, Rock Streaming gazed at the others, waiting for everyone's reactions. "Well?" he asked.

"A weapon that exists on a higher plane of consciousness is one that can be activated on a higher plane of consciousness, as well," the assassin spoke from the shadows of the cave, her soft voice carrying eerily through the enclosed space.

"The assassin is right," Bad Father said in his rumbling thunder voice. "With this and the Dreamslicer, we could establish the new territories and carve the world up for the original tribe."

"But how would we take it?" Rabbit in the Moon asked.

"By force," Neverwalk chirped, slapping a fist into his open palm.

"He's right." Good Father nodded. "Force is the surest way to gain this Death Cry that they speak of."

Cloud Singer looked at the elders, feeling the nagging question still in her mind. "But I don't understand," she said finally, bringing all her courage to bear. "How can

not-original man have made such a thing? You told us that
they had no understanding of the Dreaming, they lived
their lives only in Realworld."

Good Father smiled benevolently as he favored the
young woman with an explanation. Just one summer ago
he had been her mentor, before she had taken the warrior
vows and her final name. "Before the Little Bang That
Changed Everything, the world was a confusing place.
Other tribes, not original men but others, would explore
things they did not understand in their quest to find new
ways to hurt each other and hasten the destruction of the
world about them. The Dreamslicer, you must recall, is
their invention, not ours. They merely failed to understand
its purest application, thinking that movement from one
place to another was all important, not realizing that the
true majesty was in the getting there—the stepping
outside of worlds."

"What did they call the Dreamslicer, Good Father?"
Cloud Singer asked. "You told me once, but the name
seemed so silly that I forget."

Good Father nodded sagely. "They called it a man's
name—mat-trans," he said quietly, before turning his attention to Rock Streaming at the laptop.

"Using the Dreamslicer," Rock Streaming explained,
"we could be to Georgia in the time it takes to think—"

"No." Bad Father shook his head. "That's a three-
dream minimum, Rock Streaming. The Dreamslicer
could not handle the full journey in one step."

"Even so," Rock Streaming urged, "this is an ideal
chance to show our hand and take what we need."

"Monitor the communiqués," Bad Father said slowly.

"Make sure that they have the item in question, this Death Cry, before we take action."

"For the moment," Good Father added, "the strike force is to remain on high alert in readiness." He looked at every person in the cave with a fierce expression that brooked no questions.

With that, Good Father and Bad Father exited the cave, leaving the younger members of the strike team to ponder what would happen next.

Chapter 10

When Brigid returned to the Cheka-KGB office, Kane and Grant were on the floor, probing at the concrete and listening to the echoes as they rapped their knuckles against different sections of the room. Kane had rolled back the colorful Persian rug and wedged it by the filing cabinets. There was a patch of shiny, clean floor where it had lain.

"What's going on?" Brigid asked as the two men searched the floor.

"Started wondering about a second level to the base," Grant explained. "Thought there might be a trapdoor in here or something."

"A basement," Kane added. "Or maybe a subbasement."

Brigid looked at the stacks of paperwork awaiting scrutiny. It seemed unlikely a second level had escaped their initial search, but she could understand Kane's and Grant's frustration and inherent need to be doing something.

"Lakesh is ecstatic at our progress," she told them as she returned to the chair behind the wide desk stacked with manila folders.

Kane glanced up from the clean area of the floor. "That's something," he said amiably, before running his hands across the floor again. "There's nothing here. I had hoped maybe the desk or the rug had been used to hide a trapdoor."

"And we checked behind the cabinets for a hidden treasure trove of paperwork," Grant explained, "but there's no safe there or tucked away behind the shield on the wall."

"It's more esoteric than that," Brigid assured them, scanning the untidy room, "but it pays to check." She picked up the report before her and started skipping over the pages until she found the section about Krylograd, the mapped area of hidden human consciousness.

"Well," Kane grunted as he brushed the dirt from his hands and stood up, "someone must have written down the mental wavelength, or whatever you want to call it, that gives access to this secret room."

Brigid nodded, reaching in her pocket for her spectacles. She sighed as she pushed the glasses onto her nose, taking in Kane and the mess that they had all made of the office. Files were stacked on every surface now, and Kane had wedged the rolled-up Persian rug in the corner using an open drawer from a filing cabinet. As Brigid looked at the rolled-up rug for a moment, a smile suddenly crossed her lips and she almost laughed.

"What is it, Baptiste?" Kane asked, noticing her change of expression.

"The rug," she said. "Gosh, but we've been dumb."

She jumped out of her seat and walked across to the carpet, with Kane and Grant watching, perplexed. Carefully, Brigid unfolded a corner of the rug and examined it, her smile widening.

"What?" Grant asked. "Is there something written in the weave?"

"No," Brigid answered. "The whole design of the rug is a mandala."

Kane helped Brigid unfurl the carpet and lay it flat across the floor. Though the carpet was soiled, the vibrant design was still clear. A series of expanding golden circles and squares originated from the central point of the rug. The gold design rested on a blue background, which had probably been the color of the sky when it was weaved, though it had taken a darker color thanks to the mistreatment it had suffered over the intervening years. The design was phenomenally intricate, clearly the work of many long hours on the loom. There were smaller branches showing in different colors, and the main gold-and-blue design was highlighted in regular spots with different shades of green and red.

"Quite a work of art." Grant nodded appreciably.

"Looks like one of those Julia things that Lakesh was looking at a while back," Kane added thoughtfully.

"A Julia set," Brigid confirmed. "A mathematical extrapolation interpreted as a regular, repeating pattern of shapes coming from a central core. You're right, it's very similar, though its origin is quite different.

"The mandala is an integrated structure organized around a unifying center," she told them. "They exist in nature, as well as man-made, like this one. Generally, mandalas were a plan, a chart or geometric pattern that was supposed to represent the cosmos metaphysically, showing the universe from the perspective of man. A number of religions have used mandalas as a part of their practice for untold thousands of years."

"What do they use them for?" Kane asked.

"Meditation," Brigid told him. "Mandalas are a spiritual teaching tool, used as an aid to trance induction.

Tibetan monks, for example, would concentrate on and memorize every intricate detail of the mandala over a period of weeks or months."

Grant and Kane were both smiling now as they looked at the beautiful design on the Persian rug. "Have you just found our key?" Kane asked.

"I think so," Brigid said. "In theory, meditation on a particular mandala could set up a specific mental resonance, like using a tuning fork, only one attuned to Buddha, Allah or God."

"But the Russians have bastardized the concept," Kane suggested, "and turned it into a superweapon. Or at least a way of storing a superweapon."

"I guess the Communists weren't real big on the whole religion thing," Grant rumbled.

Kane leaned against the desk and admired the expanding pattern of squares and circles on the rug laid out before him. "You think they'd really just hide it here? In plain sight like this?"

"We walked right over it," Grant noted.

"If you hadn't moved it the way you did," Brigid said, "I doubt I'd have given it a second thought. It was there as the structure of the room, but you don't bother to look at things once you've seen them, you know?"

"So what do we do now?" Kane asked. "Concentrate on the mandala until we find enlightenment?"

"The way in which mandalas were used by the Tibetan monks," Brigid considered, "was to commit the design to memory. If that's the process required here, then we only need memorize the design to access this Krylograd region."

"But didn't you just say that took these monks weeks to do?" Grant said incredulously.

"Sometimes months." Brigid smiled. "But not too many of them had an eidetic memory like mine."

Kane laughed. "Oh, I knew we brought you along for something, Baptiste."

"Let's see if we can get the worst of the dirt and dust out of this thing before we start," Brigid decided, folding the carpet up on itself and lifting it from the cold concrete floor.

"I THINK YOU SHOULD TAKE a look at this," Donald Bry said as soon as Lakesh walked back into the Cerberus ops room.

Having worked through the night, Lakesh had just caught up on some sleep with a ninety-minute nap in his private quarters. He had reached a point where fatigue had set in and he promised himself a proper night's rest the very second the field team returned from Georgia. "For goodness' sake, Donald," Lakesh chided in a friendly manner, "at least let me sit down first."

Bry looked at him apologetically from his computer terminal. "I think this one's important."

Lakesh walked across the floor of the vast monitoring room until he stood before Bry's bank of terminals. The main monitor showed a continuously updated feed from the Keyhole comsat, with a stream of data covering conditions in western Russia and the old European territories that bordered Georgia. Bry, however, was sitting before a secondary monitor that sat to the side of his desk. On it, a sequence of data was marching gradually up the screen, the basic mechanics of the computer system itself, Lakesh realized after a second's look.

"Well," Lakesh asked, "what is it? What have you found?"

"I think we have a snooper," Bry explained, pointing to a section of code that was slowly working its way up the monitor. "See this here? That's a subroutine that has nothing to do with the communications protocols I set up when I achieved full access to the Keyhole comsat. I know this program like the back of my hand, Dr. Singh—I had to write it pretty much from scratch."

Lakesh nodded, reminded once more of how important every member of Cerberus had been to contributing to his vision.

"I had an inkling of suspicion about a week ago," Bry told Lakesh as they watched the strange piece of code disappear. "Something not quite right, a little flash on the screen like a breakdown in the signal for a billionth of a second, so slight I almost didn't see it. I put it down to tiredness. I was coming up to the end of my shift, and it had been an eventful day with the operation in North Dakota. But the more I tried to forget about it the more it nagged at me. Ultimately I decided to take the time to deconstruct and examine every line of operating code built into the system."

"Lucky you did," Lakesh assured him as the strange code reappeared as a suffix on one of the standard protocols at the bottom of the screen. "But what do you think it means?"

"Somebody else has tapped into the comsat," Bry said assuredly, "that much is clear. Why they're in our system, as well, I'm not sure, but we can probably assume it's nothing good. We may need to start thinking about what we say over supposedly secure channels from now on."

"That sounds like a wise precaution," Lakesh mused.

"Do you think you can trace back the code? Find out where it appeared from?"

Bry nodded slowly. "I can," he said, "but it won't be easy. This is a very subtle piece of programming, working as an adjunct to the main code."

"Like a virus?" Lakesh suggested.

"Far less invasive than that," Bry stated. "If I hadn't written the program myself, I doubt I would have recognized that anything untoward had happened. And if our hacker is half as good at hiding himself as he is at hiding code, well, it could take a very long time to track him down."

Lakesh nodded thoughtfully. "Assemble a team, work in shifts and make sure that you, Donald, get some sleep. I want a full report on this every two hours, either from you or your designated deputy."

Bry nodded in agreement. "I'll get myself some strong coffee and assemble a crew right away."

BRIGID SAT CROSS-LEGGED on the floor of the little office and stared at the mandala pattern on the carpet before her. They had beaten as much of the dust from the rug as they could, then hung it from two climbing hooks Grant had hammered into the ceiling. Kane and Grant had pushed the desk back against the wall to give Brigid room to sit down on the floor before the rug, and they took up chairs at the side of the room, watching her as she steadied her breathing and prepared to go into the trance.

This was a risky exercise, they knew. To some extent, all three of them hoped that it proved to be a fruitless exercise. The alternative, accessing a previously unvisited region of the human subconscious and finding the Death Cry doomsday device waiting there, seemed dangerous and threatening in the silent and unfamiliar surroundings of the hidden bunker.

Brigid sat quietly, slowing her breathing as she studied the beautiful pattern of concentric circles and interlocking golden squares before her. She knew that there were a number of ways to engage in meditation. Stilling the mind was a part of it, but a heightened awareness of physicality played a part, as well. The kundalini—the life force—could be raised during meditation, giving the subject increased focus in everyday matters.

The rebus of squares and circles seemed to swim before her eyes, its details merging, adding a depth to the image as though it were a portal, a tunnel stretching past the filing cabinets through the wall beyond.

She felt movement then, a flower opening at the base of her spine, a glowing, organic red throbbing at the core of her body. The logical, scientific part of her mind, divorced from the experience, realized that the feeling was her base chakra opening, the first step to enlightened meditation. She let the feeling of well-being wash through her, blossoming from the red flower at the pit of her spine.

The chakra located in her lower abdomen would be next, the orange-petaled chakra associated with reproduction. She let it unveil itself, immersing her in a wave of sensual intensity. She felt, for a scant few seconds, the mothering instinct within her, the desperate urge to hold the fruit of all that she believed in and fought for, all that she dreamed of.

She continued to look at the mandala as it swirled before her eyes. If it had ever been a picture weaved onto a rug, she could no longer remember. Its image had encircled her, blotting and extending into her peripheral vision, becoming her entire visual world.

The yellow chakra felt like a tiny sun as it burned beneath her navel, blossoming into a bright flame of incandescence. The intensity of the yellow flame was almost too much to bear, pulling from her solar plexus, and it made her feel as though she would fold into herself for a protracted instant. The solar plexus chakra ruled willpower, and Brigid had trouble allowing it to open, letting it chart a course without her. But she continued to stare at the fascinating picture before her eyes, and she let the chakra flower inside, filling her with her own, enviably strong kundalini.

Brigid recalled seeing an illustration of the seven chakras found in the human body, let the image drift from her mind and fall into the deep pool of the mandala that filled her eyes.

The fourth chakra was located in the heart, so still but so full of life. Brigid felt it twitch, its petals pulling apart reluctantly. The heart chakra controlled love and compassion, something that seemed to have little currency in the world that the Cerberus exiles inhabited.

OUTSIDE THE SMALL OFFICE, Grant kept his voice low as he spoke to Kane, fearing that he might disturb Brigid. He had silently indicated that he needed to speak to Kane and they had left the chairs and stepped from the room where Brigid continued to sink into a meditative trance. "You understand what's going on?" Grant asked.

Kane shrugged. "Meditating," he whispered.

"Yeah, that's what I figured," Grant said, peering back into the office. Brigid was perfectly still, her eyes wide, her breathing deep. Apart from her open eyes, she appeared to be asleep, sitting cross-legged in the middle of the low-ceilinged room. "Is it meant to take this long?"

Kane shrugged again, checking his wrist chron. "How long's it been? An hour?"

"Coming up for ninety minutes," Grant said, checking his own wrist chron. "Pretty soon one of us should check in with Lakesh, too."

"That's going to make a fascinating report," Kane said. "'So, Lakesh, Brigid's sitting on the floor looking at a rug.'"

WHEN SHE FELT the sixth chakra open, the indigo swirl in the middle of her forehead that felt like a third eye, Brigid almost shocked herself back into conscious awareness. It seared and burned like a blister, and she wanted to move, to pop it, to release the pressure.

She drew another regular breath and looked deeper into the pattern of the mandala, sinking inside it, feeling it envelop and cool her like a waterfall. The depth of the image was no longer an image at all. It was something physical, a corridor into the timeless space. And it had taken on a definite scent, a smell like freshly mowed grass in the height of summer, lush and full. It was so very inviting now. She wanted to step forward, to enter the corridor, to lose herself within the world of the mandala.

With a tingling like a pealing bell, something split the crown of her skull. The crown chakra was also called the many-petaled lotus, a violet-colored flower that spoke of enlightenment and mysticism. It didn't feel like a lotus to Brigid. It felt like a tiara, sparkling atop her head.

She felt taller now, taller than she had ever felt before, as if she could straddle the Earth. She realized that she was larger than her body; her physical limitations had been exceeded. Experimentally she flexed her hands and felt her fingertips and somehow beyond the tips. It was as if she were a light passed through a prism, split into the seven composite hues that made up the spectrum of Brigid Baptiste. She felt that she was more than those parts now, more than just the colors of the spectrum.

The seven multicolored buds within her body had flowered, each bringing a new intensity, a new level of experience. The chakras glowed and pulsed, glowed and pulsed.

Brigid looked ahead, narrowing her eyes as she tried to see the farthest point of the mandala, as she tried to see within, feeling like a runner in the starting blocks, poised to move forward. The mandala's pattern splashed into her, a breaking wave lapping against the headland of her body. But she could not see far enough. There was always further detail to take in, always more to the pattern of the square-circle-square tunnel.

With a decisive push, Brigid Baptiste stood up and entered the mandala.

Chapter 11

It was a familiar feeling, Brigid realized, familiar but long forgotten. The feeling you had when you let go of your mother's hand for the first time and wandered off. You turned and Mom wasn't there anymore, and you were kind of scared but mostly just excited, that fluttering of butterfly wings in your stomach.

She was standing but her eyes were closed. She felt her body, sensed it, flexing her fingers and wriggling her toes. She was back to normal, the same size as she had always been, no extensions beyond her normal limbs. And her feet were covered; she was wearing her boots.

She opened her eyes, the lids fluttering against the bright light, and looked down at her feet. Her tan-colored boots were there, scuffed toes and the chunky wedge heels, just as she remembered. Her denim jacket, too, over the shadow suit. Just as she remembered.

But the ground below her was no longer the painted concrete floor of the bunker. It was white, a pure white, like lightning. A bolt of lightning beneath her booted soles.

She looked up then, squinting as she adjusted to the brightness of her surroundings. She was in a corridor, ten feet from wall to wall, farther than her outstretched arms could reach. And the corridor walls were the same lightning-flash white, dazzling in their intensity.

There was nothing on the walls, nothing on the floor and, when she looked above, she saw that there was nothing on the lightning-colored ceiling, either. No markings, nothing. The ceiling was a long way above her, at least fifty feet. Despite the width of the corridor, the high ceiling made the space feel narrow, the proportions absurd.

Brigid took a single step forward and then looked behind her. There was a wall there, white like the rest of the corridor, and bulbous. A convex bud curving toward her. She reached out to it with her left hand and watched, in astonishment, as her hand sank painlessly through the wall. The way home, she realized. The corridor of the mandala had to be hidden behind the wall, awaiting her return.

She stepped forward once more, striding away from the wall and down the long, pure white corridor.

KANE AND GRANT SAT across from each other at one of the wooden tables in the empty, echoing canteen. They had found a pack of playing cards in one of the footlockers in the bunk room and they sat playing blackjack for spare ammo cases. It didn't matter who won; they had just gotten bored of waiting for Brigid to move or wake up.

The last time that Kane had checked on her, she was still sitting absolutely motionless before the hanging rug, her eyes closed and her breathing slow and deep. Five hours had passed since she had begun the meditation, and Kane had reported twice to Cerberus, taking advice from

Lakesh that they were not to disturb Brigid until the exercise was complete.

At one point, Grant and Kane had rested against the desk at the back of the office and tried staring at the mandala design on the hanging carpet themselves. After fifteen minutes, Grant had stifled a yawn and Kane had agreed that if this was enlightenment it was pretty damn boring.

"You think she's okay?" Grant asked as he dealt another hand.

Kane peered at his cards—a black seven and the king of hearts. Seventeen. "She had better be," he said, placing the cards facedown on the table's surface.

Grant checked his own hand. He held two aces and pondered whether to split them into separate hands before deciding to risk a five-card trick.

"The trouble is," Kane continued, "there's no way that we can monitor her."

"Cerberus still has the telemetrics," Grant reminded him. "They'd soon know if Brigid suffered any trauma."

"But where she is, what she's doing," Kane considered, "she's on her own. Anything could be happening to her right now and we'd never know."

"Busted," Grant wailed as he dealt out a queen atop the four cards he now had showing. "Forget about it, Kane. Let Brigid do her job. She can handle herself."

BRIGID WORKED HER WAY along the corridor for a long time. She took turns to explore both walls, but they contained no special qualities that she could discern—just solid walls, neither hot nor cold. Whatever made them glow like lightning didn't seem to be radiating any heat, as far as she could tell.

After about two hours, just walking forward, one foot in front of the other, Brigid came to a T-junction where her corridor ended at an intersecting corridor. She looked behind her and saw that strange convex wall was still there, perhaps a dozen steps away in spite of her seemingly long trek along the corridor. Something was either altering her perceptions or the nature of physicality in this place deviated from the norm.

Brigid stood there for a moment, considering the implications of that and listening hard for any sounds. All she could hear was her own breathing.

Warily she poked her head into the crosswise corridor and peered to her left. Nothing. Just another corridor, the same as the one she was in, approximately ten feet across with a ceiling high above, all of it finished in a glowing, liquid white sheen.

She turned to her right and looked straight into the barrel of an Automat held by a soldier dressed in the familiar Red Army uniform.

"End of the line, Comrade," the soldier drawled in a lackadaisical voice.

Brigid dropped to the floor, instinct taking over, and her booted right heel jabbed into the front of the soldier's leg, just below the knee. There was a loud crunch as it connected, and the soldier let out a scream as he staggered forward, plummeting to the floor.

Brigid let out her breath with a whoof as the soldier collapsed on top of her, his weight pressing against her abdomen. She shifted her position, rolling her shoulders and hefting the bigger man off her as she pulled herself across the white floor. He was regaining his composure now, and he swung the business end of the big autorifle at her as she skittered away.

Her right leg kicked out again from where she lay before him, and the toe of her boot knocked the barrel of the gun away from her, yanking the weapon from the young soldier's grip. It sailed in the air for a moment before clattering into the far wall and dropping to the floor.

Brigid swung her other leg around, kicking the soldier hard in the stomach as he clambered after her. He growled and his grasping hands reached for her leg as it arced away.

Brigid rolled on her buttocks, launching her arms behind her for balance as she leaped into a crouch, resting on the flats of her toes. The soldier scrambled away, spinning over and frantically making his way toward the dropped Fedorov rifle on hands and knees. As he did so, Brigid launched herself across the width of the corridor and came crashing down on his back, her weight shoving him chin-first into the floor with a mighty cracking sound. The soldier went suddenly very still.

Brigid reached down, feeling the young man's pulse at the neck. Weak but steady—he was unconscious but alive. Still sitting across the soldier's body, Brigid reached for the Automat, pulling it toward her by its leather shoulder strap.

She looked down then, realizing that her hip holster was still there, and she peered curiously inside to see if her TP-9 pistol was still within. The weapon seemed to exist, but only as a ghost image in the holster. When she tried to grasp it, the pistol remained intangible, and the image turned to mist as her hand swept through it.

"I have no idea what's going on," Brigid whispered to herself. "Did you speak Russian, then, lover boy?" she added as she looked at the unconscious soldier. She thought that he had. Was it her Commtact translating or was there something else going on there?

She took the Fedorov Automat rifle in her hands and felt its weight. It seemed to be right; so far as her senses could tell, she was holding a genuine Automat rifle. She looked it over. The black finish was scratched, the leather shoulder strap featured a frayed thread and was dark in places where sweat had turned the tan color to a darker shade of brown. She was briefly tempted to pull the trigger just to see whether a real bullet would come spurting from the muzzle, but she decided against it, fearing that she may alert other soldiers. Where there's one soldier there are usually others, she thought.

As she walked down the corridor that the soldier had silently appeared from, she looked back at his fallen body. "Not the best example of diplomacy," she chastised herself under her breath. Kane would have a field day if he knew, but the reaction had been instinctive and she had to assume it had saved her life.

She paced along the corridor for a short while until she saw an opening at its end through which she glimpsed a darker shape in the midst of the lightning-bright whiteness. There was movement there, too, she noticed, and voices drifted back to her ears from beyond the opening.

Warily Brigid walked forward, stepping lightly to keep

her approach quiet, the rifle held across her body. As she neared the opening, she assumed a crouch, walking the last few steps with her back against the wall and her body held low. Slowly she peered through the threshold and into the vast room that waited beyond.

The room was huge, and it was dominated by a giant metallic shape that reminded Brigid of a submarine. It was difficult to gauge the object's true size—the room seemed to stretch on forever, floors, walls and ceiling finished in the same luminescent white as the corridors. The ceiling was higher than in the corridor, and Brigid estimated it to be as high as one hundred feet or more. You could fit a small skyscraper in here, she realized. And perhaps they had.

The sleek torpedo shape was a dark color, almost black but glinting where the light caught the metallic finish. The light itself seemed to radiate from the walls, the ceiling, the floor, as it had in the corridors.

Scaffolding was arrayed around the dark torpedo, metal poles holding wooden platforms, towering into the colossal heights of the room. Figures walked along the scaffolding, men and women, some working at the exterior of the huge construction. Next to the dark shape, they looked like ants swarming around a melon.

Brigid guessed that there were about thirty people on the scaffolding. She could make out the rigid figures of soldiers standing guard with long automatic rifles cradled in their arms. Have these people been here since before the nukecaust? Have they been working on this mighty feat of engineering for two hundred and fifty years?

What she was looking at, Brigid realized, was the Death

Cry. It had to be. A weapon so vast, so powerful that it needed to be hidden in a higher stream of human consciousness.

For a moment she just crouched there, her mouth open, the weight of the rifle forgotten in her hands. And then, slowly, a fearful smile crossed her lips. She had found it.

But just what was it that she had found?

Chapter 12

Standing on the threshold of the vast room, Brigid calmed her breathing. She watched the movements on the scaffolding and around the room, counting eleven soldiers in all. They were dressed in old-fashioned Red Army uniforms, and all of them were armed with Fedorov automatic rifles like the one she held.

The room was pure white and, although her eyes had adjusted to the brightness, the illumination still seemed fierce. There were pools of shadow beneath the torpedo-like Death Cry and the surrounding scaffolding, but the shadows were gray and washed out, diffused by the bright light coming from all directions, even from the floor. With the brightness of the room, it would be very difficult to sneak around for long; there was simply nowhere to hide her presence.

As she peered along the right-hand wall, she spotted an opening at its far end, not a doorway so much as a gap in the wall stretching all the way up to the high ceiling, a hundred feet above. White on white, she hadn't noticed it at first; three people entering the vast room from this gap had drawn her attention there. She wondered where it might lead. Was there another room, an even more impressive weapon? Was this Device One or Two, with the next room containing one of the improved versions of the Death Cry prototype? One thing was certain: she wouldn't learn anything there, crouching out of sight.

She looked around at the patrolling soldiers, weighing the options in her mind. A surprise attack would only get her so far, and without Kane or Grant to back her up, Brigid didn't much like her chances against eleven armed and trained soldiers. The guard in the corridor had had an itchy trigger, and she guessed these people weren't used to visitors. Despite the esoteric location, this was a military base, she reminded herself, and she was trespassing.

She looked down once again at the Automat cradled in her hands and decided that going in armed might prove a deadly mistake. Brigid looked around for a moment, trying to find somewhere that she could stash the rifle, but the smooth walls and unforgiving lighting left her with nowhere to hide it—no nooks, no crannies, no shadows. Tentatively she pushed her hand against the wall she stood beside, wondering if there might be a trick to the surface somehow, operating in the same way as the convex wall through which she had entered this installation, a semipermeable membrane. Nothing happened— the wall was as solid as rock.

Reluctantly Brigid rested the big gun against the wall and strolled into the vast white-walled room.

A moment before, the atmosphere there had been still, an area of scientific study, quiet and clinical. Brigid felt the change immediately as the soldiers spotted her and leveled their weapons, zeroing the stranger in their sights. Brigid raised her open, empty hands above her head and tried to put on her least-threatening smile as she looked at the guns suddenly pointed in her direction.

One of the soldiers, a gray-eyed man in his midforties lifting the weight of his Automat as though it were an extension of his own body, called to her from his position above her head on the nearest of the scaffold platforms. "You would do well to explain yourself quickly, Comrade," he told her in a firm, sure voice. His voice echoed back from the high ceiling.

"I think I may be a little lost," Brigid replied, her voice loud in the otherwise silent room. After a moment, the echoes of her own words were audible. She was speaking English, or at least she thought that she was, despite knowing that the soldier had addressed her in Slav-accented Russian.

The soldier didn't seem to notice, or if he did notice he certainly didn't appear to mind. "This is a government facility. Not a wise place to be losing yourself in," he said ominously. "Would you care to explain how you got here?"

Brigid felt her smile slip and wondered whether there was any chance that Kane might appear right about now with a satchel full of flash-bangs. She needed to say something fast, something that would convince these bored, action-starved and trigger-happy soldiers that she wasn't a threat. Several lab-coated workers on the scaffolding had stopped what they were doing to watch the excitement below.

"I bring word from the people's government," she said, "from Pritisch, Sokolovsky and Yudenich." The names sprang to mind immediately, some of the ranking players in the final Soviet government before the world blew out in 2001. Pritisch was an ex-KGB warmonger who had upped the military budget tenfold in his final years of power.

"From Pritisch," the soldier repeated, lowering the Fedorov's muzzle slightly, "Sokolovsky and Yudenich? Is this right?"

"That's what I said," Brigid replied, suddenly aware that her fixed smile was making the muscles of her mouth ache. "I was sent here with a message."

Still standing on the scaffolding above Brigid, the gray-eyed soldier granted her a brief stiff smile. "And who are Pritisch, Sokolovsky and Yudenich?" he asked, raising the muzzle of his gun once more and aiming it firmly between her eyes. His colleagues surrounding her all raised their own weapons higher, and Brigid was acutely aware of their fingers brushing longingly against triggers. "Speak quickly, Comrade, I lose interest easily."

Damn! Brigid thought.

LAKESH STUDIED THE biometric data broadcast from Brigid Baptiste's subcutaneous transponder. "Her heart rate has slowed and her body temperature is a little lower than normal," he explained to Kane over the comm-link after a moment. "Over."

A silent ten-second break passed in the Cerberus ops room, and Lakesh continued to study the constantly updated feed of information. Brigid and the other members of the field team appeared to be in good health.

"So she's, what, asleep?" Kane's voice patched through

the room's speakers from across the other side of the world. "Over."

"A little more like a coma," Lakesh stated thoughtfully. "That's not a bad thing, of course. Comas can be the body's way of healing. It's not anything to worry about. Over."

"Fine," Kane replied after another short pause. "I'll keep an eye on her, make sure nothing changes physically. You still having some communication problems?" Kane asked, referring obliquely to the announcement that they had a snooper watching them. Donald Bry had passed that information along to Kane, using a stock code phrase indicating the channel was no longer considered secure. "Over."

"We're looking into that and trying to ascertain the source," Lakesh told him. "For the moment, keep to the two-hourly reports and we'll let you know when we discover anything else. Over."

"Understood. Over and out," Kane replied a few seconds later.

It was a difficult situation they now found themselves in. On the one hand, communication with the field team was essential, more so than ever now that Brigid was out of action. Kane and Grant were relying on Cerberus to update them. On the other hand, giving away any vital information over the communication link was like feeding it to the enemy, even if they didn't know who this enemy was.

"Donald?" Lakesh called, looking up from the telemetric feed on the monitor display.

He saw Bry's unruly mop of copper-colored hair pop up from behind a bank of computers on the far side of the room. "Yes, Dr. Singh?"

"What progress on our new friend?"

Bry shook his head, his permanent expression of worry seeming all the more heartfelt. "Nothing good so far," he admitted as Lakesh paced across the room to join him and his three-man decoding team. "It's like the code has been hardwired into our own. Disentangling it could take weeks. The nearest metaphor I can come up with is of cancerous cells."

Lakesh shook his head slowly back and forth. "And have you had any success with finding where this hack set out from?"

Bry turned to Skylar Hitch, a timid woman in her twenties who stood a mere five feet tall. Hitch had light coffee-colored skin, black hair and hazel eyes, and despite her timid attitude she was a wonder with computers. "With the lack of operational satellites left in orbit," she explained, "it shouldn't be that hard to triangulate where our cutter came from, because he can't bounce his signal around to disguise it. However, with the way the coding works, it's proving hard to isolate it enough to begin a proper trace. Every which way I've tried, it's ended up triangulating on the Bitterroot Mountains. Probably this room," she added after a moment's thought.

"So you're going around in circles," Lakesh concluded.

"We're looking into the possibility," Donald Bry added tentatively, "of actually adding something to the code, building on it rather than trying to isolate it. Brewster's trying to figure out a way to do that without upsetting the link."

Lakesh nodded. "As quickly as you can," he instructed them.

BRIGID TRIED NOT to show any sign of the rising fear in her gut as she began reeling off names of Soviet political leaders. "Gorbachev? Gromyko?"

The gray-eyed soldier showed no sign of acknowledgment beyond the slightest shake of his head.

"Kuznetsov, Chernenko, Yuri Andropov?" Brigid tried, the names spilling easily from her phenomenal memory.

A grim slash had replaced the soldier's smile, and he still showed no sign of recognition of the names of Soviet state presidents from the closing decades of the twentieth century. How long had these people been there, out of contact with the real world?

"Joseph Stalin?" she tried hopefully. Surely they couldn't have been there since the 1930s. That was almost three hundred years ago.

"I think," the soldier said as his cold stare bored into Brigid's eyes, looking for a trace of fear, "you have outstayed your welcome, little miss."

This was it, Brigid knew. This was where the quest ended. Unless...

"And I think," she told the people in the vast white room, turning her gaze away from their gray-eyed spokesman, "that you people have been in here for a hell of a lot longer than you realize."

The room fell silent, with only the ghostly echoes of Brigid's statement providing any noise at all. Then, as she stood there, surrounded by armed soldiers, she heard the hiss of whispering voices. The voices came from farther along the scaffolding. She couldn't make out the words, but she knew the tone—frantic and urgent.

Suddenly a man's voice broke the tense silence, loud

and clear. A lab-coated man, with a head of dark hair that was graying above the ears, came into view from farther along the same scaffolding rig that the gray-eyed soldier stood on. "Let her speak, General Serge," the whitecoat said. "There may yet be truth to the lady's story, and the very least we can do is show her a little hospitality before you execute her."

So far so good, Brigid thought. Apart from the "execute" part, of course. Hopefully she could hold that off indefinitely.

Slowly, a little too slowly for Brigid's comfort, the gray-eyed general lowered his Fedorov rifle and ordered his troops to do the same.

The lab-coated man stepped across to a ladder propped up beside the high scaffolding and made his way carefully down to ground level. Once he reached the white floor, he turned and limped slowly across to Brigid, extending his right hand. "My name is Dr. Djugashvili," he told her, and Brigid felt her eyes widen involuntarily in surprise. Was this the same Dr. Djugashvili who had written those reports about Device One in 1922? This man was still quite young, perhaps in his late forties or early fifties; he could pass for a contemporary of Mohandas Lakesh Singh, certainly. "Perhaps you would prefer to answer the same questions that the general posed without a rifle pointed at you." He gestured around at the soldiers who watched restlessly from the circle they had formed around Brigid.

"Dr. Anastas Djugashvili," Brigid said, looking for the flash of either recognition or confusion in his eyes, "it is very definitely an honor to meet you at last."

The lines around Djugashvili's eyes creased as he smiled. "You have me at a disadvantage, Miss…?"

"Baptiste," Brigid told him, "but, please, call me Brigid."

SITTING ALONE IN THE CANTEEN, Grant gazed around the shadow-filled room, playing the beam of the penlight across the walls and wooden tables. Near the back wall, well away from the room's sole door, two skeletons were slumped over.

Grant walked over to take a closer look at them. They were dressed in ancient clothing, a lab coat and a soldier's uniform, moth-eaten and slowly disintegrating to rags beneath a layer of gray dust. They looked still, almost serene, and Grant crouched on his haunches to get closer still.

When he had arrived there with Kane and Brigid, none of them had taken much interest in the skeletons. The bunker was a graveyard, and hardly the first one that the Cerberus field team had seen. But now, left alone while Kane made his two-hourly contact with Cerberus, Grant started thinking about the bricked-up entryway, the skeletons that remained in the bunks and several other rooms.

From the shape of the pelvis, the lab-coated skeleton was a woman, wearing light trousers. There was no visible ID, no indicators as to who she was, her age when she had died, anything. Same for the soldier, just a serial number on a card tucked into his inside breast pocket.

There were no signs of trauma, no bullet holes or broken bones. It looked to Grant as though these people had simply died in their sleep. He remained crouched by the skeletons, thinking about the figures in the bunks, wondering if they had died the same way. A shiver slowly ascended the length of his spine as he thought of that: a whole facility falling asleep, never to awaken. Like something out of a fairy tale.

Slowly Grant drew a steadying breath and eased himself back into a standing position. "What happened here?" he muttered to himself.

The thought of these people dying in their sleep reminded Grant of how tired he was feeling. He and Kane had taken catnaps since they had secured the facility, but the toll of simply waiting, ever alert, was showing.

Grant rubbed his eyes and looked across to the skeletons on the floor. "Sorry, guys, but I don't think I want to end up like you just yet," he told them, but the humor sounded forced to his own ears. He shook his head and paced across the room to the open doorway and the unlit corridor outside. "Come on, Kane," he muttered, glancing at his wrist chron. "This place is starting to give me the creeps."

"BAPTISTE?" DR. DJUGASHVILI said thoughtfully.

He led Brigid around the side of the massive metal construct to the high-ceilinged corridor she had noticed off to the right-hand side of the colossal, white-walled room. She tried not to show too much interest in the dark torpedo shape that dominated the room as he limped beside her, aware that every eye in the room was on them. The weapon was breathtakingly impressive, as long as a preskydark aircraft carrier and finished in a sleek, metallic black that seemed to absorb the pervasive glow of its white surround. She wanted to stop to examine the gigantic construction, but was aware that now was not the opportune time to express her interest.

Brigid walked with Djugashvili along the corridor that seemed to stretch forever. It was hard to get a sense of location with the white walls, white ceilings, white floors. When she tried to stare into the distance, Brigid felt as though she had lost her depth perception. There were occasional gaps in the walls, and Brigid saw that these led into smaller, white-walled rooms. Eventually Djugashvili stopped before one of these doorways and encouraged Brigid to lead the way inside. She was wary of entering, conscious that it could be a trap, until she realized Djugashvili was simply being a gentleman.

"Normally I would hold the door for a young lady such as yourself, but sadly we have no doors here."

Inside she found what was unmistakably an office despite the alien nature of the design. A flattened, glistening lightning bolt stretched from one wall like an operating table, acting as the desk. Behind it was a molded L-shape, again in white, that served as a chair. There were several other large blocks in the room, and Djugashvili gestured to one of these as he took up his place behind the desk. The ceiling was much lower in this room, perhaps just twenty-five feet above them, and a pure white shelf ran the length of one wall, holding a line of lever arch files, battered and spilling over with paperwork. The files had been labeled sequentially using the Cyrillic alphabet, and Brigid idly noticed that the sequence running М-Н-О was missing.

"Baptiste?" Djugashvili repeated, the glint of metal fillings showing along the upper left side of his jaw. "This is French, no?"

Brigid smiled. "As a matter of fact, I'm from Irish stock originally, care of…" She stopped. Should she mention the United States of America, the old enemy? "Care of all over, really," she finished lamely.

"A globe-trotter?" Djugashvili asked, intrigued. "And what brings you to this little piece of Russia? You said something about carrying a message from the people's government."

Brigid wondered where she should begin to explain to a three-hundred-year-old man. "It breaks down like this— it's time to use the weapon, the Death Cry." She had said "Death Cry," the name that she and Kane had attributed to the information from the U.S. surveillance files, but it came out of her mouth as something else. "The Call of Death," maybe, or perhaps something entirely different. Whatever she was speaking wasn't speech at all, more like communion.

Dr. Djugashvili waved a hand before his face as he tried to articulate his question. Which was a strange thing to do, Brigid thought, an old habit that meant nothing in this level of reality. "Where precisely is this instruction coming from, Brigid? This question is perplexing me somewhat."

"When was the last time you had communication from your superiors, Dr. Djugashvili?" she asked, a horrible realization forming in the back of her mind.

"It must have been…" He paused, trying to remember. "I'm not sure. I would need to check our records. But you haven't answered my question."

"No, I haven't," Brigid agreed. "What year is this, Doctor?"

"Year?" he repeated. "Well, I hardly think that has anything to do with…" He stopped as he saw the look of concern in Brigid's eyes. She was staring at him, and her smile was gone.

"Perhaps you would indulge me by answering one of my questions before I answer yours," he suggested, and Brigid nodded. "Do you know where you are?"

"My understanding of the situation," Brigid told him, "is that we are on a higher level of consciousness, in a region dubbed Krylograd by the staff of Project Chernobog—your staff."

"Krylograd." He laughed, resting his elbows on the desk and knitting his hands together. "I've not heard that expression in a very long time. Dear Laynia—Dr. Krylova," he corrected himself, "left us many months ago now. She died. It was a very sad thing."

"I'm sorry," Brigid said automatically. "I only knew her through her research. She came across as a brilliant woman."

"More than brilliant," Djugashvili agreed. "Her understanding of the human mind was exceptional. A completely lateral manner of studying the human experience." Djugashvili looked older to Brigid in that moment, the weight of the years showing in his face.

"What happened?" Brigid probed, wondering for a moment whether she had said such a thing aloud.

"It is a fair question." Djugashvili nodded. "Since you know where you are, you must have realized that the rules here are different. Death is…it's a very hard thing to explain here," he began, and Brigid noticed that he was rubbing at a scar that ran across the inside of both of his wrists. The scar had a chain-link pattern. "There was an argument with the general, something he felt was against the remit of Project Chernobog and, well, the best way that I could describe this—scientifically, you understand—is that she *dissipated*. It was like a mist, a fog where a person had been but moments before."

Brigid nodded, remembering the experience of the nonexistent TP-9 pistol in her holster.

"We collected her," he explained sadly, "gathered the mist as best we could and added it to the device. The Death Cry."

Again, Brigid had heard "Death Cry," but that wasn't what he had said. It was as if the Tower of Babel had never fallen; language no longer had barriers in this plane of existence. "So she's a part of the weapon?" Brigid said, her voice coming out as little more than a whisper through no conscious effort of her own.

"We are all part of the weapon," Djugashvili stated solemnly.

Brigid wanted Djugashvili to explain what that meant, but she stopped herself, focusing on the primary question she needed answered. "What year is this, Doctor?" she probed again.

"Yes." He smiled, rubbing absently at his brow. "The year. It has been a long time since I last had contact with the world. Outside of this facility, many months," he explained, an ingratiating smile crossing his lips, "a long time since I last saw a newspaper, you understand."

Brigid nodded encouragingly.

"I think," Djugashvili said ponderously, "I think it is 1928 or perhaps 1929 by now. It is still winter, I am certain of that. I feel the cold in my old bones," he reasoned tri-umphantly.

Brigid nodded, trying to absorb what this would mean. This man, this whole astral factory, was stuck in time, toiling there under the deluded belief that only a few months had passed since they— She stopped herself. Since they what? she wondered. Up-leveled? What had they done to end up there, permanent residents of the astral plane? "When did you come here?" she asked finally.

"It was in the spring just gone," Djugashvili replied, "1928."

That meant that this man, this whole group had no knowledge of the nuclear holocaust, of skydark. Heck, this man didn't even know about the Second World War, which had defined the players that led to the nukecaust. Joseph Stalin had just assumed power when they had ascended to this higher plane. Which either meant that time ran much slower there or that the whole plane played tricks on the human sense of its passage. Either way, Brigid realized, it would be dangerous for her to remain there any longer than absolutely necessary.

"There have been some changes," Brigid said care-fully, "since you left the corporeal world, some of which may come as a shock."

The doctor nodded thoughtfully, and then his attention was drawn to something behind Brigid, and she looked over her shoulder, following his gaze. Standing in the doorway was the gray-eyed General Serge along with a half-dozen men from his battalion. Standing beside the general was the sentry whom Brigid had knocked out in the corridor, a nasty purple bruise forming on his chin beneath a split lower lip. The general had drawn a Tokarev pistol from the holster at his belt.

"I think you had better start with who really sent you, Miss Baptiste," the general announced sternly.

"What is this about, General?" Djugashvili asked, shocked.

"She knocked out Krementsov, left him for dead," Serge explained, the gun and his hard stare locked firmly on the seated Brigid. "I believe Miss Baptiste is a counterrevolutionary sent here to retard the progress of Project Chernobog. And once she's told me exactly what I want to know, I plan to shoot her for the dog she is."

Chapter 13

The atmosphere in the white-walled office was electric as Dr. Djugashvili, General Serge and Brigid Baptiste all waited to see who would make the next move.

The general's pistol was held steady as he spoke again. "Well, Miss Baptiste, I'd suggest that you start talking."

"If you're planning to shoot me like a dog anyway," Brigid said, "it's hardly an incentive for me to tell you anything now, is it?"

A thin, terrible smile crossed Serge's lips, a sadistic expression that held no compassion or humor. "Oh, I think you'll appreciate that there are worse things that can happen to a young woman than being shot. Far worse things." The smile held for a second longer before he gestured with a slight raise of his pistol. "Now, get up. Your little heart-to-heart with the good doctor here is at an end."

Djugashvili began to say something, but stopped when he saw the flash of anger in Serge's eyes and noted the barrels of Fedorov Automat autorifles that had been leveled at him by the soldiers through the open doorway.

Brigid rose slowly from the white stool that she had

sat upon, watching General Serge and his soldiers warily, trying not to make any sudden moves. Once she stood, the general tilted his head to the doorway. "Outside," he instructed her.

Brigid stepped toward the door, watching Serge's flint-gray eyes. The general waited by the door and indicated that she was to precede him into the bright corridor. As she passed Krementsov, the young soldier she had knocked out, his arm snapped out and his hand was suddenly entangled in her red-gold hair, pulling her head backward.

"You broke my tooth, you dog," the soldier growled. "Don't think that this makes us even."

Brigid grunted, straining to her tiptoes as Krementsov yanked at her hair. She watched from the corner of her eye as he swung a low punch toward her with his free hand. The punch slammed into her belly, knocking the wind out of her in a rush, and he released her hair. As soon as Krementsov let go of her, Brigid collapsed to her knees, alternately coughing and dry-heaving as she tried to get her breath back.

"You see, Comrades," she heard General Serge tell his men as she knelt there, her eyes struggling to retain focus. "Enemies of the revolution are weak. We have nothing to fear from them." Suddenly his hand was upon her, pulling at her elbow, forcing Brigid to stand. "Come now, kitten," he whispered, "time to play question-and-answer."

With that, Brigid Baptiste lurched from the room, surrounded by armed soldiers, with the general pulling at her elbow.

WHEN KANE RETURNED through the wide ventilation duct, Grant indicated the skeletons in the canteen and spoke of his growing sense of unease.

"Look at them," Grant insisted. "What did these people die from, Kane?"

Kane shrugged. "I dunno," he grunted, looking across to the small kitchen area that sat behind a low counter. "Food poisoning maybe?"

"Sure," Grant snarled. "You know what I think they died from? Death. I think they died from death, you know?"

Kane laughed. "You don't die from death. There's a cause of death, you don't just…"

"Look at them again," Grant insisted, tension rising in his voice. "They didn't die of anything. They just sat down and willingly turned into worm food."

Kane knelt and examined one of the skeletons. He reached his hand out to touch it, thought better of it and reached for a discarded spoon that had been left on the table beside him, using that to prod at the long dead body.

"See," Grant urged. "No marks, no entry or exit wounds, no broken bones, no head trauma. Believe me, Kane, I looked."

Kane nodded as he used the thin handle of the spoon to turn the skull. "What about the people in the bunks? Did you take a look at them?"

"Not close-up," Grant admitted, "but I'd offer even money on them being the same."

"At least," Kane agreed absently as he used the spoon to push the dusty rags of the lab coat to one side. In the thin beams of the penlights, the shirt beneath looked a dull brown color and it began to shred as he pushed the spoon against it, disintegrating beneath its touch. He looked at the exposed ribs of the lab worker, dull, yellowing bone strips that had once protected the lungs. After a few moments he glanced up at his field partner. "You have a theory?" he asked.

Grant's white teeth showed in the dim light as he offered his tight smile. "Could have been something airborne, but then why would they brick up the place but leave the ventilation shaft open? Doesn't make much sense," he reasoned. "Even though you were being cute, that idea of food poisoning isn't so far-fetched. But, again, the bricked-up door—which was done from the inside, remember—seems pretty extreme, and it's one fast-moving case of sickness to take out the whole installation. There must be close to thirty skeletons in this bunker."

"Plus," Kane added, rising from the debris-strewed floor, "almost everyone is fully clothed. With the bunks, we can safely assume that people slept here. I figure the very least you'd do is take off your lab coat or field jacket if you needed to lie down and die."

"So they sealed themselves in and then what?" Grant wondered. "Suicide pact?"

"Using what?" Kane asked. "Poison? It doesn't ring true to me."

"Me, either," Grant agreed. "We need to take a proper look at the bunked skeletons, though. Could be there's something we're not seeing."

"What we're not seeing is the obvious," Kane stated, glancing again at the twin skeletons in the corner of the room. "We don't know what the Death Cry is, we don't know how it works, but we've speculated that it has the potential to destroy an Annunaki mother ship."

"You think this is a test gone wrong?" Grant asked. "But if the effects were that immediate, why would there be so many troops in bed rather than, I don't know, monitoring things?"

"It wasn't a test," Kane theorized, thinking on his feet. "Something went wrong, or…" His voice trailed off, and Grant saw concern mar his friend's features.

"What is it?" Grant asked after a few seconds of silence.

"What if access to this Death Cry thing is flawed?" Kane proposed, pacing quickly to the doorway and into the corridor, with Grant following behind. "What if they could get to it, but they couldn't get out again?"

"You mean they were trapped in meditation?" Grant pondered. "But with no food, no water, their real-world bodies would atrophy and ultimately perish."

"Baptiste told us that this mandala thing was designed to be all-encompassing. It is meant to be your sole focus, a way to rewire the brain. How did she describe it?" Kane tried to remember as he rushed along the corridor. "A tuning fork attuned to Buddha or Allah or God."

"So you think they bricked-up the main entrance before they were all absorbed by the resonance of this tuning fork?"

"I think that was probably the job of the last two soldiers on the premises, maybe even our canteen couple back there," Kane said, turning back to address Grant over his shoulder. "The last things they did was brick-up the entry and bunch-up the rug to try to disguise its pattern, make sure no one gave it a second thought."

"Before going into the meditation themselves," Grant finished.

"Remember what Baptiste was saying about the Tibetan monks committing these designs to memory?" Kane said. "That's how they would have done it here. Everyone knew the design, lost themselves to it, went wherever it is the thing was designed to take them."

Grant continued Kane's reasoning as he followed him into the small, brightly lit office with the brass Cheka-KGB shield on the wall. "Which means—" he began.

"Which means Baptiste in trouble," Kane finished for him.

THEY HAD TAKEN HER to another room, once again constructed of the lightning-bolt-white material. A series of white pipes ran across the room at about nine feet above the bright floor. What the pipes contained, Brigid couldn't begin to guess. Perhaps they were just cylindrical bars, shapes that held nothing at all.

General Serge watched with a grim smile on his lips as two of the soldiers produced a metal chain from an alcove in the back of the small room and wound it around Brigid's wrists, binding her hands before her and leaving a long length of chain trailing along the floor. Once that was done, one of the soldiers tossed the length of chain over the pipes to a soldier who stood across from him, waiting to catch it. Without a word, the catcher yanked the chain and Brigid was drawn backward and up, her arms stretching over her head, until she hung from the pipe by the chain, the outstretched toes of her boots just two inches from the floor. It was an uncomfortable

Get FREE BOOKS and a FREE GIFT when you play the...

LAS VEGAS
GAME

Just scratch off the gold box with a coin. Then check below to see the gifts you get!

YES! I have scratched off the gold box. Please send me my 2 FREE BOOKS and gift for which I qualify. I understand that I am under no obligation to purchase any books as explained on the back of this card.

366 ADL ENWS

166 ADL ENX4
(GE-LV-08)

FIRST NAME	LAST NAME

ADDRESS

APT.#	CITY

STATE/PROV.	ZIP/POSTAL CODE

7	7	7	Worth TWO FREE BOOKS plus a BONUS Mystery Gift!
🍒	🍒	🍒	Worth TWO FREE BOOKS!
🔔	🔔	☘	TRY AGAIN!

Offer limited to one per household and not valid to current subscribers of Gold Eagle® books. All orders subject to approval. Please allow 4 to 6 weeks for delivery.

▼ DETACH AND MAIL CARD TODAY! ▼

© 2007 WORLDWIDE LIBRARY ® and ™ are trademarks owned and used by the trademark owner and/or its licensee.

The Gold Eagle Reader Service — Here's how it works:

Accepting your 2 free books and free gift (gift valued at approximately $5.00) places you under no obligation to buy anything. You may keep the books and gift and return the shipping statement marked "cancel." If you do not cancel, about a month later we'll send you 6 additional books and bill you just $31.94* — that's a savings of 15% off the cover price of all 6 books! And there's no extra charge for shipping! You may cancel at any time, but if you choose to continue, every other month we'll send you 6 more books, which you may either purchase at the discount price or return to us and cancel your subscription.

*Terms and prices subject to change without notice. Price does not include applicable taxes. Sales tax applicable in N.Y. Canadian residents will be charged applicable provincial taxes and GST. Credit or debit balances in a customer's account(s) may be offset by any other outstanding balance owed by or to the customer. Offer available while quantities last.

If offer card is missing write to: Gold Eagle Reader Service, 3010 Walden Ave., P.O. Box 1867, Buffalo NY 14240-1867

BUSINESS REPLY MAIL

FIRST-CLASS MAIL   PERMIT NO. 717   BUFFALO, NY

POSTAGE WILL BE PAID BY ADDRESSEE

GOLD EAGLE READER SERVICE
3010 WALDEN AVE
PO BOX 1867
BUFFALO NY 14240-9952

NO POSTAGE
NECESSARY
IF MAILED
IN THE
UNITED STATES

position, with all of her weight pulling at her shoulders, but Brigid was physically superior to a normal woman, strong enough to handle this punishment without complaint, at least for a little while.

Once she was strung up, the gray-eyed general ordered all but two of his men to leave the small room. Then he leaned back against the wall beside the door and silently admired Brigid as she hung there like a piece of meat, his eyes slowly working their way up from her toes to her face, lingering for a long time on her hips and torso, feasting on her curves. Brigid watched him, seeing the predatory glint in his eyes, trying her best to relax her muscles as she hung uncomfortably from the chain.

Finally the general's voice broke the silence. "You are quite a woman, I think," he said.

"Thank you," she said, offering a smile.

"I think we will have much fun before you are dead, yes?" he continued, pulling a pair of leather gloves from his pocket and putting them on.

She fixed her emerald eyes on his, determined to show no fear. "I'm always up for fun," she told him.

He stepped forward then, and his gloved fist was a blurring motion before her as he swung a heavy punch into the left side of her face. Brigid felt the blow ringing through her nose like a sneeze that wouldn't come, and the vision in her left eye blurred over with hot, salty tears. Before she had time to recover, the general swung again, his left fist driving a fierce jab into her stomach in the same spot that Krementsov had hit her less than ten minutes before. Above her, the chain creaked as she rocked back and forth, hanging from its length.

As she continued swinging, inhalations painfully pulling the muscles in her stomach, Brigid felt something trickle down her face and realized that her nose was bleeding from the left nostril.

BRIGID BAPTISTE WAS STILL sitting on the floor before the desk, cross-legged, facing the rug hanging from the pitons that Grant had hammered into the ceiling. In the unforgiving illumination of the xenon flashlight, two things were made starkly clear: her eyes were closed and there was a glistening line of blood trickling from her left nostril.

"Come on, Baptiste," Kane said, kneeling before the redheaded woman, his voice rising. "Don't get yourself stuck in some stupid head game now."

Kane reached forward, his hands grabbing Brigid's shoulders, ready to shake her awake, but Grant stopped him. "Remember what Lakesh said," he admonished. "We're not to disturb her, right? This is way out of our field of expertise, Kane. I think we had better report this and make our next move under advisement."

Kane looked up at his friend, his face full of anguish, and finally he nodded. "She had better be okay," he stated.

As Kane knelt there, looking at the trickle of blood coming from Brigid's nose, a purple-black bruise erupted over her left eye, forming from nowhere.

Grant pointed to the ceiling, but Kane wasn't looking at him. "I'll go upstairs and file the report while you stay here and watch her," he said. He walked backward to the door, his eyes never leaving the two people on the floor, before turning and exiting the room. After a moment,

Grant's face reappeared in the doorway. "And Kane?" he said. "Until we hear different, you take a hands-off approach to this, no matter what you see, right?"

Kane nodded, not bothering to look back. "Get going, I'll hold the fort." He and Brigid were anam-charas, soul friends for eternity. Watching her being tortured like this, her body being marked as if from within, hurt Kane, as well. But it hurt most that, for now at least, there wasn't a damn thing he could do about it.

"I HAVE QUESTIONS," General Serge stated, standing before Brigid's blurry left eye, "but I believe you will need softening up before we get to those, Miss Baptiste."

"Why don't you just try asking them?" Brigid asked, blinking back the tears from her eye and looking at General Serge as he stood less than two feet away from her, his face on a level with hers. "I'll gladly cooperate."

"No—" he shook his head "—let's do this my way. The questions can wait a little while, I am sure."

Brigid had the man's measure then, as if she hadn't guessed before now. Hurting people, torturing and killing them—that was just a sport to him, a way to while away the hours. The scars on Dr. Djugashvili's wrists hinted that he had been subjected to the same torture as this. The story about Dr. Krylova's death at the general's hands offered another hint. Brigid's answers regarding her counterrevolutionary status were secondary to the sport, the game he wanted to play with this new piece of meat.

"General," she addressed him firmly, "it would be of much benefit to you and your men if I could speak with Dr. Djugashvili immediately, and I have no objections if you feel that that should occur here in your presence. But you must understand that there is more at stake than the security of Soviet Russia."

That grim, humorless smile crossed his face once more as he looked at her, and his gray eyes played over her body once more. "We can get to that in good time," he told her. "There is no need for impatience, kitten. First we can have our fun, okay?"

She gritted her teeth as he swung another punch at her ribs, a boxer training with a punching bag.

GRANT WAS STILL IN THE ventilation tunnel when he tried his Commtact. "Grant to Cerberus. Grant to Cerberus, you there?"

By the time he had pulled himself halfway up the rope that dangled from above, he heard Lakesh's voice piping through his skull. "Receiving you, Grant, loud but not too clear. What's going on? Over."

Grant lifted himself over the lip of the barred vent and climbed out into the fresh mountain air. It was well past midnight outside, the sky a rich, deep blue, a sprinkling of stars overhead. "I'm on higher ground now," he explained before confirming that the signal was now clear once more.

"We may have a new problem," Grant explained. "Something's happening to Brigid, some kind of physical trauma. We think it's related to the way the people died here. Over."

There was a delay until Lakesh's response came through. Grant scanned the horizon, watching as a few wispy clouds languished by the mountain peaks.

"Where is she now, Grant?" Lakesh asked. Then he

added with clear significance, "*Specifically*. Over." Grant had been warned that the communication channel was no longer secure, Lakesh's request to be specific meant that he should break security protocol if necessary.

"Physically she's still meditating in the office, but we presume her mental essence is elsewhere, I'm guessing with what we came looking for. The question is, can we wake her?" Grant asked. "Over."

IN THE CAVE IN THE tall rocks, somewhere in the Australian outback, Rock Streaming crouched before the laptop as the communication piped through its tiny but powerful speakers. Two other people were in the cave with Rock Streaming. Rabbit in the Moon crouched on his haunches near a rocky wall beside Rock Streaming, checking at his own computer monitor, while Good Father stood close to the doorway, his head bowed and his stance crooked.

The screens showed a live image of the Caucasus mountain range, delayed by approximately fifteen seconds as it was bounced across the Earth. A strip of tarmac in the shape of a hangman's noose could be made out to the center left of the image, and the sleek shapes of two bronze-hued manta ray–shaped vehicles could just be discerned beside the trees if one looked carefully. Rock Streaming's fingers played across the compact keyboard for a moment, and the image wavered before moving in closer and picking up a dark speck beside the Manta craft that could have been a man in the twilight, but could just as likely have been a wolf or the fallen limb of a tree.

The man's voice, the one who had identified himself as Grant, came over the speakers again, as clearly as though he were in the room with them. "Physically she's still meditating in the office, but we presume her mental essence is elsewhere, I'm guessing with what we came looking for. The question is, can we wake her? Over."

Rock Streaming didn't turn his attention from the computer, but he heard Good Father take several steps closer from behind him. "The woman is clearly in this other realm," Rock Streaming clarified, his voice low.

"Which means she's with the weapon," Rabbit in the Moon stated firmly. "Now's the time to move, Good Father."

Good Father remained silent as the communication continued to play out.

"For the moment," the other speaker stated, "I have to strongly advise against it, Grant. We have no idea what sort of trauma that might cause, and our biometric data here shows that she's in no immediate danger. Her heart rate fluctuates a little, but it's well within acceptable limits. Nothing out of the ordinary, Grant."

From the corner of his eye, Rock Streaming saw that Good Father was nodding. "Lock the picture, as well as the biodata feed," Good Father said as the conversation continued from the laptop's speakers. "Block their live feeds so that we may enter unnoticed."

Rock Streaming nodded, his fingers playing across the keyboard once again as he accessed a sequence he had previously set up with Rabbit in the Moon for this very eventuality. The live feeds that provided satellite imagery and biometric data were now looped to provide a reasonable facsimile of a continuing feed. "This won't stand up to too much examination," Rock Streaming warned, "but unless they're looking for it, it should fool them."

IN THE CERBERUS OPS CENTER, Lakesh watched the feed from Brigid's subcutaneous transponder as his conversation with Grant continued in staggered bursts.

"What about going into the zone with Brigid?" Grant asked. "Could me or Kane do that maybe?" To Lakesh, Grant was sounding increasingly desperate as he spoke around the subject, retaining as much security as he was able under the circumstances. "Over."

"It's the magic-eye picture argument," Lakesh explained. "Magic-eye pictures were a phenomenon at the end of the twentieth century, where a three-dimensional image of, say, a sailboat could be seen in a two-dimensional pattern, but only if the viewer was able to defocus their eyesight sufficiently. Some people could do this with ease, but for others the pictures never appeared. It is my contention that without the proper mental discipline, you and Kane would be ill suited to enter the zone, as you put it. You may never see the sailboat. Over."

Lakesh heard Grant bite back a curse before he responded properly. "We're kinda stuck playing the waiting game, then, is that what you're telling me? Over."

Lakesh nodded sadly, conscious of trying to keep the concern out of his voice. "Brigid's transponder will alert us if there's any need for action, and either Reba or I am here monitoring that at all times now. I know it's frustrating, but however it may look, there's no sign here of physical trauma, Grant." Lakesh watched as the heart rate dipped back to its normal level, a little slower, in fact, suggesting that Brigid was at rest. "Hold your nerve. Over."

During the gap in communication, Lakesh took in the

satellite image of the Caucasus Mountains. Looking closely, he imagined that he might be able to identify a speck that could be Grant talking to him, close to the grounded Mantas, but he couldn't be certain.

"Understood, Cerberus," Grant agreed over the Commtact. "Kane might take a bit of convincing, though. Over and out."

"Yes," Lakesh agreed, "good luck with Kane. Over and out." With that, he walked back to study the data from the transponders, tapping the screen to expand all three feeds from his field operatives. Heart rates, blood pressure and brain-wave activity all remained reassuringly normal. There was nothing to worry about, Lakesh told himself as Domi arrived carrying two mugs of steaming herbal tea, one for him and one for herself.

BRIGID GROANED as Krementsov kicked her for the sixth time beside her right hip. General Serge had left the younger man to the task, instructing him to get as much payback as he felt was reasonable for the loss of his front tooth while he dealt with another matter. Krementsov had punched her in the gut about a dozen times, then began walking around her as she hung from the pipes, kicking her from different angles and laughing when she cried out.

Finally Krementsov stepped back, looking at her bloodied face as she struggled to raise her head to look at him. "Are all you counterrevolutionaries so weak?" he asked her, laughing.

There was no answer and she knew it. It was just sport, another round of the same game that General Serge had played. "Let me speak to Dr. Djugashvili," she told him, her voice straining where her throat felt raw from vomiting. "Please," she added after a moment, her bright emerald eyes locking with his.

"Maybe in a while," the young soldier agreed, clearly not caring one way or the other. "I'm sure that the general will decide when."

At that, General Serge returned from whatever assignment had taken him from the little, fiercely lit room. Walking across the room, he dismissed Krementsov and the other sentry with a casual wave of his hand before standing before Brigid and clutching her beneath the chin, forcing her to look at him. He smiled when he saw the bruises on her face, the blood trickling from both nostrils and the gobs of spittle that clung to her chin. "You've been having quite some fun without me," he said, leering, "but now, kitten, I think it's time you started talking."

"Please," she breathed in a hoarse voice as he held her face tightly in his grip, "get me Dr. Djugashvili."

"He doesn't give the orders in this facility, Miss Baptiste," General Serge told her, his gloved fingers digging into the flesh of her bottom jaw.

"But he's the only one likely to understand what trouble you're all in," she replied.

Chapter 14

In the sacred tribal hut, Neverwalk watched as the members of the strike team prepared themselves for the oncoming mission. Following the briefest of discussions with Good Father immediately after the most recently overheard broadcast, Bad Father had given the order to move out. It was clear that they needed to act on their information now, or fear either discovery or losing their chance of recovering the astral weapon for their own use.

Including Neverwalk, there were now six people in the armory hut, stashing weapons about their person, readying themselves for the long walkabout through the Dreaming.

Rock Streaming appeared calm. He wore his long duster open to reveal an undershirt that left his tattooed shoulders bare. Tucked into his kangaroo-hide waist holsters were two boomerangs carved of razor-sharp titanium, weighted and potentially lethal. Neverwalk had seen Rock Streaming fell an eagle from the sky on one occasion, and loose a koala from the branch it clung to by cleaving clean through its clinging arms on another, both at a distance of one hundred or more paces. Rock Streaming had brought a portable computer with him, and as the others suited up he continued to refine the programs that they might need in the forthcoming battle with these Cerberus warriors.

Rock Streaming's cousin and blood brother, Rabbit in the Moon, wore a tattered jacket in vibrant blues and greens along with his low-slung combat pants. Rabbit in the Moon had elected to remain bare-chested, proud of his tattooed circuitry, twin homage to the old days and the new ways. He was checking the thin shafts of each of his arrows before adding them to the quiver he would carry on his back. The compound bow, a two-hundred-year-old tungsten-steel artifact, waited at the desk beside the arrows, its weight and targeting system perfectly attuned to Rabbit in the Moon's hawklike vision.

Cloud Singer had stripped down to her abbreviated combat wear—the bandage of white material that covered her breasts, the thin white strips that wrapped her knuckles and held her wrists firm, the white skirt ending at midhip and the bandagelike strips wound around her otherwise bare feet and ankles. She carried a hollowed stick that sang when it cleaved the air, the only weapon she required other than her tightly muscled body.

Good Father looked tense as he waited close to the door of the little hut, bull roarer in hand, cup dangling at the end of its limp string. Good Father had taken to using his gnarled walking cane once more, hollow at its tip and holding a dash of hot powder, enough to irritate a surprised opponent into making a foolish mistake. He wore a loose, short-sleeved shirt in a checkered pattern of washed-out red and black along with baggy shorts, leaving his ancient arms and legs bare. He had settled on a pair of sandals to protect his feet, cushioning his steps but still open to the elements.

Dressed in dark pants that ended high above his ankles, his hardened feet bare and his long, brown-black toenails curling, Bad Father stood at the other end of the armory, stocking up with throwing weapons, boomerang and yo-yo.

Neverwalk himself preferred the yo-yo, though had yet to test his ability in genuine combat against a human opponent. He carried a light version of the weapon, carved wood on a string of toughened emu hide. He had displayed much prowess with the yo-yo in mock battle, entangling the limbs of lesser opponents, as well as knocking a female kangaroo senseless from his hiding place in a tree before stealing her joey for food. However, for this, his very first field mission, he would primarily be tasked with the role of lifter and handler, carrying Rock Streaming's laptop on his back and replenishing weapons if required.

"What we do today," Bad Father rumbled in his voice of thunder, "will secure the original tribe's role in this dangerous new world." The members of the strike force stopped what they were doing and looked at him; even Rock Streaming stopped tapping at his computer program. "This is the next step on the long road to supremacy for each member of the tribe."

"You have all trained hard," Good Father added after a moment, picking up where his equal had left off. "The portents are good. We shall succeed in this matter—I have no doubt. The weapon they speak of in their communications, this Death Cry, will be ours before the next moonrise."

"Let none stand in the way of the original men," Bad Father hollered.

Everyone in the enclosed room bowed their heads respectfully as Good Father and Bad Father silently left the little hut and waited for the strike force to join them outside.

Neverwalk stood beside Rock Streaming as the programmer powered down his laptop and slipped it into the harness that Neverwalk would strap across his back. "Do you really think that we can win?" the boy asked, the tremor of fear in his voice.

Rock Streaming looked the young warrior squarely in the eye, standing tall and proud. "We must," he told Neverwalk. "The not-original men have ruined the world, destroyed nature, destroyed themselves. We are the last hope of humankind, as our kind have always been. But without the weapons to enforce what is right, to annex and hold the Dreaming, we will ever face opponents guided only by stupidity and selfishness."

Cloud Singer's head turned at this, overhearing the explanation. "We come to create new fiefdoms to rule," she said. "Are we not ourselves selfish?"

"Rulers come in many stripes," Rock Streaming told them both with a smile. "To make things better must never be wrong."

Rabbit in the Moon slung his quiver over his back and folded the compound bow into its holster along its side. "The written future promises ultimate victory for our tribe," he assured Cloud Singer and Neverwalk.

The young woman nodded at that, before turning to the doorway and walking out of the hut.

Neverwalk added spare arrows to the long pockets in his combat pants and placed the sharpening stone inside his jacket. Then he followed the two warrior men from the hut as they left to join Good Father, Bad Father and Cloud Singer.

Other members of the tribe waited outside in silence as the warriors prepared for their long journey through the Dreaming. Bad Father had described it as a three-dream minimum, but Rabbit in the Moon had plotted a different course, emerging in Africa before trekking the second leg of the journey. With the Dreamslicer, the attack would come as a complete surprise to these Cerberus people, snatching the weapon from right under their noses.

The midmorning air was warm outside, the sun reaching its zenith. Many of the original tribe members had come to proudly watch their warriors depart.

An area at the edge of the settlement had been marked out using pebbles, twin rings beside one another, one small and one large. Good Father stood in the smaller ring, his old eyes closed in contemplation, his chest slowly rising and falling as he drew deep, calming breaths.

Bad Father waited in the second, larger circle. The other warriors joined him, imitating his serene calm but aware that his gaze held fiery rage as it watched them enter the circle. Bad Father was ever impatient with his pupils, despite his apparently endless patience with the world around him. Three months ago, on a mission to the Russian territories, Bad Father had become too impatient with a female warrior called Dashed Accomplice and elected to leave her behind. Without access to the bull roarer that engaged the Dreamslice technology embedded in her skull, Dashed Accomplice had no way to return home to the outback and had been stranded somewhere in Russia.

Dashed Accomplice's failure to return meant Cloud Singer was promoted to take her place on the strike force. Such an example served as a stern reminder that dawdling would not be tolerated.

They stood across from one another, a five-pointed star within the circle. Once everyone was in place, Good Father began to spin the bull roarer, unleashing the full fury of its droning, ugly song as he raised it above his head and increased its revolutions. The instrument sang, a banshee shriek that carried far into the arid land that surrounded them. Its echoes bounced off the huge rock formation in the distance where the cave was located, the rock formation atop which Rabbit in the Moon had sparred with Cloud Singer for the entertainment of the original tribe.

As the drone of the bull roarer cleaved the air, Neverwalk felt the tingle at the base of his skull where the implant had come to life, fired up and awaiting his instruction. He watched Bad Father, allowing his consciousness to be overwhelmed with the bull roarer's ceaseless note, waiting for the signal to depart.

Suddenly Bad Father bowed his head, feeling more than hearing the tone of the bull roarer rise and fall, dancing across the spectrum to find its level. And swiftly, he raised his right arm and flicked it down again, like an official starting a race, and the six of them disappeared into the Dreaming. Both circles were now empty, just the trace of their footprints in the sand.

Neverwalk felt it as exquisite pain, that sensation at the top of his spinal column as the implant flipped him into the Dreaming. Its smell was familiar, the scent of dreams.

Neverwalk had closed his eyes automatically in an attempt to stave off the nausea that crept up on him when he entered the Dreaming like this. The others were with him, a few steps ahead, making their way across the deserted plain, their footsteps the only sound other than the soft sussurus of the wind across the shale beneath their feet.

Cloud Singer turned back, beckoning him to join them. "Hurry, Neverwalk," she said, and her voice was something musical now, the source of her beautiful warrior name. "Don't get left behind."

The Dreaming could be hard to navigate. Some of the tribe were experts at finding their way to the part of the Dream that they sought. Rabbit in the Moon had always shown an uncanny sense of tracking across the Dreaming. Good Father had said he was an instinctive dreamwalker.

Rabbit in the Moon dashed ahead, with Bad Father keeping pace at his heels, and the others trotted behind. Good Father remained with the group, spinning his bull roarer overhead as he jogged, ensuring none of them would get lost or left behind. The frequency of the bull roarer determined access to the Dreaming, as well as the length and type of the journey therein.

Neverwalk watched as Cloud Singer took a deep breath before she loosed a high-pitched note from her throat. The note welled deep within her, trilling loud and long, cutting the silence all around them. As the note burst forth, she took to the air, not in the manner of Rabbit in the Moon, all muscle energy and brute force. Instead, Cloud Singer stepped into the air the way a person would step onto a raised hillock, the way a goose lifted into the air as though it were just another part of the ground, angling away from the flat horizon. Cloud Singer stretched her arms out at her sides, her body forming a straight line from toe to neck, her head raised to look forward, her mouth wide as the exquisite note sang forth.

Up ahead, Rabbit in the Moon bent in a crouch, amassing energy before leaping high into the swollen sky like a firework, almost touching the rushing clouds as he lunged into the heavens, with Cloud Singer immediately altering her trajectory so as to follow him.

Bad Father went up in the air behind Rabbit in the Moon, apparently with no effort at all, just hooking into Rabbit in the Moon's slipstream and being carried into the air, too.

With their feet still on the shale-sprinkled ground, Good Father urged Rock Streaming and Neverwalk to ascend with the others.

Rock Streaming turned back to Neverwalk. "Come, little brother," he said, "we have much to do." Then Rock Streaming continued to turn, twisting into the air, like a seed fluttering on the wind.

Neverwalk prepared himself, finding his mental center just as he had been taught. A hop, a skip, a jump and he was airborne, too, gathering speed and feeling the wind in his face as he lunged after his companions. He thrust his arms forward to cut through the air as if diving. Looking over his shoulder, he saw Good Father, sitting cross-legged, the walking cane resting across his lap as he glided low over the ground. No longer in his hands, Good Father's bull roarer continued to spin, keeping pace with his flight above and a little behind his right shoulder.

Neverwalk turned away, tucking in his head to cut down on drag as his body moved faster and faster, cleaving the skies of the Dreaming.

Travel through the Dreaming was almost instantaneous, covering ground at speeds impossible in Realworld. Two hundred feet or two hundred miles—it was all the same in the Dreaming.

There was ground, then indigo sea below them, rushing past at a blur, eerie because it was soundless, lit by a sky that held the tint of green, the color of plants, of life.

Suddenly Rabbit in the Moon indicated below, dipping from his high altitude just beneath the rushing clouds, speeding like a meteorite back down to Earth, a trail of fire left in his wake across the sky. Neverwalk dipped to follow the other members of the strike team, his body holding the arrowhead shape as it cut through the air. The sea disappeared as he approached it, replaced by the rush of land colored the yellow of sand.

Beneath him Bad Father, Cloud Singer and Rock Streaming brought themselves in to land, their feet slapping against the dirt. Neverwalk spun his body, thrusting his legs forward, bent at the knee to take the shock, and suddenly he was on solid ground once more, stumbling as his speed slowed. He staggered across the ground for fifteen steps, feeling the jarring impact through his knees before finally falling down to a stop. A few paces behind him, he saw Good Father lower himself to the ground, grabbing the handle of the bull roarer as it whirled through the air beside him.

The others looked across the dirt to him as Good Father helped his young apprentice up from the soil. It felt like flecks of dried rice there, little pieces of ground that could get caught under your fingernails. And it was empty and silent. The only living things in this world, the world of the Dreaming, appeared to be the strike force.

"We're here," Good Father explained as Neverwalk let go of his hand and stood quietly beside him. The spinning of the bull roarer slowed, and with it the furious rushing of the clouds above them.

The burst of fire came again then, jarring Neverwalk at the top of his spine where the implant resided, forcing him to close his eyes to hold back the tears of pain. When he opened his eyes they were in a desert, three bony goats looking up at him, the rising sun still low in the sky.

"Africa," Good Father stated.

They were back in Realworld. The whole journey of seven thousand miles had taken less than ten seconds.

Chapter 15

"The trouble that *we* are in?" General Serge mocked as he looked at Brigid's helpless form hanging from the chain before him. "I fear that your assessment of the situation is back to front, Miss Baptiste," he told her with a braying laugh.

Brigid gritted her teeth against the pain in her stretched muscles, the aches where her body had taken punishment at the hands of Serge and Krementsov. "Be that as it may, General, I really must insist that I speak with Dr. Djugashvili," she told him firmly.

"You are hardly in a position to insist upon anything," Serge shot back hotly, anger rising in his voice.

At that moment, a voice came from the doorway as Dr. Djugashvili himself took a half step into the room. "I think that, with all due respect, we would be wise to listen to her, General," he said quietly, his determined look adding weight to his words.

The general turned to pierce him with his fierce gray-eyed glare. "Must I remind you that I am running this facility, Doctor?"

Djugashvili held his gaze, and Brigid wondered if this was the first time that the doctor had actually stood up to this bullying military man. "Even you are not immune to the ravages of time, General," he stated, "which is the message that I fear Miss Baptiste here came to give us."

Serge exploded, his face flushing red. "What are you talking about? You accept the word of, what, a counter-revolutionary, Doctor? A spy?" General Serge's hand fumbled to unclip his holster, and he seized the Tokarev pistol and thrust it into Djugashvili's belly. "Perhaps you are in league with her. Is that it, Anastas?"

Djugashvili shook his head, his once firm tone turning to whining. "Please cease this foolishness, General, for all our sakes," he requested. "The barbaric treatment of the woman avails us nothing. If she is, as you suspect, a counterrevolutionary, then you may execute her at your leisure. But if she has come here with information, we would both be fools to dismiss it out of hand without so much as listening to her tale."

Brigid urged Djugashvili to say more, to press his point, but he had made his stand and she could see his body slowly retracting into itself as he took up his traditional position of cowering before the ogrelike general.

A half minute passed as General Serge pressed his Tokarev against Djugashvili's gut. He finally relented, pulling the weapon away and holding it firmly in his hand. "Fine," he snapped. "We shall listen to her, and then we shall decide on the appropriate course of action."

Serge turned to Brigid and raised the pistol to aim it at her head. "You, Baptiste. Speak," he instructed.

Djugashvili took a step forward into the room. "Come now, General," he said, "look at her. Your men have been—" as Serge turned his fierce glare back to the doctor, Djugashvili judged the words carefully "—very efficient," he finished. "We must let her sit, clean her wounds. And I imagine that she is thirsty also." He looked at Brigid and she nodded.

"I'm not interested in her well-being, Doctor," the general growled.

"Perhaps you should be," Djugashvili responded ominously.

Brigid could see the conflicting emotions cross the general's face. He was a brute who only truly understood brutish behavior, and the notion of allowing his prisoner any comfort, however minor, unsettled him greatly. "Fine," he barked after a moment. "My men will unchain her and we shall conduct the interrogation in your office, Comrade."

Brigid breathed a sigh of relief. It was a step in the right direction at least.

GRANT RETURNED FROM his discussion with Cerberus to find Kane waiting for him in the doorway to the little, brightly lit office. When he looked past Kane he saw Brigid was still in her cross-legged position on the floor, her eyes closed with her chest rising and falling slowly as she breathed. Beneath her nose, her face was cobwebbed with blood, and a trail of spittle drooled from her slack mouth. The beginnings of a black eye had formed over the left side of her face, and he could see a reddening patch of skin over her right eye where a bruise was forming.

"What did Lakesh say?" Kane demanded anxiously as Grant walked into the office.

"He says everything is fine," Grant stated, hardly believing his own words as he looked at the battered face of his seated colleague. "Transponders show Brigid's in no actual danger. All this stuff may look bad, but it has to be superficial."

"Superficial my ass," Kane spit. "Something is very seriously messed up here."

Grant dipped his head. "Sure looks that way," he agreed. He leaned closer to Brigid and saw there was blood along the edges of the fingernails of her right hand. He wondered what other damage she had suffered that he couldn't see.

"We both know that Lakesh can be a tricky bastard," Kane stated. Lakesh had had a hand in orchestrating Kane's and Grant's hasty exit from their previous lives as Magistrates in Cobaltville, which was just one example of the underhanded techniques he had used to pursue his personal agenda. "You figure if he wants this Death Cry badly enough he'd tell us not to disturb Baptiste despite the consequences?"

Still looking at Brigid's bloody face, Grant considered Kane's words for a moment before he shook his head. "Lakesh is a pretty straight shooter these days, especially when it comes to Brigid," he reasoned.

"But a leopard never changes its spots," Kane reminded him.

"Yeah," Grant agreed, "and I can believe that Lakesh would throw us to the lions if it meant getting something as important as a weapon to stop the whole war. But I don't believe that's what's happening here."

Kane stood beside the open door, his breath loud in the silent underground base. "I can't look at her like that and still think straight," he admitted before turning away from Brigid's bruised and blood-streaked face. He left the room and paced down the unlit corridor, finding his way in semidarkness down the little flight of steps that dropped the sunken base lower into the mountain.

Grant remained crouching by Brigid, studying her wounded face before he stood and followed Kane. When he reached the doorway he saw Kane turn back from just outside the canteen, a grim smile on his features.

"What about if the readings are wrong?" Kane suggested as he walked back toward Grant.

"Say what?" Grant asked.

Kane tapped at his inner wrist as though searching for his pulse. "What if the transponders are supplying bogus information and Lakesh doesn't realize it? What then?"

Grant shook his head. "I don't know, Kane. Is that likely?"

Kane walked up the small flight of steps and joined his partner at the doorway to the lit room. "Take a look at her and you tell me," he said, gesturing to Brigid. "Does she look in good shape right now? Honestly?"

Grant looked across the room at Brigid, then back to Kane, concern creasing his brow. "Even if that were the case, would it make waking her any less dangerous?"

Kane sighed. "Well, there's the rub."

BRIGID SAT IN SILENCE in Dr. Djugashvili's office as a handsome young lab technician called Yuri dabbed antiseptic on her cuts. She had removed her jacket to look at her arms, but other than the ridges in her wrists where the chains had cinched into her flesh, they had remained blessedly free from harm. Her legs and torso, she could feel, were a different matter, but she wasn't about to do a striptease for the lecherous General Serge now that she was finally in a position where he might actually listen to her.

Brigid winced as Yuri dabbed at the cut over her right eye, muttering to her that a nasty bruise was already taking hold. "I'm sure it will not leave any lasting damage," he told her thoughtfully. "It would be very sad to mar such a pretty face."

Brigid felt herself blush and she looked down at her lap for a few seconds, avoiding eye contact with the handsome lab assistant. "Thank you," she said quietly.

Besides herself and the lab assistant, General Serge and Dr. Djugashvili sat in the room, the general breathing loudly through his nose. Two sentries had been placed outside, standing on either side of the open doorway.

Djugashvili had complained that they were unnecessary. "She's just a lone woman," he told Serge. "What harm can she do?"

"She very nearly killed Krementsov," Serge reminded him in an ominous rumble. It wasn't true—she had only knocked Krementsov out, and that had been in self-defense, but she was very much regretting her reaction. Had things gone differently, might Krementsov have brought her to the general as a lost soul found walking the bland corridors of the vast astral factory? Somehow she doubted that Serge would have done anything differently.

"Okay, enough," Serge snapped, dismissing Yuri as he attended to Brigid's cuts. "Come, Miss Baptiste, join us."

Brigid shifted on her lightning-bright chair and edged a little closer to the general and Djugashvili at the desk. "I should begin by thanking you for your hospitality, General," she said without a trace of irony.

The general nodded and allowed her to continue. "Before our own discussion, I was speaking with Dr. Djugashvili concerning the status of this research facility."

"You mean that you were probing him for information on this facility." General Serge looked knowingly at Djugashvili, sitting on the other side of the desk.

"No," Brigid replied, "you misunderstand. I was trying to establish what year he thought it was."

"It's 1929," Serge responded immediately. "This is preposterous. What point are you hoping to make with this foolishness, Miss Baptiste?"

"It's not 1929, General," she told him, holding his gaze with her own. "Not by a long shot."

Serge looked to Djugashvili, who nodded briefly in encouragement. "I fear that what she says is true, General," he stated.

"So," the general continued, addressing Brigid once more, "what year is it, then, Miss Baptiste—1930, 1931?"

"This facility," Brigid said, deliberately addressing Djugashvili as she spoke, "has somehow become trapped in a mockery of time. When you came here in the spring of 1928, you gave up your physical bodies for a continued existence in this astral realm, hidden in an upper level of human consciousness."

"She knows too much," Serge growled through gritted teeth. "I shall shoot her now and be rid of the witch."

Djugashvili raised his hand in a halting gesture. "Let her speak, General."

Brigid took a deep breath, wondering whether her audience was ready for the proverbial bombshell. "It is the twenty-third century," she told Djugashvili and Serge, "and the world has changed beyond recognition."

"The twenty-third—" Serge spluttered in disbelief.

"At the start of the twenty-first century, about seventy years after you began your work here—" Brigid gestured around at the lightning-bolt surroundings "—a brief but deadly war erupted between the two most powerful nations on the planet, Russia and the United States of America. The war brought untold devastation, culling the global population and leaving the once fertile environment a deathland. Two hundred years later, we finally discovered why."

Dr. Djugashvili had edged forward in his seat as he listened to Brigid's recital, and even General Serge had quietened his bluster.

"The nukecaust was orchestrated by an alien race called the Annunaki. We are still piecing together the full story, but as we understand it the Annunaki have long prized the Earth as a playground full of wonderful toys to corrupt and manipulate. Those toys are us—the human race." Brigid looked at them, grateful that these people had been indoctrinated into a firm belief in aliens as a threat. "Evidence of the Annunaki's dabbling in human affairs reaches back over millennia—they were responsible for the Great Flood that appears in the Bible, and their influence on human affairs has been wide-reaching and almost always deadly. They have come back to subjugate humankind and use them as slaves or…I don't know what."

General Serge placed a hand on his brow and rubbed at his eyes thoughtfully. "You spoke of two great nations, Russia and the United States of America, going to war," he stated. "Which nation do you represent, Miss Baptiste?"

"I represent the resistance movement that opposes the Annunaki in their most recent incarnation as the overlords," she told him. "Borders are irrelevant."

"America, then," he decided. "You think I am stupid?"

"I think you need to listen carefully," Brigid corrected. "This facility, Project Chernobog, was tasked to design and hide a weapon that can be used against a significant supraterrestrial threat. That threat has arrived, and if you want to play patriot games with an outdated notion of national borders that has had no relevance for almost three centuries, then I'm going to have to assume you're just too damn scared to do your job, General."

General Serge's left hand whipped out and he slapped Brigid across the face, knocking her from the stool. "Watch your tongue."

As Brigid got up from the floor, the side of her face stinging, she saw Dr. Djugashvili stand up behind the desk and address General Serge. "It seems to me, General, that the young lady has a point," he stated firmly.

"And what point is that, Doctor?" Serge snarled, watching Brigid reseat herself.

"We have had no communications with the outside world in many months," Djugashvili pleaded, "and if, as Miss Baptiste proposes, time is running differently for those within this facility, then it is entirely plausible that the reason for this is a massive world upheaval about which we know nothing."

"But this concept," Serge wondered, "that time is somehow stuck in this facility…"

"When asked, I told Miss Baptiste that I thought it was perhaps 1929," Djugashvili explained fearfully, "but when I thought about it I could not, for certain, say that this was the case. It is like trying to remember a dream, trying to pin three-dimensional facts on a two-dimensional picture. Time and memory seem to be somehow ephemeral, unreal."

"These concerns have never bothered us before," Serge stated.

"They bothered Laynia Krylova," Djugashvili stated, "before you killed her. That was why you shot her, wasn't it? She had begun to ask questions that you didn't have answers to."

"You would do well to remember where you are," the general said ominously, his hand playing with the catch on his holster, "and who is in authority here."

Djugashvili sat back down, taking a steadying breath. "I am sorry, General."

Brigid spoke up again as the general glared at Djugashvili. "I think it's time to exercise your authority, General," she told him, "and bring the Death Cry into play."

GRANT LOOKED AT BRIGID'S static form in the bright light cast by the xenon beam as he considered the dilemma. "I don't know, Kane," he admitted. "My fear is that by waking her we could make a bad situation worse."

Kane stood beside him, looking down at their deathly still companion. "She's still breathing," he decided. "That's got to be a good sign."

Grant pointed at the cut on Brigid's forehead where the

bruise was forming above her eye. "Looks like her wounds are scarring over, and she's no longer losing blood."

"She vomited earlier, while you were away," Kane told him. "Just a little, but I cleaned it up."

"Maybe we should clean up the cuts, too," Grant proposed, "so long as we don't disturb her. If the transponder's not giving Cerberus accurate data, then waking her might be a good thing. I just don't want to disturb Brigid if she's on the verge of a big discovery."

"Agreed." Kane nodded.

"So we clean her, we monitor her visually, but we don't wake her," Grant concluded.

"It blows, but it's a plan I can live with," Kane declared.

"Let's hope she can," Grant muttered. "Do you have a medi-kit in that bag of yours?"

Kane reached for the satchel he had left on the desk pushed against the wall with the bronze Cheka shield on it. "A roll of bandage weave, needle and thread," he explained. "Probably enough for this," he added as he looked at Brigid's battered face again, dread welling inside him.

"Kane," Grant said, then repeated it louder, grabbing the man by the shoulder and turning the ex-Mag to face him. "There's a medi-kit in the Mantas. I'll go get some antiseptic and see what else I have. I'll be five minutes, okay?"

Kane nodded gratefully. "I'll time you."

With that, Grant turned and headed for the ventilation shaft once again, wishing he could offer Kane some kind of reassurance.

A RESTLESS DOMI PROWLED into the Cerberus ops room as the members of the afternoon shift took their positions at the monitoring equipment. Lakesh was dozing, stretched out on three seats that he had pushed together at the side of the room, determined to be nearby if there was any change in the status of the Russia field team. Reba DeFore, the Cerberus medic, had taken her place monitoring the computer display that showed the data feed from the subcutaneous transponders.

On the far side of the room, Donald Bry, Skylar Hitch and two other computer jockeys were working through pages of printouts, examining the material line by line as they searched for a way to break the hack that had infiltrated the Cerberus satellite feed.

Domi saw that Brewster Philboyd had taken Bry's usual spot at the communications desk, and she walked silently across the room to speak with him. "Any word from Kane?" she asked, startling Philboyd from his monitoring work.

"Domi." The big man gulped, nervously adjusting his glasses as he looked at her. "I didn't hear you come in."

"No shoes." She smiled, lifting one of her shapely, white-skinned legs from the floor and pointing her bare foot at his face, toes outstretched. "Good and stealthy!"

Philboyd smiled at that. "We heard from Grant an hour ago, but I haven't heard anything from the field crew since then." He glanced at the clock. "No big deal—we don't expect a report for at least another hour," he assured the albino woman before turning back to the satellite feed and adjusting the monitoring filters.

Domi leaned across the desk, catlike as she took in the

changing feed from the Vela-class satellite. "That's the same picture," she told him.

"What?" Philboyd asked, confused.

"I saw that picture." She tapped the glass of the monitor where a small window showed the overhead surveillance feed of the Caucasus Mountains in Georgia. "About an hour ago when I brought Lakesh tea." She looked across the room and saw that the cup of herbal tea sat, untouched, beside Lakesh where he dozed.

"Yeah," Philboyd said, "this is where Kane's team is, the Caucasus Mountains. We're keeping a close watch in case anything approaches. Hopefully we can get a message across if anything does happen."

"But this is the picture from an hour ago. Look," she said, pointing to the dark shadow close to the Mantas, "that's Grant when he spoke to Lakesh. He was just wrapping up when I came in last time."

"That's just a shadow," Philboyd assured her, but he expanded the window to look more closely.

"The picture is moving," Domi told him as she watched the wind rustle the leaves of the trees in the image, "but it's been looped somehow."

Philboyd frowned, pushing his nose close to the screen. "How can you be sure?"

"I can't," she said, "but if that's Grant it means that something is very wrong with the feed, and the rest stands to reason."

"I still say it's just a shadow," Philboyd grumbled, "a branch or something, maybe a rock." He tapped keys and enhanced the picture, drawing the dark blemish into focus. It was indistinct, but it certainly looked like a man seen from overhead. He turned his head, realizing that Domi was right beside him, close enough to kiss.

"Grant," she told him, her red eyes burning into his like flaming embers.

Philboyd turned away from her and pushed himself up out of his chair. "Dr. Singh, Donald," he shouted, "you really need to come look at this."

Chapter 16

General Serge shook his head. "I'm sorry, kitten," he told Brigid, "but your story is beyond ludicrous. A trick, a fairy tale to fool us into unchaining the Death Cry for the use of the enemies of Russia."

Dr. Djugashvili spoke immediately after the general had finished. "I disagree," he said. "Miss Baptiste's story is eminently plausible. Incredible, certainly, but plausible. To my mind, General, this fits with the facts."

"What facts?" Serge bellowed. "Three hundred years in stasis? No contact with the outside world? I see no evidence of this. You said yourself, Doctor, that the year is 1929."

"No," Djugashvili argued, "I said that I *thought* it was 1929 but that, upon reflection, the salient points of my memory and my sense of time's passage seem to be incomplete or unreliable. This facility was placed outside of normal reach, and we have nothing to go on, no objective, scientific facts with which to verify the woman's story."

"And that is all it is," Serge insisted, his fingers playing ominously with the catch on the pancake holster at his belt, "a story. A story to trick us into handing over the Death Cry to our enemies."

Stalemate, Brigid thought. They could go in circles

forever, arguing the same basic point. And unfortunately, forever was about how long it would take if what Djugashvili had told her was true, all the while her believing perhaps a few hours or days or weeks had passed when in fact it was another three hundred years.

"Would you like to know how the Annunaki started the war in 2001?" Brigid asked, addressing General Serge.

The general scoffed. "This race of supraterrestrials that you speak of? Do tell, how did they start the war?"

"There were a lot of smart men in power," Brigid told him, "men like you, General, who believed in national pride and the importance of defending their integrity as much as their borders. And every last one of those smart men, on both sides of the iron curtain, was so damn paranoid that he was all too willing to press the button that launched the missiles and bombed the whole planet back to the Stone Age." Brigid fixed him with her stare.

General Serge visibly swallowed as he absorbed her words. After a significant pause, Serge finally spoke once more. "Paranoid, you say?" he asked and Brigid nodded. "You are cunning, exploiting our fears in this way, but ultimately I choose not to fall for your deception, Brigid Baptiste." As he spoke, Brigid saw General Serge flip open the holster's flap and withdraw his Tokarev pistol.

"Don't do that," she told him, glancing at the gun.

"I think it would be for the best, don't you?" He smiled that awful, humorless smile once again.

Dr. Djugashvili gasped as he watched the general raise the pistol at Brigid on the other side of the desk. "General," he stated, his voice quavering, "this is madness. You cannot follow this course of action without—"

"Without what?" Serge snapped, handgun held firm and his eyes not leaving Brigid.

"Evidence," Djugashvili replied. "Science demands that you disprove her contention before you execute her."

"I am a military man," Serge dismissed, "not a fool scientist." With that, he placed the barrel of his Tokarev between Brigid's eyes. She felt the cold steel push against her forehead, her mind racing as she tried to come up with another solution.

LAKESH YAWNED AND stretched the kinks out of his muscles as he studied the image from the Vela-class satellite feed. Brewster Philboyd had transferred the picture to the biggest screen in the room, blown up to full size. Every thirty seconds, a caption flashed up in the bottom left of the image reading "Live feed," but Domi's observation had now put that contention into question.

Lakesh turned to Donald Bry. "What do you think, Donald?"

Bry gazed intently at the image on the screen. Philboyd and Domi waited for his response, Philboyd sitting at the keyboard that operated the large screen. "I'm not sure," Bry admitted after a few moments' thought. "There's definitely movement—you can see the wind catching the leaves, and there's no obvious join where the image has been looped. *If* it has," he added, turning to face Lakesh. "However, it's certainly not beyond the realm of possibility."

Domi grunted in disgust. "Stupid tech-heads, never good at making decisions. No instincts, have to analyze everything."

"I just don't want to be jumping at shadows because

of a paranoid notion someone's put in my head," Bry explained reasonably to Lakesh, casting a significant look at the albino woman.

"It's not paranoia," Domi assured Lakesh, dismissing Bry's implication. "That feed is on a fixed loop, repeating itself every minute plus."

"If that is the case," Lakesh announced, acting as mediator between the opposing viewpoints, "then we would need to decide on a course of action."

The voice of Skylar Hitch, the computer expert who had been seconded into Donald Bry's investigation team, cut through the room. "It is the case, Dr. Singh," she called, waving a sheet of computer printout above her head as she stood up at her desk. Everyone in the Cerberus ops center stopped what they were doing to hear what Hitch was about to announce. She moved across the room to join the group at the satellite monitor feed, feeling increasingly self-conscious.

"Um," she began, her voice nervous and loud, "I've isolated the hacker's coding. He's in the comm network, in the satellite feeds, and it looks like he's taken control of the transponder relays, as well."

Reba DeFore, currently monitoring the transponder feed, gasped and turned her attention back to her monitor, tapping several keys to bring up the enhanced details for Brigid, Grant and Kane.

Lakesh quickly scanned Skylar's printout before handing it back to her. "Well," he said levelly, "this certainly puts an interesting spin on things."

All around him, the crew in the ops room began asking questions and discussing the implications, but Lakesh ignored them and addressed DeFore at her terminal. "Anything?" he asked her.

She shook her head. "As far as I can tell, this is a normal feed," she admitted. "There's no indication that anything's being tampered with."

"Our hacker's probably looped a sequence from earlier," Lakesh concluded, "the same way he's dealt with the surveillance feed."

The rest of the room was quiet now, looking to Lakesh for instructions. Donald Bry, a man who always wore an expression of worry, had gone visibly pale. "Lakesh?" he asked.

Still looking at DeFore's screen, Lakesh took a deep breath and turned to address the ops room. "Okay, people," he said in a loud, commanding voice, "we are officially deaf and blind. Our ability to track our own people has been compromised, and we can no longer rely on the data that we are receiving. We have a field team out there that requires our support and assistance and that may well be in more danger than we realize.

"What we do know is that, though tapped, our communications to the field team still appear to be in working order," he continued.

Bry held up his hand, stopping Lakesh in midflow. "Couldn't those communications have also been faked?" he proposed.

Lakesh looked to Skylar, who was still holding her printout and looking slightly uncomfortable at having been the center of attention. "Miss Hitch?" he encouraged.

"It's possible," she acknowledged with a grim nod. "I don't know what the likelihood of that is, though."

Sitting just behind Skylar, Brewster Philboyd attracted Lakesh's attention with a raised finger. "Wouldn't we know if the Mantas had been moved?" he suggested.

Lakesh replied, addressing his answer to the audience in the ops center. "Let's not assume anything. From here on in we are to act in complete isolation. Line-of-sight confirmation on everything."

There was a brief rumble of contention from a few people in the room, and Lakesh heard the audible mutter of "impossible" from off to his right.

"Is that understood?" he asked, and was greeted by a lackluster assent from everyone in the room. "Donald, Skylar—I need you to purge the whole system of this hack. I don't care what it takes, and I don't care what we lose."

"But, Lakesh…" Bry began, and Lakesh cut him short.

"No buts," Lakesh told him. "If we built it once we can build it again, if we programmed it once we can program it again. Just get this thing out of the Cerberus mainframe."

Bry nodded, and Hitch followed him back to the desks where his team members were already discussing the problem as they brought up program data on their terminals.

"Brewster, Reba," Lakesh continued, "for the present, your feeds are useless. If you can come up with any possible ways of working around this, let me know."

"We might be able to piggyback off the Keyhole satellite and create a secondary feed for the transponders," Philboyd theorized.

"Then look into that," Lakesh told him. "For the present, monitoring duty is suspended with the exception of communications."

Lakesh strode across the room, taking another look at the bogus satellite feed showing the Caucasus Mountains. He felt suddenly very vulnerable as he saw the flashing "live feed" indicator pop up for a few seconds.

Domi stepped across from her position leaning against one of the desks and placed an arm around his waist. "Is it the end of the world again?" she asked Lakesh, and he saw the mischievous smile play across her lips.

"No, dearest," Lakesh admitted, "I guess not."

Domi kissed him lightly on the cheek then pulled away, giving him a significant look.

"What is it?" Lakesh asked. He had known Domi for a long time, as first a friend and later his lover. He knew that look.

"I'm going to join Kane," she told him firmly. She saw that Lakesh would protest, and she shushed him. "No, I'm going. Someone needs to tell them what's happened. 'Line-of-sight communications'—that's what you said."

"The effort that has gone into this," Lakesh warned her, "means there's a good chance there's going to be a wealth of trouble there in the mountains."

Domi offered a broad smile. "All the more reason to send backup," she told him, letting go of his waist and heading for the exit. "I'll go to the armory while you figure out the closest operational mat-trans point on your big map here. Okay?"

Lakesh nodded. "Since when did you start giving orders?" he asked her as she walked through the doorway.

Domi turned back and showed him a coquettish grin. "Oh, you love it, really," she told him.

Lakesh smiled as the door closed behind the petite frame of his lover. She was right. It wasn't the end of the world. Not for them. But he couldn't speak for Brigid, Kane or Grant.

"CONTACT HEADQUARTERS," Brigid ordered, the Tokarev still pushing against the bone between her eyes. "Speak to your superiors."

General Serge shook his head ever so slightly. "No, Miss Baptiste, I don't need their permission to execute a counterrevolutionary dog like you. I am the ultimate authority in this facility. I have no need to verify my actions with my superiors."

"I understand that, General," Brigid told him, holding her nerve as the cold steel pushed against her head, "but in speaking to them you will disprove my story and be able to shoot me in good conscience." She knew it was the wrong thing to say the very second that the words passed her lips. This man had no conscience.

Serge spoke quietly then, looking Brigid firmly in the eye. "It has been nice meeting you, kitten."

Dr. Djugashvili spoke up before Serge had finished the sentence. "Do not pull that trigger, General," he insisted. Brigid looked hopefully over the general's shoulder, imagining that perhaps Djugashvili had a pistol of his own stored in his desk, but he was empty-handed. "I am of the firm opinion that we should contact the KGB and confirm the situation in the corporeal world before we execute the woman."

"And why is that, Dr. Djugashvili?" Serge snarled.

"Because if what she tells us proves to be true," he responded, "then your counterrevolutionary is the only link we have to the outside world."

Silence followed the doctor's statement, and Brigid felt her heart leaping in her chest as she waited for the next move. Finally General Serge relented, lowering the Tokarev from Brigid's forehead but still training it on her. He rose from his seat and walked across to stand beside the open doorway to the white-walled room, the weapon still pointing in her direction.

"You have friends on the outside world, Miss Baptiste?" Djugashvili asked, and Brigid nodded. "And they will be sympathetic to our situation?"

"My friends are one of the few bastions of human resistance to the alien threat, Doctor," Brigid assured him. "If you and the general are courageous enough to use the Death Cry weapon in battle against the Annunaki, then you will be hailed as heroes. I promise you that." She had used the word *courageous* deliberately, hoping to appeal to the military man's pride.

Djugashvili looked to General Serge for a decision, and hesitantly Serge nodded. "We shall contact headquarters," he explained before turning and exiting the room.

Brigid caught Djugashvili's eye and whispered, "Thank you," as they waited together in the office.

She heard Serge's voice giving instructions to the two sentries just outside the door. "I have a brief errand to attend to. Chain the woman up until I return."

Brigid's heart sank. The two sentries marched into the

room and took her by the elbows back to the room with
the crisscrossing pipes. She was back precisely where she
had started.

LAKESH TURNED AS DOMI entered the ops center at a
fast trot.

She had changed her clothes and was now wearing a
parka coat with a faux-fur collar over a cream blouse and
dark, full-length trousers and boots. The parka was a muddy
leaf color, all the better for blending into the background
trees of the Caucasus Mountains. With the coat open,
Lakesh could see that she had her trusted Detonics Combat
Master .45 holstered in a shoulder rig along with a viciously
sharp blade in a leather sheath on her belt. She hefted a
compact Uzi in her hands, feeling its weight for comfort.

"Not your usual choice," Lakesh said as he noticed the
Uzi.

"It's just a little something for the masses." She
shrugged. "Never know who I'm going to bump into."

Worry crossed Lakesh's features and he began to
express his concern but was stopped by Domi's gentle
touch on his arm. "It'll be okay," she whispered. "A little
change of scene is all. With bullets."

Nodding, Lakesh pointed up to the large map of the
world that covered one wall of the ops center. He had set
the Mercator relief map to show specific points at his
commands, and he flipped a control switch to dim the
lights so that his instructions were clear. "Our field team
is here," he explained as a throbbing green circle appeared
close to the old Russian border. "The most efficient way

to get you there would be by the interphaser, but there's no energy vortex in the vicinity of our friends."

Domi nodded as she looked at the map, encouraging Lakesh to proceed.

"We've located an old Soviet naval base here, just outside a fishing town called Poti." An amber light sparked to life beside the throbbing green circle, touching on the Black Sea. "Our tests show that a working mat-trans exists in the base, although we cannot be certain that the base itself is empty. We'll send you to this mat-trans and, if you run into any resistance, you are to jump back immediately. *Immediately,* Domi—you hear me?"

Domi saluted playfully. "Aye-aye, skipper."

"I'm serious about this," Lakesh warned her. "Now, Poti is perhaps twenty-five miles west of your final destination, which means you'll have some territory to cover once you get there. We're going to try to get a message through to Kane's team and see if he or Grant can come find you in one of the Mantas. But as you know, we can no longer guarantee the veracity of communiqués in this regard, so it may be that you're on your own."

Domi nodded. "I understand."

Lakesh stepped back and reached for a bundle of papers in a sealed, stay-dry pouch. He handed the pouch to Domi. "Here's a map of the area, as well as a second map showing operational mat-trans units in a two-hundred-mile radius from your landing point, in case you need to exit via a different route," he explained. "The main map shows the terrain with markings for the best route and your final destination. There may be some climbing involved, I'm afraid, but let's hope that Kane or Grant can come find you before that."

"Yup," Domi agreed, taking the stay-dry pouch and rifling through its contents.

"We've also included several satellite photographs of the immediate area," Lakesh told her, "which may be useful if there are any discrepancies between the old maps and the current lay of the land. From our most recent surveillance sweep, the area is mostly unpopulated once you get away from the coast, so you shouldn't run into any trouble. *Shouldn't* doesn't equate to *won't*, of course."

"Of course." Domi smiled.

Lakesh led the way to the antechamber that held the mat-trans unit. Farrell was already there, prepping the unit for use, and he silently acknowledged Lakesh and Domi as they approached.

"If there is any trouble," Lakesh warned her, "I want you back here straight away. Just a swift jump there and back, nothing more. Okay?"

"It will be fine," Domi assured him as she zipped up the parka coat and settled the hood down behind her neck, its faux-fur brushing against her earlobes. She stepped into the armaglass-walled unit, and Farrell pulled the door shut behind her, sealing her in the room.

A few moments later, a rising hum was audible and mist rose from the vents as the mat-trans unit prepared to blast Domi's atoms across the map and into faraway Georgia.

Chapter 17

"God hears the pleas of all of Her children," Minister Petrovna told the congregation as she stood before them in the cavernous church hall in Poti. She wore the ornate robe of office, a red dress with a golden star-field pattern stitched across it, and the miter that added almost two feet to her height.

The meeting hall was cold, despite the mild weather outside, and her congregation looked miserable and desperate. They numbered fewer than forty now. The whole town of Poti had been whittled down by disease and famine and the burning hunger they all held inside, and they had pinned their dwindling hopes on God. For Minister Petrovna, at least, business was booming.

A hand went up in the middle of the gathered group. The hand was attached to a thin arm and the arm belonged to Donatas, a twenty-five-year-old fisherman whose family, the minister knew, was on the brink of starvation. At twenty-five, Donatas looked like a man in his fifties. "When will we eat?" he pleaded desperately. "When will God bring us food?"

Minister Petrovna smiled reassuringly. "Soon," she replied, addressing the whole congregation. "An angel will come from the heavens to bring us God's bounty. I have seen this in my visions."

Petrovna really had seen this in one of her visions, although the validity of the visions of a woman on the very edge of starvation might be brought into question were it not that her congregation was also subject to the same hallucinations due to lack of protein.

Their coastal town was self-reliant and resourceful in the tough and unforgiving world of the long, postnukecaust recovery. But something had poisoned the fishing waters, a rainstorm that belched toxins into the water and the lands all around. The plants had continued to grow, the fish had continued to swim, but they were bad plants now, bad fish. The contamination was rife, and the vast community had been cut down to a tenth of its number in the space of a few months.

In such trying times, people turned to Minister Petrovna for advice and salvation, and she had done her best to assure them that all would be well, as their pets and then their children and their old folks wilted away before their eyes.

Once upon a time, the church hall had been a part of the naval base on the shores of the Black Sea. But the ships had long since gone, the sailors dead and forgotten. The old usage had made way for the new. Minister Petrovna had inherited the church from another minister in a gunfight that had left the man of the cloth bleeding in the street for three days before he finally passed away. By mutual agreement, it was decided that Minister Petrovna clearly had God's will behind her and that the old man had been nothing more than a fraud and a fool. While she may be the chosen of the Almighty, Minister

Petrovna chose to remain heavily armed. As it was written, God protected those who heavily armed themselves.

The congregation was getting restless, she could tell. They wanted food, not promises. "God's bounty," Minister Petrovna called, raising her voice above the hubbub, "is rich and She is generous. She has helped us all to survive for this long—we, Her faithful. This test of our faith is almost at an end."

Despite her rhetoric, no one could have been more surprised when, at that very moment, there was a sudden flash of lightning from the stained-glass wall behind the minister. The glass was a smoky violet in color and had been there for as long as anyone could remember. The stained glass surrounded a storage room, just a box with a tiled floor. In all of her days there, Minister Petrovna had never seen the room flash with lightning.

She paced across to the glass-walled room, watching as a wave of fog seemed to fill the room before parting to reveal a bulky figure inside where there had been no one before.

Minister Petrovna stood outside the door to the room, her congregation waiting eagerly behind her. As they waited, the figure inside the room made its way to the door and worked the lock from the inside.

When the door opened, a woman stood revealed, dressed in a bulky, green coat that ended in a fur-lined collar. The woman had short, close-cropped hair and her face was a beautiful combination of high cheekbones covered in smooth, iridescent skin. And the woman was white as snow, her hair and her skin a dazzling alabaster.

Minister Petrovna knew immediately what the beautiful woman was. "Welcome, angel," she said.

As Grant made his way back through the wide, sludge-filled ventilation shaft with the medi-kit from his Manta, he heard a voice patching through over his Commtact: "Kane? Grant? Do…read? Ov—" It was Brewster Philboyd.

"This is Grant," Grant responded. "I hear you, but the message is coming through broken. I repeat, your message is broken. Please stand by, and I'll let you know when I'm on higher ground. Do you copy? Over."

Grant stopped in the tunnel, the small metal box of medical supplies held loosely in his left hand as he waited for a response from Cerberus.

There was a brief pause, then Philboyd's voice came stuttering over the Commtact once more. "…sage received, Grant. Will be wait…ver."

Grant sprinted to the low end of the ventilation shaft, shouting for Kane's attention. As he was lowering himself through the busted grille into the underground Soviet base, Kane appeared in the doorway of the room, microlight in hand.

"What is it?" Kane asked urgently.

"I've just had a message from Cerberus," Grant explained, passing the medi-kit across to Kane. "Sounds urgent. I'm going topside to get a proper signal. Will you be okay taking care of Brigid?"

Kane flipped open the lid of the medi-kit, glancing at the supplies inside. "I'll be fine," he assured Grant. "Any idea what they want?"

"Dunno," Grant said, shaking his head. "Just heard

Philboyd trying to raise us. Breaking protocol, so I'd assume it's pretty urgent."

"You want me to come up and speak to him?" Kane asked.

"Stay with Brigid," Grant told him. "It's where you want to be. If they need to speak to you I'll shout down. Okay?"

Kane thanked his friend and urged him to get going. "Baptiste seems stable anyway," Kane added as Grant clambered back through the broken grate of the air shaft.

"Good," Grant acknowledged as he disappeared into the huge ventilation pipe once more.

DOMI OPENED HER EYES, and found herself slumped on the floor of a mat-trans unit. Beyond the armaglass walls, she could see figures moving.

Carefully Domi righted herself, forcing her muscles to move as she climbed up from the tiled floor. All around her, wisps of smoke were dissipating where the mat-trans unit was powering down, and she could see battered boxes and crates full of ammunition and books on the far side of the room. Mat-trans travel was an altogether unpleasant experience. Domi stood in the middle of the chamber and took and held a deep breath, letting her nausea pass. Then she made her way to the door and disengaged the lock to let herself out.

She was greeted by a crowd of people, at least thirty of them that she could see, all of them looking tired and disheveled. Standing at the front of the group, smiling benignly, was a middle-aged woman wearing a long red dress and a tall hat.

"Welcome, angel," the woman said, staring at Domi in wonder.

Behind the woman, the crowd shushed to silence, and Domi realized that everyone in the room was watching her, awaiting her next move, their feral eyes glinting and sharp teeth displayed.

Despite Domi's assurances to Lakesh, it wasn't fine. Not by a long shot.

BRIGID BAPTISTE WAS STABLE, hanging limply from one of the lightning-white pipes in the part of the astral complex that she had come to think of as the torture chamber. It was the second time in an hour that she had been made to hang like this, a chain wrapped tightly around her wrists, binding them together and causing her to lose the feeling in her fingers. Or was it an hour? she wondered. Was it a day, a week, a year? She knew now that this place disrupted a person's sense of time, and the thought that she might have been hanging there for months rather than minutes, that Kane and Grant had perhaps deserted her decaying body, worried her greatly.

No, she told herself, they would never leave her like that. Kane would find a way to transport her back to Cerberus and have Lakesh and Reba DeFore look at ways to keep her alive until she woke up.

But how did one wake up from this astral weapons factory? Was it even possible to do so?

She remembered the strange concave wall with its permeable surface. It had seemed that she could pass through it, but she hadn't put that to the test. Perhaps it was a valve, a one-way filter that she had traveled through but could never use for a return trip.

"Damn!" she grumbled to herself as she hung there, completely still, conserving her energy. Djugashvili would know, surely. But what if Djugashvili did know, and what if it transpired that there was no way to return? What if Krylograd, the astral factory or whatever they were calling this place, what if it was fundamentally flawed, a dead end that could never be escaped? What if that was the reason that the Soviets had never revealed the existence of the Death Cry?

DID THAT WOMAN IN THE crazy hat just call me an angel? Domi wondered as she spun into the crowd behind the lady in the red dress. It seemed a pretty crazy thing to say, but maybe it was a mistranslation from the Commtact. She couldn't hear what the woman said after that; her words were blotted out by the rising cheer from the crowd.

The crowd certainly seemed pleased to see Domi; they greeted her with open arms. But there was something sinister about the whole occasion, an undercurrent that Domi felt instinctively.

"Look at her beautiful fingers," a disheveled woman close to Domi cried as the crowd pawed at her, pulling at the parka she wore.

"Give me some room," Domi said. "I can't breathe."

The crowd ignored her. They were probably unable to understand her words anyway, Domi realized as they huddled closer.

The woman in the hat and the red dress was shouting

again, giving instructions to the mob. "Everybody will get a piece of the angel," she assured them. "Hold her down," she said as she produced a meat cleaver from somewhere in her long, layered dress, "while I make the first incision."

The disheveled woman who had been admiring Domi's fingers suddenly pulled at the albino woman's wrist, yanking her closer and snapping her teeth as she tried to bite Domi's pinkie finger.

Domi made a fist and the woman's sharp teeth clamped down on a knuckle. Across from her, a man was trying to pull Domi's left arm behind her back, trapping it. Domi bent, loosening the man's grip and rolling him over her shoulders.

Cannibals, she realized, or something very much like. She'd touched down in a great big gathering of the vile bastards. And it was clear that they were hungry for albino meat!

GRANT STOOD BESIDE THE broken ventilation grille as he spoke to Cerberus over the Commtact. Brewster Philboyd had been replaced by Lakesh, who explained the situation in brief.

"We have significantly more than just communication problems," Lakesh told him, "and it seemed judicious to send another agent to join you in the field. Over."

"Understood," Grant acknowledged, before waiting for Lakesh to give him the details. "Over."

"Domi has jumped to a mat-trans unit in the old naval base in Poti. The coordinates have been forwarded to the Mantas. Do you think you can track her down, Grant? Over."

Grant thought about it for a few seconds. "Couldn't you patch through her transponder signal?" he asked. "I could lock in on that and pick her up in next to no time. Over."

There was the standard pause over the Commtact as the communication was bounced from the satellite to the Cerberus redoubt in the Bitterroot Mountains and back. "That may be problematic," Lakesh explained. "We can try, but we've been having trouble with the transponder signals," he admitted. "Over."

Grant thought of Brigid and the conversation he had been having with Kane not so long ago about the apparent discrepancy of her condition and the transponder data's interpretation. "Patch it through," he decided, climbing into the cockpit of his Manta, "and I'll assume it's with a pinch of salt. Over and out."

As soon as the communication with Cerberus was finished, Grant hailed Kane, hoping the signal would penetrate into the underground bunker enough to explain the situation. "Kane? I've got a rush job on," he stated. "You hear me?"

Kane's voice came back to him over the Commtact, stuttered with asthmatic pauses. "—eceiving y— —at's happening?"

"Domi's here," Grant said as he went through the preflight routine. "I repeat, Domi's here. Needs a taxi service to pick her up from the airport. I'll be back inside an hour," Grant told him. "Do you copy?"

"One hour," Kane replied. "Gotch—"

With that, Grant powered the Manta into the skies and headed west toward the blip on his heads-up display that represented Domi's location in the coastal town of Poti.

VOICES FROM THE DOORWAY made Brigid look up. The two sentries who had brought her there had taken up posts outside the open door. Now they were talking to another man, and as Brigid listened she recognized the voice of Yuri, the young lab technician. A moment later, he walked through the door carrying a bottle of ammonia and a roll of gauze.

"I wanted to take another look at your wounds," he explained quietly, offering Brigid a shy smile.

"That's very kind," she told him, struggling to keep her head raised to maintain eye contact. Her muscles were screaming with pain from fatigue and discomfort.

The lab assistant removed the cap from the ammonia before placing a balled rag over the top and tipping it upside down. Once the rag was soaked he began dabbing at the cut above Brigid's eye, cleaning the wound of debris. It stung, but Brigid endured it in silence.

Once Yuri had finished cleaning the wound, he examined it closely, nodding with satisfaction. "It shouldn't cause you any trouble," he told her, keeping his voice low, "just a bit of swelling. You have another cut on your cheek," he told her as he added ammonia to a new cloth.

"You're very thoughtful," Brigid said as he worked at the graze that ran down her left cheek. She looked closely at the man; he couldn't have been much more than nineteen or twenty years of age. He had thrown his whole life away, albeit unwittingly, on this fabulous project.

"Dr. Djugashvili tells me," Yuri began, trying to appear matter-of-fact, "that you have come from the future."

Brigid smiled. No, she thought, you're stuck in the past.

But it didn't bear explaining. "It's true," she responded, "a long way in the future. The twenty-third century."

"It is incredible," Yuri said. "A modern wonder. My mother would never believe such a thing possible, that I, her son, met a visitor from the future."

"Your mother must have seen a lot of change," Brigid said. "You must miss her."

"Not so much," Yuri told her. "Mostly I miss my brothers and sister. My mother would have much difficulty comprehending where it is that I work. This whole research facility is an exceptional construction."

"I can't argue with you there," Brigid agreed.

Yuri smiled tentatively as he worked at the cut on Brigid's cheek, apologizing for the stinging sensation that the ammonia water caused. "The future—what is it like?" Yuri asked finally.

"It's…" Brigid began, and then she halted, considering her words. Finally she spoke once more. "The future is very different from what you remember, Yuri. There was such a flurry of achievement in the twentieth century, it must have seemed that the miracles would never stop coming. But one day it ended, literally in the space of a few hours. There was an atomic war, a war of such incredible destruction that it stunted humankind for two centuries."

"But where you are from," Yuri asked as he recapped the ammonia bottle, "what is that like? What is it like to live in the future?"

"It's a struggle every day," she admitted. "Did Dr. Djugashvili tell you why I'm here?"

"He says that you have come requesting our charity," Yuri told her.

She nodded, and it started the chain that held her swinging slightly. "Man may have fought the war that started the twenty-first century, but it is an alien race called the Annunaki who have reaped the benefits," she explained. "We have struggled with their opposing army, which has superior technology—aircraft and guns and things that you couldn't begin to imagine. The device that you have constructed here, the Death Cry, could change the face of that war. With it, we could end two hundred years of exploitation, millennia of manipulation."

"You believe that the Death Cry could do this?" the young man asked.

"I have read Dr. Djugashvili's original reports," she told him. "I think it's worth a try."

Yuri nodded, considering her words. "My mother saw many changes in her homeland," he said after a few moments' thought. "She said that brave men changed things for the better."

Brigid considered the young man's subjective age. His mother would have lived through the October Revolution, the dethroning of the czar, the rise of the Soviet Socialist Republics. He himself was probably too young to remember those changes, just a child when Russia's identity and her people's way of life had changed so utterly. Yuri himself had a strange kind of immortality in this realm, a useless kind of eternity that meant nothing ever changed for him and the other people working there. "I need brave men," she told him, "men who can make brave decisions."

"You have come here at great personal risk to fight for what you believe in," he told her. "I think, perhaps, that all brave men are not men at all, Miss Brigid," and she felt the blush rise in her cheeks.

THERE WERE SO MANY PEOPLE surrounding Domi that there was no chance of pulling her Detonics pistol clear of its holster or getting the 9 mm Uzi out of her coat.

The tired-looking woman in the filthy clothes was grasping for her wrist again, eyeing her fingers. Domi's fist drove forward, caving the woman's nose in a burst of blood. She spun on her heel, surveying the mob around her.

Upward of thirty people surrounded her, their feral eyes watching her closely. All of them looked emaciated, their faces sallow, their limbs thin. She doubted that any of them had much strength left, but they could overwhelm her by sheer numbers. And the leader, the woman in the red dress and tall hat, she looked pretty handy with that meat cleaver.

Something glinted in the corner of Domi's vision and she spun just in time to see a bearded man swinging an ax toward her head. She ducked and the heavy blade swished through the air above her, the attacker stumbling as his blade unexpectedly met nothing but air. Domi thrust her left leg forward in a sweep, hooking the man behind his ankle and pulling him over onto his back with a crash.

The rest of the crowd stepped back warily, watching the albino stranger with newfound caution. Domi leaped up from the dusty floor, holding her empty hands open for all to see. "I mean you no harm," she told them in a loud voice. "I'm not here to hurt you. It's just a misunderstanding."

The woman in the tall hat, clearly the group's leader,

snarled and shouted something that the Commtact translated as "Kill the meat angel." The rallying cry was taken up by other members of the mob as they closed ranks and moved toward Domi from all sides, giving her no chance to escape.

Domi's gaze darted across the mob, trying to find a way to break through. She could see windows along one wall and a set of wide double doors toward the end of the vast room. Other than the mat-trans, that doorway was the only exit from this place. Hanging above her, attached to the ceiling, was some kind of metal hook, a big thing that had once been used to lift moored boats for repair work on the underside of their hulls. The hook was attached to some kind of mobile crane, pitted all over with orange spots of rust.

As the crowd surged forward, Domi crouched, then leaped into the air like a coiled spring, her hands reaching for the hook that was nine feet off the ground. She grabbed it, yanking herself up as the mob reached for her, pulling herself just out of reach.

She stood atop the hook, looking down at the angry group. Their eyes and teeth glinted along with the smattering of blades that many of them had now produced. She could go up, use the thick chain that held the hook to reach the top of the crane, and from there climb into the rafters of the high-ceilinged chamber. That was a possible way to keep moving, but where would it lead her? She would still be stuck in the room, the crowd beneath her. Could she break a window maybe and get out that way?

As she balanced on the hook she heard a loud report, and a bullet zinged past her head. One of the crowd was shooting at her! It was time to move.

Domi clambered up the chain, arms and legs wrapped around it as she pulled herself up into the dark rafters of the room. There was another report, and a handful of buckshots slapped into the chain just below her feet, making the hook sway in a little circle.

Still clinging to the chain with her knees, Domi swung her body outward and grabbed one of the wooden rafters that crisscrossed the room, pulling herself up onto it. More shots were being targeted her way, ripping through the air and taking chunks out of the rafters around her. Balanced on a rafter, she hunched into a ball, making as small a target as she could while the bullets embedded themselves into the ceiling above her. Domi reached into the parka and pulled out the Uzi. "Screw this," she muttered as she flipped off the safety catch and reeled off a stream of bullets at the crowd.

The 9 mm bullets zipped through the air, felling two of the crowd members and clipping a third before the crowd dispersed, running in all directions from the immediate area that Domi had targeted. She watched them scamper away, eyeing her fearfully as they backed into the shadowy corners of the vast boathouse.

A noise drew her attention, and she turned to see the woman in the hat and red dress had produced some kind of hunting rifle from who knew where. The laser targeter put a red spot on the ceiling by Domi's head as she tried to locate the albino woman through the rifle's sight. Domi ducked and began running across the thin bar of wood that she was balanced on as the woman fired her first shot.

"Kill her," the woman shouted triumphantly. "Kill the meat angel!"

I've been an angel for less than five minutes, Domi thought grimly, and already everybody wants to clip my wings.

A second shot from the rifle slapped into the rafter, splintering the wood just a step in front of Domi's left foot. As the bullet struck the rafter, she slipped, her arms windmilling as she struggled to keep her balance. Another bullet cut through the air, whizzing past her ear and into the ceiling just above her head.

Domi recovered her footing and surveyed the crowd beneath her, trying to pick out the woman in the tall hat. A volley of bullets streamed past her a little farther along the rafter as other members of the hostile group took aim at her. Domi held down the trigger as she blasted a stream of shots randomly toward the floor below her. Cries and screams came back as the crowd panicked once more.

One voice came translated over the Commtact, louder than the others: "Tough damn angel you called down, Minister."

Domi recognized the screeching voice of the woman in the hat as she replied, "But all of God's own taste heavenly, make no mistake about that."

Domi sprinted the length of the rafter and turned as she spotted a long beam that reached toward the windows. It was light outside, early morning.

Suddenly the loud, angry bellow of a shotgun cut the air and a great chunk of the roof beam disappeared just as Domi was about to step onto it. Her foot trod into thin air, slipping through the gap as she overbalanced. She threw her arms out as she sailed over the edge, letting go of the Uzi as she desperately reached for something to hang on to. Her right arm wrapped around a roof beam, pulling her body after it. She slammed into the roof beam with the top of her chest, driving the breath out of her in a weighty gasp.

Domi hung there, twenty feet above the floor, trying to recover her breath as a crowd of feral cannibals circled beneath her like sharks scenting blood.

GENERAL SERGE STOOD at the radio unit in the communications room of the astral factory feeling despondent. He had been trying for thirty minutes to hail the monitoring facility in Stalingrad to no avail. It was inconceivable that no one was on monitoring duty, whatever hour of the day or night it might be there. Utterly inconceivable.

As he sat staring at the silent radio unit, Serge became aware that someone was watching him from the open doorway to the lightning-walled room. He turned to see Dr. Djugashvili, his face a picture of concern. "Anything, General?" Djugashvili asked.

"I posted sentries and asked not to be disturbed," Serge growled, shooting Djugashvili a fierce look.

"I told them that I needed to see you immediately concerning a personal medical matter," Djugashvili explained hesitantly. "You have been in here for a long time, General."

"It appears," Serge said steadily, "that there may be a fault with our communications equipment, Doctor."

"You have been unable to raise headquarters?" Djugashvili asked.

"That is correct," Serge told him. "We will get Yuri to look at the radio set and see where the fault lies."

"Listen to yourself," Djugashvili barked, his voice

loud in the vast, empty room. "Excuses. You are making excuses. After everything that the woman told us, you are making excuses, trying to rationalize her story away as though it could not possibly be fact."

"She may have sabotaged our equipment," Serge told him evenly.

"I do not believe that," Djugashvili spit, "and neither do you, General. If her story is true, then we have been stuck here in this awful, soulless place for three hundred years. And we have nothing to show for it but dead colleagues and a weapon that no one has ever asked us to use. Until today."

"*If* her story is true," General Serge agreed, his emphasis showing his skepticism.

"I see no reason to doubt her story," Djugashvili announced firmly, "and I believe that we should now proceed forward, albeit with caution."

"Yes," General Serge whispered as he produced the Tokarev pistol from its hiding place in his lap, aiming it at Djugashvili, "with caution."

With that, Serge pulled the trigger and the gunshot sounded harsh in the empty, echoing room as the bullet ripped through Djugashvili's body between his second and third ribs.

Djugashvili didn't even have time to cry out, the shot was so sudden. He just slumped to the floor, mouth open, clutching at the wound in his chest as his blood stained the lightning-white floor of the room.

"And now, Dr. Djugashvili," General Serge announced as he rose from his seat, "I shall deal with your counterrevolutionary friend for good." Pistol in hand, he strode from the room.

Chapter 18

Still hanging from the pipes, Brigid cocked her head as she heard the sudden pop.

"What was that?" Yuri asked, turning to the open doorway of the room.

"Gunshot," Brigid said with the certainty of experience.

Yuri turned to her, a shocked expression on his face. "Do you think?"

Brigid nodded. "Yuri, you have to help me now," she told him quietly. "You must get me down from here, untie me."

"But," Yuri began, but Brigid cut him off with a stern look of her emerald eyes.

"Everyone's life in this facility is in danger," she told him firmly. "If you do not help me now, everyone here will die."

Yuri looked at the chain that held her to the pipe. The chain was looped over the pipe and attached to a hook on the far wall at Brigid's back. It would be a simple job to free her. He glanced over his shoulder, looking for the sentries he knew were waiting just outside the door. "I do not know that this is the right thing to do, Miss Brigid," he admitted sorrowfully.

"I believe that General Serge has just done something very, very stupid," she whispered, "and if you don't get me out of here, I think he'll continue doing stupid things until everyone in this facility is dead, yourself included."

"Why would he do such a thing?" Yuri asked, consternation furrowing his brow.

"Please," Brigid urged, "there's no time to discuss this. Get me down from here before—" She didn't bother to finish her sentence. The large figure of General Serge was standing in the open doorway flanked by the two sentries.

"Do continue," Serge encouraged, gesturing to Brigid with his handgun.

"What happened?" she asked forcefully as Yuri backed away from her and stood against the wall, as far from the discussion as he could get, too terrified to push past the general and his sentries.

Serge smiled that awful, humorless smile of his. "A little difference of opinion," he told her. "Nothing to concern you."

As the general raised the pistol in his hand, Yuri cowered from the military men, pushing himself against the back wall.

"Where is Dr. Djugashvili?" Brigid asked. "I think that I should speak with him. Right now."

Serge took a step forward, weapon pointed between Brigid's breasts, just inches from her sternum. "He is indisposed, kitten," Serge told her, the malicious smile still on his lips.

Brigid could feel her heart pounding faster now, the

pulse pumping in her ears as the gun was held on her. "Did you contact your superiors as we discussed?" she asked, struggling to keep the tremor from her voice.

"That need not concern you any longer," Serge stated ominously, and Brigid watched as his gray eyes narrowed infinitesimally. It has to be now, she realized.

The general was pulling the trigger as Brigid moved, pulling herself upward from her pendulum position and kicking her legs out before her. There was a flash of light and a loud recoil as the gun went off, but the heavy heel of Brigid's boot had already knocked into the general's wrist, throwing his aim.

She saw the look of shock on his face as the bullet went wide, drilling into the white wall off to Brigid's left. The twin sentries were lifting their Fedorov rifles now, even as General Serge regained his position and swung the pistol back toward her, targeting her face as she dangled at the end of the chain.

The general pulled the trigger for a second time just as Brigid's face disappeared from his line of sight and she dropped to the floor. Immediately afterward, a volley of shots followed from the sentries' weapons, splitting the air above her as she fell.

Yuri, she realized. He had unhooked the chain once he had eased himself, unnoticed, to the back of the interrogation room.

She was on the floor now, wrists still clamped together, and she kicked upward, driving the pointed toes of both boots into the general's groin. He grunted in pain, dancing on the spot for a split second as the sentries' bullets whizzed around him.

"Cease-fire," the general shouted, his voice suddenly strained. "Cease-fire!"

As the sentries stopped shooting, Brigid rolled to her knees and swept her bound hands outward, flicking the long chain cord like a whip. The chain cut through the air, and its heavy links slapped across the face of one of the young sentries, cuffing him across the ear with a blossoming of blood.

She spun to her feet, glancing behind her to make sure that Yuri was still safe at the back of the room. As she whipped around to her attackers once more, Brigid's left leg stretched out, booting the general full in the face with a weak but effective roundhouse kick. The general howled, staggering to one side as Brigid's foot came back down on the solid floor. Immediately she used the energy to kick off from the floor, driving forward with her shoulder down, right elbow pointing outward.

It was messy, brutal and quick, but her elbow connected with the side of the general's head as he reeled from the kick. She thumped the fleshy part of his face between the eye and ear, knocking him backward. She had to disarm this psychopath. That was the first priority. And, after that, she had to disarm the others and get a gun for herself.

It was insanity. She was tired, still bound by the chain and three armed enemies were just a shout away.

General Serge crashed to the floor, his jaws clacking loudly together and the breath spurting out of him like a burst balloon, his right hand letting go of the Tokarev pistol. One of the sentries was shouting, ordering Brigid not to move, telling her he would shoot, but she just ignored him as she scrambled across the floor and grabbed Serge's handgun.

Less than a second later the gun was in her hands, pointing at the sentries as a bullet from it split the air between them.

"You are both going to be as still as statues," she told them, "because my patience has totally run out."

Both sentries stopped moving, looks of abject terror on their faces. Their fear was a palpable thing, more so than Brigid expected. They were clearly terrified of being shot.

"Yuri," Brigid called out, still holding the gun on the two soldiers, "are you there?"

Yuri's voice was quiet, timid, as he struggled to speak. "Yes, Miss Brigid. I'm here."

"You got any leaks? Any blood?" she asked.

"No," he told her.

"Good," she said. "I need you to disarm these gentlemen." As she said it, Serge began to shift beneath her, struggling back to his senses. Brigid coldcocked him with the gun, a swift blow to his temple before training the pistol on the two soldiers once again. "Don't either of you try to be clever now," she warned.

As Yuri took their autorifles from them, another figure walked into the doorway and Brigid saw that it was Dr. Djugashvili. He seemed to be limping more profoundly than before, and when Brigid glanced at him momentarily she realized that he was clutching his chest, his hand red with blood.

"Doctor," she gasped, "what happened?"

"The general," Djugashvili explained, staggering into the interrogation chamber, "had some trouble raising headquarters, exactly as you suggested."

"Are you…? What happened?" she asked, still watching Yuri take the Fedorovs from the sentries.

"I fear we do not have long," Djugashvili said in a strained voice.

Brigid looked at him properly then, and what she saw took her breath away. His face was drawn and pale, and a fine mist was floating from his skin, hair and clothes. Where his hair had been dark with gray streaks, it now seemed as though it was made of water vapor, gradually evaporating in a misty halo around his head.

"What happened to you?" Brigid asked, standing now and making her way toward him, the gun still trained on the disarmed sentries. As she got closer, she saw that his skin was breaking up, as though he were constructed of little flakes stitched together. When she glanced down at his white coat, shirt and tie, she saw the same thing was happening there, too.

"The general shot me," Djugashvili stated, and Brigid heard Yuri gasp as he used another chain to tie up the sentries.

"But what…?" Brigid began, unable to find the words to finish her question.

"This place." Djugashvili nodded sagely, untying the chain that held Brigid's wrists together. "Come, we have little time left."

Brigid followed Djugashvili out of the room with Yuri trailing behind her carrying a Fedorov rifle under each arm.

THE SLEEK, BRONZE-HUED Manta soared through the air toward the Black Sea. Sitting at the controls, Grant studied the heads-up display as he banked in a wide arc toward Poti, dipping below the clouds.

The shells of buildings jutted into the sky like fangs, and the tarmac roads were overgrown with grass and weeds. As Grant brought the Manta lower, he spotted the group of buildings that had once served as a Soviet naval base. They were dilapidated now, smashed windows and missing chunks from their roofs and walls.

According to the sensors, Domi was in the largest building in the complex, her transponder signal steadily winking on the visual overlay inside Grant's helmet.

CLINGING TO THE ROOF BEAM, Domi watched as the townspeople circled below, their keen eyes urging her sylphlike body to fall.

"I want her toes," one man cried, brandishing a mason's hammer in his hands.

"A leg," another shouted. "Look at her delicious, long legs."

A woman shouted over them, waving a chopping knife over her head. "I'm going to eat the angel's face. Gonna drink her eyes."

Domi forced her grip on the beam to tighten as she tried to pull herself back up, but it was an impossible task from that angle.

The woman with the tall hat was holding her sniper rifle loosely in her hands now, confident that Domi was about to lose her grip. "Come on, angel," she encouraged, "come down and feed us."

Domi swung her body around, letting go of the beam for a fraction of a second and dropping two inches before she grasped the beam once more, this time with both hands. She gritted her teeth as she pulled herself up, getting her chest over the beam before resting against it, the weight on her stomach, her legs still dangling over the side.

"She's trying to fly, I think," someone cried, and the others laughed.

"Shoot her down," the woman in the hat instructed, resting the butt of the sniper rifle against her shoulder and taking aim at the albino woman once again.

Domi vaulted onto the roof beam as the bullet cut through the air and ripped a chunk of wood from the beam beside her. She looked across to the line of windows, still halfway across the vast room from her current position crouching on the thin beam.

Another shot whipped by her, shattering a disused light fixture and showering Domi with splinters of brittle plastic.

Domi unzipped her coat and reached in for the Detonics Combat Master .45 that she wore at her shoulder. Swiftly, she popped her head over the edge of the rafter and located the woman with the sniper rifle before whipping her head back in as another bullet whizzed toward her. As the bullet drilled into the roof above, Domi flipped over so that she was resting flat on the beam, her right arm dangling over the side, Combat Master in hand. A series of bullets streaked past her, several clipping at the empty folds of the parka, as she sought her target. Then, Domi fired the Detonics and the bullet raced away behind a burst of explosive, arrowing to the ground and splitting the woman's tall hat—and skull—in two.

The leader in the ornate red dress dropped her sniper rifle and screamed, her hands reaching up to the sides of her head as her hat slipped and blood began to pour down her forehead. The woman was wailing loudly as she tried to hold her head together. Domi fired a second shot, and the bullet pounded through the woman's eye and into her brain, silencing her with a final, hideous yelp. As the woman fell to the floor, Domi started to select more targets. Those with ballistic weapons were her first priority; the knife wielders could wait.

She drew her arm back behind the wooden shield of the roof beam as an angry cry came up from the mob and another volley of bullets sprayed the air around her. Domi felt the thin beam that she was resting on shake with the impacts, and she saw chunks splinter away all along its length. She heard a creak and realized that the beam had lost integrity and would split or snap if she didn't remove her weight shortly.

Her ruby eyes scanned both ends of the roof beam and the area all around it. There was a cross beam about ten feet along from her at the end that her feet were pointed at. The cross beam looked relatively undamaged and capable of supporting her weight.

Lifting herself up like a cat, back arched, Domi rolled to her feet, her left arm out to steady her. Bullets zinged all around as Domi sprinted along the thin beam, one foot directly in front of the other, and then she heard the loud explosion of some kind of antiaircraft missile launcher cut the air.

She leaped the corner gap to the cross beam as a rocket blasted behind her, turning the beam that she was just standing on to so much firewood. Smoke clogged the air, and the ceiling above where the missile hit was now on fire, a small circle of red-orange flames flickering to life.

Ultimately a child of the Outlands, Domi had seen plenty of people like these, well-armed and crazy as rabid dogs. Seeing their leader die before their eyes had sent them into a killing frenzy, their own safety no longer a concern.

Domi danced along the beams, trying to keep moving toward the windows as bullets zinged around her. She reeled off a series of shots at the crowd as she ran, no longer taking aim, just trusting that her bullets would find targets.

As a second missile burst into the air with a cacophonous roar, Domi heard a voice in her head. She struggled to distinguish the voice as the symphony of violence exploded all around her.

"Domi, do you copy? I repeat, do you copy?" It was Grant, speaking over her Commtact.

She switched to broadcast and spoke softly. There was no need to shout, despite the racket all around—the Commtact could pick up and add sound to subvocalized conversations if need be. "Grant, this is Domi. I read you."

There was relief in Grant's voice as he spoke again. "Domi, I'm just over the Poti naval base in the Manta. My display says you're inside. That right?"

"I think so," Domi answered, realizing that Grant had to have been told about the tech problems that Cerberus was having with the transponders.

"There's a wide skirt of concrete here that I can land

on," Grant told her. "Southeast corner of the complex. Think you can get there?"

Domi leaped from the beam she was running along as a third missile rushed toward it. As the roof beam disintegrated, Domi took to the air and landed on a parallel beam, struggling for a moment to keep from toppling. "I'm in what looks like a ship-repair center," she told Grant over the Commtact, "but I'm having a little trouble."

"What kind of trouble?" Grant asked, concern in his voice.

"Hungry locals mistook me for dinner," Domi told him. "Now they're trying to flambé me with a rocket launcher."

"Crap!" Grant spit. "I'm bringing the Manta down now. What do you need me to do?"

"Hang tight and I'll come find you," Domi said as she skipped along the beam between another hail of gunfire. "And, Grant—keep the engine running, okay?"

"Roger that," Grant responded.

BRIGID BAPTISTE'S BODY remained unmoving in her trance while Kane watched her. Occasionally, he noted, her breathing sped up and he could see her eyes darting back and forth rapidly beneath her eyelids, but she gave no indication of being in pain or distress, and no further wounds had appeared that he could see. Having tidied up and bandaged the cuts on her face, Kane decided to leave Brigid alone in the brightly lit Cheka office while he took a look at the bunks.

The bunk room was quite large but felt small because

of all of the high beds within it, lining each wall. Kane counted twenty-four units to each wall, so the room contained forty-eight beds in all. A little over half the beds were occupied; there were twenty-seven skeletons in the room. Each was fully dressed, eleven of them in military uniform, their Fedorovs still clutched across their chests by skeletal fingers. Like the pair in the dining area, there was no visible sign of cause of death; it looked as if they had just lain down and gone to sleep.

Kane brushed the beam of his microlight across the walls of the dark, silent room, feeling uncomfortable and somehow expecting something to move, to jump out at him. Whatever had happened there had better not be about to happen to Baptiste. He wouldn't forgive himself if it did.

NEVERWALK SAT IN THE SAND, watching the emaciated goats and sucking on a pebble as he waited for his next instruction. The first dreamwalk had proved a strain for Good Father, and he had needed to sit down on a little outcropping to catch his breath. Until he was ready, the strike team had to wait.

Bad Father was standing over Good Father, speaking softly to him, words that didn't carry to Neverwalk's position. As he watched, Good Father pushed hard against the gnarled walking cane and got back to his feet, dismissing Bad Father's proffered hand.

"We are ready," Bad Father announced, encouraging the group to gather around.

Rock Streaming slammed the lid of his laptop shut, and Neverwalk bent over and he slipped it back in the carry case on his back. "Their communications are veiled," Rock Streaming told everyone significantly. "They suspect tampering."

"Do they know anything about us?" Bad Father rumbled gruffly.

Rock Streaming shook his head. "They have not identified the source of their woes yet."

"Will they?" Good Father asked urgently.

Rock Streaming's gaze took in the other warriors around him. "I cannot adjust the coding while we are in the Dreaming," he said. "If they were to crack it now there is a possibility…"

"*What* possibility?" Bad Father snapped, his voice raised.

Rock Streaming shook his head. "Hard to say," he admitted, "but I suggest we keep moving while we still have the advantage of surprise."

"Agreed," Bad Father and Good Father stated in unison.

During the stopover in Africa, Cloud Singer had etched out twin circles in the sand with the end of her pole, mirroring those at the edge of their tribal village in Australia. Good Father took up his position in the smaller circle while the other warriors gathered around Bad Father in the larger disk.

Good Father whipped the bull roarer above his head, spinning it to begin the long ululation.

And they were gone.

DOMI'S ARMS PUMPED as she ran the final fifteen feet of the roof beam, bullets slicing through the air all around her and patches of flame licking at the ceiling. The bank of windows was ahead of her now, and she raised her

Detonics pistol and fired repeatedly at the central panes of glass, shooting them out in an explosion of shards.

"She's making a run for it," one of the crowd hollered, "trying to fly back to heaven."

"Kill her," a woman screamed. "Don't let our angel meat escape."

Domi turned her head back, pulling the fur-lined hood of the parka over her head with her left hand as she dived through the shattered window. Glass flew everywhere as she crashed through the opening, knocking the crossbars of the window frame with her as she fell toward the ground fifteen feet below.

She could hear the wind rushing about her, then suddenly there was a jarring impact as she slapped against the ground and tucked into a roll, whirling across the hard concrete as broken glass tinkled all about her.

Shoving the hood back, Domi turned, the Detonics Combat Master up and ready, like an extension of her arm, pointing at the building she had just exited. She could see flames licking at the holes made by the rockets. As she watched, three heads appeared in the windows as her pursuers tried to clamber out. She loosed a shot, and the head in the center turned into a cloud of blood, bone and brain matter while the other two ducked back down out of sight.

There was a crash off to her left, and she turned to see a set of double doors burst open in the building. A crowd of armed townspeople ran after her. Still crouched, Domi squeezed the trigger and dropped out the lead runners. The others just kept coming, firing shots and waving knives and axes that twinkled in the morning sunlight.

Domi spun, launching into a run straight from her

crouch, the pistol still clutched in her right hand. She looked up at the sky to locate the sun, heading in its direction to find Grant and the Manta.

There was a huge dirty white building running right up to the sea, and Domi dashed toward it as the cries of the mob behind her grew louder. As she reached the corner of the building a wad of buckshot slapped against the wall beside her, and she tripped and fell to the hard concrete with a shriek. Lying there, Domi turned to push herself upright, and she saw that the lead cannibals were only a dozen paces away.

Domi took careful aim with the Detonics, conscious that she would need to reload momentarily. Two of her pursuers went down, screaming as they took the force of the bullets in the abdomen and shoulder, respectively. Behind them, the crowd stopped for a moment, unsure what to do.

Domi pointed the gun at a mustached man in ragged, blood-soiled clothes as he stepped forward, wielding a sledgehammer in his hands. She pulled the trigger. Nothing. Her gun was empty.

Domi leaped from the ground and sprinted away from the group, head down, arms pumping, the now-useless weapon still clutched in her hand. The crowd was just behind her now. She could hear rapid breathing over her shoulder, footfalls mirroring hers on the hard concrete of the ground. She reached into her open coat and fumbled for the spare ammo she had stashed in the inner pocket. Come on, she urged herself, come on.

Domi felt something then, the brush of a hand as someone reached for the bouncing hood of the parka.

"I have her!" a man crowed, but the braggart had spoken too soon.

Domi twisted to elude his grasp and looked up to see the familiar bronze metal shape of the Manta as she rounded the far side of the large white building. Relief soared through her, relief and joy as she recognized Grant sitting in the cockpit, the hatch open and pushed back. He held a long shaft of black metal in his hand—his Copperhead subgun.

Domi threw herself on the rock-hard ground, rolling to take the impact on her left shoulder. As soon as she hit the ground, she heard the rapid drumming of the Copperhead as Grant unleashed a storm of 4.85 mm steel-jacketed death into the mob. Domi put her arms over her head, covering her ears as the slugs drilled into the startled crowd of hungry killers. It was over in less than ten seconds, Grant standing in the cockpit spraying the area behind Domi with bullets.

As spent casings tinkled against the swooping wings of the Manta, Grant scanned the horizon, spotting more people running their way. "You want a lift?" he shouted as Domi rose from the ground and jogged toward the Manta.

She smiled at him, ruby-red eyes catching the sun's rays. "Hell, yeah," she told him.

Grant waited, Copperhead poised, as Domi leaped into the seat behind his. "You okay, Domi?" he asked, not looking behind him.

"Yeah," she told him. "Let's just get out of here, okay?"

Grant unleashed another burst of rapid-fire from the Copperhead, forcing the approaching group to back away, before he closed the hatch and quickly ran through the pre-flight sequence. "Seem like a friendly bunch," he muttered as he pulled at the throttle and the Manta lifted into the air.

"Bastards wanted to eat me alive," Domi spit, watching the town of Poti disappear below them.

"Yeah," Grant said, "you've got to learn to choose your friends better."

THE STRIKE TEAM STEPPED OUT of the Dreaming and found itself in a forest in the mountains, the cool, fresh air whistling through the trees. Its members spread out, weapons at the ready, checking their surroundings warily.

Neverwalk stayed close to Good Father as he leaned against his walking stick and kept to the shadows. Cloud Singer and Rabbit in the Moon rushed ahead to check that the area was secure.

Ahead of them, Neverwalk could see a clearing and a single-story building, just a box really, built of concrete with slit windows all around. Over the far side of the building were more trees, and just before them was a wide, sleek metallic object finished in a glistening bronze that glowed like fire in the rays of the early-morning sun. Neverwalk recognized it from the Vela-class satellite feed as one of the vehicles that the Cerberus people had traveled there in. But hadn't they used two of the graceful aircraft to get there?

"Good Father," Neverwalk said, keeping his voice to a whisper, "look. One of their vehicles is missing."

Good Father looked to where Neverwalk was pointing, nodding when he noticed the lone metal-shelled craft sitting there.

"What does it mean?" Neverwalk whispered urgently.

Good Father held a finger to his lips, shushing the boy. Rabbit in the Moon dashed back to the others, his compound bow in one hand. "The area is clear," he assured them. "No one is around."

Bad Father stroked his beard thoughtfully as he looked around the clearing at the overgrown road. "They spoke of a burrow," he said slowly. "Beneath our feet."

As the strike force made its way toward the clearing, Cloud Singer cried out from the end of the blacktop opposite the low concrete building. The road was shaped like a hangman's noose there, a little circle for turning large vehicles, and an old, rusty truck was parked at a lurch, its wheels rotted through. "Here!" Cloud Singer shouted, pointing to a patch of weed-covered ground at her feet.

The team jogged across to look, and Cloud Singer gestured to a wide, circular grille of rusty bars, partly obscured by the undergrowth. On one side of the circle there was a space where a large hole had been cut and a thin cord snaked from the hole, snaking into the grass until it attached to a climber's piton that had been driven into the ground.

"They came this way," Rock Streaming decided. "Do we follow?"

Good Father unhooked the bull roarer from his belt and looked to Bad Father and Rabbit in the Moon. "We'll get there through the Dreaming," he stated, and the two navigators agreed with nods.

The five of them gathered around Good Father, forming a rough circle as the bull roarer gathered speed above his head. After a tingling of the implants at the base of their necks, they all emerged in Realworld.

In this instance, Realworld was a close-walled tunnel, almost entirely dark apart from a light source shining from a rectangular opening at the far end. As one, the strike team called on the electrochemical polymer lenses that appeared over their eyes on nictitating membranes, and suddenly the corridor was revealed to them clearly, as though well lit.

"Silent now," Bad Father hissed as the bull roarer stopped spinning. "We're in the lap of the enemy."

Neverwalk swallowed, and it felt hard and jagged in his throat. He watched as Cloud Singer and Rock Streaming moved ahead, warily checking the open doors to the left and right of them.

KANE HAD FOUND A LOCKER in the far end of the bunk room and was running the beam of his microlight over the contents: books and magazines, personal letters stuffed in old envelopes. Suddenly he cocked his head, thinking that he had heard something.

Kane stepped away from the locker and made his way back to the open doorway of the room, covering the beam of the microlight with his hand. He waited by the door, listening.

He had heard something, just for a second, a kind of moaning. A ghost maybe? Crap, this place is giving me the heebie-jeebies, he told himself as he drew his hand away from the front of the microlight.

Then he heard something else, a light scampering, so quiet it was almost not there at all. That wasn't his mind playing tricks on him; his point-man sense was damn sure of that even if his conscious, rational mind was trying to deny it.

Kane doused the beam and placed his dark glasses

with the electrochemical polymer lenses back over his eyes, granting himself artificial night vision in the dark complex. Silently he paced toward the door, his feet kissing the tiled floor.

Once he reached the doorway he pushed his back against the wall and listened for sounds in the corridor beyond.

He had heard the footsteps of at least two people, quietly moving along the corridor. Warily Kane leaned forward and popped his head around the door frame for a fraction of a second, peeking down the length of the corridor with the polymer lenses over his eyes, creating light where there was darkness.

His head whipped back behind the doorjamb, eyes closed as he assessed what he had seen. There was a group at the far end of the narrow corridor. Kane couldn't say how many, but not more than ten, maybe as few as three.

Crouching, he leaned against the door, his wrist tendons flinching as he slapped the Sin Eater into the palm of his hand. Then he popped his head out once more, looking up the corridor and assessing the situation. Five—no, six people. One of them was a woman, leading the others, a stick or pole in her hand. Next to her was a man, a long coat similar to Grant's billowing behind him, some kind of bent blade in his hand.

Kane ducked back again, looking around for another exit that he knew wasn't there, just an instinctive reaction to being trapped as the strangers approached.

The weight of the Sin Eater pistol in his hand was just another part of Kane's body, not even a consideration in his mind. But he looked at it then and he thought of

Brigid Baptiste, three doors away from him and lost in meditation.

Diplomacy, Kane reminded himself, stepping into the corridor and preparing to introduce himself. He flicked on the microlight beam and waved it along the corridor, hoping he hadn't blinded anyone. "Um...hello?" he called.

Before Kane realized what was happening, an arrow whizzed through the air and clapped against the flashlight, knocking it from his hand and killing the beam. A second shaft whistled toward him, and he dodged his head back as it slapped into the wall behind him.

"Looks like negotiations are over," Kane muttered as he raised the Sin Eater.

Chapter 19

Brigid Baptiste turned to Dr. Djugashvili as they rushed down the pure white corridor toward the main room of the astral complex.

"We must launch the Death Cry," he told her, gritting his teeth as he limped along at her side.

"The soldiers will never let us do such a thing, Doctor," Yuri called from behind them. The lab assistant had slung one of the rifles over his shoulder by its strap and he hefted the other in his hands, poised to shoot anyone who followed them.

"We'll have to convince them," Brigid said, shoving the Tokarev into her hip holster, where it seemed to overlay then replace the ghostly image of the TP-9. "Yuri, hand me a rifle."

Yuri passed the one that he held across to her, then shirked the other from his shoulder and rested it in his hands while she covered their advance.

"We don't have much time," Djugashvili said, his voice strained.

"Why not?" Brigid demanded. "What's going to happen?"

"I won't be here to help you for very long," he told her.

"What do you mean?" she asked, glancing at him

before turning her attention back to the corridor ahead of them. Djugashvili seemed to be disintegrating. Flecks of his face were blowing away, rising into the air like the embers of a wood fire before disappearing into nothingness. A mist of washed-out black billowed from his head where his hair had once been, and his limbs seemed to smolder, billowing like smoke as he swung them to march onward.

"I don't understand. What's happening to you?" Brigid asked.

"Do you remember what I told you about Laynia Krylova?" Djugashvili prompted.

"You told me she was shot, that she became a mist, a fog before your eyes," Brigid replied, feeling her stomach tighten in horror. "You're not… You can't be…"

Djugashvili nodded wearily. "General Serge shot me in the chest," he told her, pulling his bloody hand away from the wound that sat just to the left of his breastbone. Brigid saw the hole in his chest, the charcoal burn on his shirt where the bullet had driven through the material into his body. "I think perhaps he has clipped my heart." There were tears running down Djugashvili's face now as he explained what had happened.

"How can this be?" Brigid asked, her mind demanding reasonable answers, rejecting the evidence before her. "How can guns work here? How can they even exist here?"

"Laynia," Djugashvili explained as he limped forward, "was quite brilliant. She deduced a way to bring solid items here—our files, the materials we would need to work on the Death Cry itself. Quite, quite brilliant."

"And so she brought the guns?" Brigid asked.

"Soldiers do not travel without guns, Miss Baptiste," he told her sadly. "It was a prerequisite of the project, before we could even begin working in this astral factory."

"But what happens to your consciousness?" Brigid asked. "When you die, I mean."

Dr. Djugashvili smiled at her then, a kindly, forgiving look. "That is a question that has taxed minds far superior to mine or yours, I suspect."

Brigid realized that, up until now, albeit subconsciously, she had been treating this like a dream. An incredibly vivid, detailed and downright painful dream, but a dream just the same. Something that she could wake up from. Seeing the doctor breaking apart as they spoke made her acknowledge there was something fundamentally wrong with her assumption, that if she was killed there perhaps she wouldn't simply wake up to try all over again like some character in a video game.

The three of them had reached the end of the corridor, and Brigid peeked out at the colossal weapon that dominated the vast white-walled room. She counted nine soldiers there, including Krementsov, who had subjected her to that sadistic beating in the interrogation room. There were a dozen white-coated laboratory assistants going about their business at the hull or shell of the huge weapon itself.

Brigid turned back to the others and told them what she had seen. "How does the weapon work, Doctor?" she asked him. "Is there a control panel? Do we launch it or do we get inside it, like a vehicle?"

"We need to be inside the Death Cry to move it to the

corporeal world. Once there, we can unleash its scream at a single designated target," Djugashvili told her solemnly as Brigid watched more parts of his face and hands flaking away, revealing nothing beneath but some substance that looked like dust or sand.

"Scream," Brigid muttered, shaking her head. "What the hell does this thing do?"

"It obliterates life," Djugashvili told her, "with surgical precision."

FACE HIDDEN IN THE pilot's helmet, Grant suddenly shook his head and muttered, "Oh, no, no, no."

"What?" Domi asked, sitting behind him in the cockpit of the Manta. "What is it?" They were swooping through a range of mountains now, beautiful, pristine territory that reminded Domi of the wilds around the Cerberus redoubt where she would often go hunting.

"I just did a scan of the underground bunker, Project Chernobog," Grant explained. "Shows eight bodies beneath the surface. Warm bodies. Living folks."

Domi counted off on her fingers: "Kane, Brigid, plus six mean Russians who just thawed out?"

"Dunno who they are, but I'm going to go out on a limb and say they are trouble with a capital *T* and probably a capital *R,* too," Grant rumbled as he aimed the Manta down toward a clearing in the trees.

Below, Domi could see a small track of road and, snuggled between the trees at its edge, another Manta aircraft—Kane's.

"I explained that someone has systematically blocked and altered the feed data that Cerberus has received on this operation," Domi said, referring to the conversation they had had on the brief flight over as she brought Grant up to speed. "These people could have been waiting right outside, unseen by the satellite, just out of sight, waiting for you to leave before they made their move."

"Exactly," Grant growled, "a whole pot roast of trouble." He brought down the Manta, bumping it on the ground and unlatching the cockpit seals as he tossed his flight helmet to one side. "Keep your eyes open, Domi—we're going in."

KANE POPPED INTO THE corridor and reeled off a few shots from the Sin Eater, deliberately aiming over the heads of the newcomers. So far as he could see, they didn't even flinch, which told him a couple of things. These people were fantastically aware of their surroundings, and they were exceptionally disciplined warriors, despite appearances to the contrary.

Kane ducked back into the bunk room as another arrow whizzed through the air in his direction, its point missing his retreating shoulder by just six inches. He stood with his back to the wall, his breathing steady, the Sin Eater held high, ready for the next attack.

"If you people weren't sure," Kane called out, turning his head to the open doorway, "those were meant as warning shots. Now, I'm certain that if we all talk about this we can figure on some kind of agreement to our mutual benefit. What say you?"

The complex went silent and Kane could detect no movement from the hallway beyond. Then a deep, rumbling male voice called out from the far end of the corridor. "You are to hand over the weapon, the Death Cry, to us. That's the beginning and the end of the negotiation."

Well, that certainly makes things clear, Kane thought as he listened for signs of movement beyond the open door. "I'm going to have to say negative to that request," Kane shouted, his back still pressed to the wall, "on account of my not actually having the Death Cry."

"One of your people has it, Cerberus man," the rumbling voice called back down the corridor. "You will place your gun on the floor now and you will provide us with access to the Death Cry immediately."

Kane was startled by the brashness of his unseen opponent. Whoever they were, they knew that Kane's crew were representatives of Cerberus and, furthermore, that the Death Cry had already been accessed by one of them—Baptiste. The speaker had a definite accent, kind of nasal, but he hadn't sounded Russian. Not American, either.

As Kane pondered his next move he heard Grant's voice coming through in fits and starts over the Commtact. "…you reading me, buddy? I'm with Domi…"

"Repeat," Kane subvocalized after a moment. "Didn't receive your full transmission, Grant. Please repeat."

HAVING RAPPELLED DOWN the climbing cord, Grant stood in the sludge and muck of the ventilation shaft, waiting for Domi.

"…peat," Kane's voice said over the Commtact. "…ceive…full transmission, Grant. Please repeat."

"I said me and Domi are coming down the shaft now,"

Grant said over his Commtact. "We'll be with you in under a minute. You copy?"

"Copy that," Kane responded. "I've got some company dow—"

"Yeah," Grant replied. "We know."

At his side, Domi let go of the cord and splashed down into the mud before freeing her Detonics Combat Master from its holster. "You ready to do this?"

Copperhead subgun held two-handed, Grant gave her a look. "They might be friendly," he reminded her.

"Law of averages on that one?" she asked in a piqued tone.

"Yeah," Grant agreed, "but let's try not to get kill crazy unless and until, okay?"

"Hell, Grant, you take the fun out of everything," Domi cussed as she sprinted beside him toward the far end of the sludge-smeared shaft.

"FOR YOUR ATTENTION, Dr. Singh," Donald Bry said as he stood beside Lakesh's chair in the center of the Cerberus operations room and handed him a paper report of roughly two dozen pages.

Lakesh flicked through it for a few moments. "Summarize it for me, Donald."

"We've managed to break the coding on the hack, and control of the satellite feed is now back in-house," Bry explained, pointing to an unmanned screen that showed a live feed of a clutch of islands in the Pacific. "Skylar's just retooling the feeds from the transponders now, bypassing the errant code that had masked them. We've cracked it, Doctor," Bry added triumphantly.

"Good work," Lakesh said, offering Bry a faintly self-conscious thumbs-up. "Can you call up a live image from the Caucasus Mountains? I want to check on our field team right away."

"The satellite's repositioning as we speak, sir," Bry assured him. "Is there anything else?"

"Communications security?" Lakesh asked. "And where did this hack originate, do we know?"

"We think it's Australia, but we haven't been able to triangulate it as yet," Bry explained. "As for communications security, my team is still working on that. Hope to have a solution in three to four hours." With that, Donald Bry strode over to the unmanned communications desk and resumed his regular position behind the monitor.

"Donald?" Lakesh asked as he placed the unread report on his desk for later examination. "Once the field team is back safely, I want you to get a good eight hours' sleep before I see you back in that seat again."

"Once the team is back," Bry admitted, "you won't be able to stop me."

Lakesh smiled, feeling content and safe once more. The crisis was not over yet, but it felt somehow that the major problems had been solved or sidestepped. He rose from his seat and joined Reba DeFore and Skylar Hitch as they examined the new feed data from the transponders.

Kane's heart was pumping fast, while Grant's and Domi's transponders showed signs of their agitation. Brigid, thankfully, appeared calm, almost as though asleep.

KANE LOOKED AT HIS Sin Eater, considered the arrows that
had been fired at him even before he had spoken, considered the fragile state of Brigid Baptiste two doors away
from him and decided that negotiating with these people
was off the agenda.

He leaned against the wall, throwing his voice into the
corridor beyond. "If you want to stop shooting arrows at
me I'll happily discuss the situation," he shouted, "but if
you won't do that I'm obliged to tell you that I'm fully
prepared to disable or kill you people if necessary.
Consider that fair warning."

The corridor remained silent, no response forthcoming,
until Kane became aware of that strange moaning again,
the sound he had mistakenly imagined was a ghost when
he had first heard it a few minutes earlier. It was an odd
sound, like a combination of groaning and humming. The
noise was continuous, though as he listened Kane noted
that it was getting subtly louder and softer, as though its
source was revolving, first approaching, then retreating.
And, though it was continuous, it was not a single note—
it seemed to shift up and down the scale, covering three
or four different notes like a swelling wave. "What the hell
is that?" Kane muttered as he listened to the alien sound.

No time to worry about it now. Kane sidestepped,
pushing his body flat to the wall, and swung his gun arm
out into the corridor, his head peeking past the open
doorway.

Two figures were running down the corridor toward
him, their heads low as they rushed forward. The first was
a trim, dark-skinned woman dressed in strips of cloth and
carrying a long, thin shaft. The strips of cloth were light

against her dark skin, and thick, braided hair swung over her shoulders in a peacocklike spread. The second was a man, also dark skinned, tall and with a muscular, athletic physique. The man's long coat billowed around him as he rushed forward. The man appeared to have some kind of curved blade in his hand and, as Kane watched, he tossed it in his direction from thirty feet away.

The blade seemed to spin around itself, end over end, and as it passed the brightly lit doorway of the Cheka office, Kane confirmed that it was metal or metal coated. It wasn't a blade at all; it was a boomerang.

Kane fired two quick bursts from the Sin Eater before ducking back into the room as the boomerang whizzed by him. The boomerang clipped against the back wall of the corridor, tossing up a flash of sparks before whipping back along its approach path and into the waiting palm of the long-coated thrower.

His head back outside the doorway, Kane saw that his shots had missed both parties and, without consciously thinking it, he aimed another stream of bullets at the man and woman as they closed the gap. The bullets raced along the corridor, straight into the two of them, but incredibly they were no longer there. Kane blinked, wondering if his night-vision lenses were damaged, giving him a false impression of the situation in the darkened corridor. But, no, there they were again, five steps closer than before, as though they had been there all along.

Kane held down the guardless trigger of the Sin Eater, unleashing a long stream of bullets as he sprayed the corridor before him in a chest-high, left-to-right arc. The bullets ricocheted off the walls and raced down the corridor, but the approaching pair of warriors had disappeared once more.

This is madness! Kane thought as he stood there, holding the Sin Eater steady on the corridor before him. Maybe he was in a meditation state, like Baptiste. Maybe all of this was a dream. People don't just disappear.

As he thought that, Kane saw the man reappear right in front of him, standing in a semicrouch and thrusting the heel of his palm against the barrel of the Sin Eater, knocking it to point at the ceiling as Kane clutched it, forcing Kane backward with the power of the blow.

Kane staggered three steps back before the back of his knees caught the lower bunk bed behind him and he toppled over. The man in the long coat had followed him into the room, swinging his boomerang at Kane's face and chest like a knife. Kane let himself fall backward into the bunk, below the swinging, sharp-edged boomerang, and kicked out with his left foot, catching his attacker with a glancing blow to the gut. The man danced backward, moving with the momentum of Kane's kick so as to retain perfect balance.

Kane pushed himself up, his left hand slapping against the rib cage of the skeleton occupying the bunk that he had fallen upon as he lunged from the bed. The woman was in the room now, too, holding the pole in a fighter's stance, her eyes focused on Kane despite the darkness of the room.

They have night vision, too, Kane confirmed as he raised his Sin Eater at her and pulled the trigger. Even as the 9 mm bullets left the chamber he saw her disappear, winking out of existence, out of his line of fire. And now the man was upon him again, sweeping the long tails of his coat at Kane's face to distract him and following through with a backward thrust of the hand holding the boomerang. Kane felt a cut open on his cheek as the boomerang passed, barely grazing him but still stinging like hell.

What are these people? Kane wondered as his foe pressed the attack.

As soon as they had descended to the lowest part of the ventilation shaft, Grant and Domi placed their dark glasses over their eyes and switched to night-vision mode, letting the lenses gather and amplify all the available light.

Grant placed the Copperhead subgun on the sill of the shaft as he lowered himself, feetfirst, through the vent that gave access to the underground complex.

"Didn't these Russians believe in fucking doors?" Domi asked in an irritated whisper.

"There's one entrance and they bricked it up," Grant told her quietly before disappearing through the gap. His hand reached back for the Copperhead and, after a moment, he stated, "Clear," in a low tone.

The waiflike albino woman crouched on the edge of the sill and slipped through the gap like a sheet of paper disappearing through the gap beneath a door. A moment later, Detonics Combat Master in hand, she was standing at Grant's side in an unlit room full of dead machinery.

Grant indicated Domi's pistol. "You bring anything bigger?" he asked in a whisper.

"Had an Uzi submachine gun," she told him, "but I fed it to my hungry friends back in Poti. Well, you know what they say—it's not the size of the gun that matters…"

"No, it is," Grant told her as he took a two-handed grip

on the two-foot-long Copperhead. "Otherwise I'd have come here armed with a blowpipe and spitballs."

With that, he stalked up to the open door with Domi at his heels. When he reached the doors he stopped, gun held high, stilling his breathing so that he could listen to the sounds of the corridor and the complex beyond. There was a strange sound coming from nearby, a kind of whirring, moaning noise that Grant couldn't place. He asked Domi if she had any idea what it was.

"Whirlybird?" she suggested, spinning a finger in the air to indicate a helicopter.

Grant shook his head. It wasn't possible to get a chopper inside this complex, even if there was a way to get it down here. "On three?" he mouthed to Domi, tilting his head toward the doorway.

Domi nodded, then did a silent countdown in front of them with her free hand. When her ring finger appeared, Grant rushed into the corridor, Copperhead leveled, with Domi a step behind him and to his right.

There were four people standing there, directly in front of them. Closest to them was a man of a similar build to Domi. He had dark skin and scraggly hair, and was likely still in his teens. Behind him, an older man— much older—stood with his hand over his head, spinning some kind of object at the end of a cord. It was the object that was making the strange noise that bled through the complex. Another older man stood farther along the corridor, his back to Grant and Domi. Beside the second older man stood a younger man with an athletic build and wearing a tattered jacket of different shades. He held a large bow in his hands, sighting along it down to the far end of the long corridor, away from Grant and Domi.

"I want everyone to freeze right where they are," Grant instructed, raising his voice to be heard over the rotating noisemaker, "unless they want to taste seven hundred rounds a minute."

As Domi watched, the four men turned as one, and the young man who was closest to her and Grant flicked his wrist almost casually. Domi saw the circle whip out from his hand, not much larger than the boy's fist, speeding toward Grant on the end of a string. Before Grant could react, the object spun around the nose of his Copperhead gun, whipping around it with the cord trailing behind. Grant had time to pull the trigger once before the gun was torn from his grasp as the boy pulled at the cord. The gun was already off target, the stream of 4.85 mm steel-jacketed rounds ripping into the wall, cutting chunks from it as they embedded.

Grant was yanked forward as the gun was pulled violently from his hands, blocking Domi's line of fire for a crucial few seconds.

"Grant, get down," she screamed as the man with the compound bow spun and leaped in their direction, loosing an arrow at them as he did so.

The arrow zipped over Domi's head as she arched backward, blasting shots from her Detonics Combat Master at the bowman. Too swift and no time to adjust her aim after Grant had blocked her line of fire, Domi's shots went wide and the man continued his leap, landing before Grant and holding the bow in one hand as he drew back the other for a punch.

As the bowman's left foot connected with the ground, he swung the punch, skimming off Grant's shoulder as the huge ex-Mag swerved to avoid the blow. Grant backhanded the man across the face, knocking him backward, and followed up with a swinging left hook. The tattooed bowman deflected the punch with the arch of the tungsten bow, feeling it shake in his hand as the energy of Grant's blow rang through it.

Grant continued his attack, jabbing with his right fist as the bowman weaved out of his way. Suddenly the bowman was upon him once more, the open palm of his left hand reaching out to slap Grant high on the chest in a seemingly effete gesture.

The tattooed warrior stepped back, a malicious grin on his face. Behind him, the whole corridor had disappeared, replaced with some kind of open, windswept plain. Grant looked around, wondering what had happened as the man literally disappeared before his eyes.

STILL IN THE CORRIDOR, Domi watched Grant and the warrior in the shabby jacket wink out of existence. Less than a second later, as Domi's mind was still trying to make sense of what she had just seen, the man reappeared. But Grant was gone, nowhere to be seen.

Something freaky just happened, Domi realized, and if I'm not careful it's likely to happen to me, too.

The Detonics Combat Master in her hand was already belching fire, bullet after bullet rocketing out of its muzzle as she tried to keep up with the movements of the tattooed warrior. It was only a narrow corridor, he didn't have much space to avoid her, but he ducked beneath her shots and through an open doorway to Domi's left.

As she rushed forward to follow him, the teenage boy with the yo-yo flipped his wrist and the little weight at the end of the cord whizzed out, hitting Domi in the bicep with a force that she could feel even through the padded parka coat.

She spun back, realizing that she was outnumbered and needed to whittle down the enemies as swiftly and systematically as possible. As she did so, one of the old men—the one without the spinning, screaming thing whirling above his head—launched a yo-yo of his own at her and Domi balked. His weapon was larger than the boy's, like two metal saucers on an axle.

Domi ducked as the spinning metal blades ripped toward her and watched as they hurtled at the wall behind her. The old man pulled back his arm with a flick of the wrist, and the projectile stopped in midair before racing back along the cord and into his hand.

As THE MYSTERIOUS ululation in the corridor grew ever louder then quieter, Kane swung his left fist toward the boomerang man's face. Just as the punch was about to connect, Kane heard a whistling noise behind and below him and he was suddenly struck by something solid in the back of his legs, toppling him over onto his back. He slapped against the floor, shoulders first, the rest of his body crashing down like an avalanche, knocking the breath out of him with a grunt.

Kane looked back as he tried to right himself. The woman was there again, wielding the stick like a bo staff, holding it in one hand as she waited for his next move. This close she looked young, her face unlined, her mostly bare body dotted with tattoos. The tattoos looked strange, like circuitry but swirling, round arches, like something organic.

Kane got up from the floor on one knee, pulling himself back to a standing position as he regained his breath. "I don't want to hurt you," he told the woman. "Either of you."

She smiled, baring a set of wide, straight teeth as she looked at him. "You're not going to," she told him, self-assured.

"We can talk about this," Kane warned her, lifting the Sin Eater to point at her again, "or you and your pal here can keep outracing bullets until, y'know, you don't."

Kane was aware that the other warrior, the man in the duster with the boomerang, was standing a few feet behind him. "Why don't you just hand over the astral weapon," the man told him, "save yourself a lot of hassle."

"Like I already said, I don't have it," Kane growled.

The woman in the strips of cloth gave no warning but just flipped her staff, swinging it up from under, between Kane's legs, where it slapped against his inner thigh, just missing his groin.

"Oh, it's like that, is it?" he snarled as he pulled the trigger of the Sin Eater and blasted bullet after bullet into her face, inches away from him.

But again the bullets didn't hit; the woman was already gone, with no hint of her ever having been there.

From Kane's right, the man swung the razor-sharp boomerang at his face again, and Kane scooted backward to avoid being hit. The man's other arm swung toward him then, and Kane saw that he had a second, metal boomerang in that hand, just as sharp as the first.

Chapter 20

Kane skipped back along the rows of bunk beds, ducking and weaving out of the way of the man's lunging attack. As he did so, Kane analyzed the situation. Gun's useless, Kane realized. These people either move too fast or they're holo-projections with solid aspects or…or I'm losing it!

GRANT COULD STILL HEAR the ululation of the spinning thing that the old guy held, so, in one sense at least, he couldn't be far from the corridor. Grant had checked every one of the twelve rooms in that Soviet underground bunker, and this place was nothing like anything he had seen there. It felt empty, a dead place full of nothing.

As he looked around, he saw someone appear a little way from him, just popping into existence from nowhere, no discernible door opening to facilitate entry. It was a woman, dark skinned and dressed in white strips like bandages, about forty feet ahead of him, roughly the distance to the canteen and bunk room if he'd still been in the complex.

Grant ran toward her, his feet kicking up little puffs of dust across the hard, baked soil. "Hello?" he shouted. "Hello, miss?"

The woman turned to him, arms outstretched, keeping her center of balance low like a martial artist. She had a pole in one hand, a thin stick that was almost as long as she was tall.

Now just ten feet away, Grant held his hands up, showing her that they were empty as he slowed his approach to walking pace. "I'm not going to hurt you," he told her, reassuringly. "You have any idea where we are?"

She pivoted then, ducking low and lunging with the pole, whipping his feet out from under him as it whistled tunefully through the air. "Welcome to your eternity, Cerberus man," she told him as he crashed to the ground.

Anger rising, Grant looked up. But the woman was already gone.

AS HE CONTINUED TO BE driven back, Kane glanced over his shoulder, aware that he was rapidly approaching the rear wall of the room. There was an air duct up there, attached somehow to the big ventilation shaft that ran above the installation, its wire grille silted up with more than two hundred years of muck and dust.

Maybe I can't shoot these people, Kane concluded, but I can still shoot everything else here.

With that, he swung the Sin Eater toward the grille and held the trigger down, unleashing an arc of steel-jacketed slugs. As the bullets tore into the vent, Kane held his breath and dropped aside.

Dust and sludge spurted out of the broken vent as the bullets split a line across it, bursting forward and spilling into the face and upper body of Kane's boomerang-wielding attacker. The man spluttered and wiped at his eyes with the back of his hand automatically, his attention diverted. As he stumbled across the tiled floor, Kane lunged forward, tackling the man full across the abdomen and plowing both of them to the floor.

The man was hacking and coughing, trying to clear the debris from his throat and lungs as Kane drew back his empty left hand and made a fist.

"Dis—"

His left fist slammed into the man's jaw with a loud crack.

"—appear…"

And again.

"From this!"

Beneath Kane's blows, the man slumped back, his mouth opening and his head lolling. "Be thankful I didn't shoot you," Kane told the unconscious form as he stood and shook dirt from his hair. As he did so, the woman reappeared, her face a mask of intensity as she watched her foe from just inside the doorway.

"So," Kane called across the room, "are we going to negotiate or are we going to fight?"

The young woman looked perplexed for a moment, a frown crossing her brow. Then, without a word, she rushed forward, whipping her staff at Kane's face as he danced backward out of reach.

She swung the staff again, and it sang as it cut through the air. Kane sidestepped, moving just beyond the reach of the swing. Then, as the staff continued through its arc, Kane's left hand darted out and grabbed it, stopping it with a sudden jolt. Still holding the other end of the long shaft, the woman staggered and let out an annoyed grunt between gritted teeth. Kane raised the Sin Eater toward her as he clung to the near end of the staff, muscles flexing as he pulled the girl to him.

CLOUD SINGER SAW the muzzle of the gun rising toward her face, and she let go of the staff and lunged backward, kicking out as she flew through the air. Her heel knocked the gun aside but no shots were fired; her opponent was holding back.

"Do you think we are playing?" she asked him as she landed in a crouch. "You had an opportunity to shoot me and yet you let it slip through your fingers."

"Yeah," the tall, lean man replied, tossing her fighting staff aside. It clattered against one of the bunk beds as he continued speaking. "I could have shot your partner, too, but I'm trying to give you a chance to reconsider things before I wind up having to kill you."

"You're a fool, Cerberus man," Cloud Singer spit as she activated her implant once more and stepped into the Dreaming for the space of a single breath. She sprinted across the open plain, noting that the other Cerberus man, the one with the dark mustache, was just getting up off the shale-covered ground behind her. Then the implant at the base of her neck fired once more, and she was back in the bunk room, seven steps from where she had been two seconds earlier, behind Kane, wrapping her left arm around his throat.

"WHAT TH—" Kane cried as the woman's arm tightened around his throat. Where had she come from? A moment ago she had been standing in front of him and yet now she was behind him, putting pressure on his windpipe in a seemingly impossible surprise attack.

As she held him, Kane felt her pivot and suddenly her knee was slamming repeatedly into his side, knocking him off balance, trying to use his own weight to snap his neck. He keeled over, crashed on one knee, and he clawed at her grasp with his left hand.

With his other hand, the one holding the Sin Eater, Kane pointed behind him, trying to locate her. Her arm darted out, knocking the weapon aside as he pulled the trigger. With a loud recoil, the bullet went wide of its target.

Gritting his teeth, Kane tried to roll forward, pulling the girl's arm away from him with as much strength as he could muster. Suddenly she let go and he lost his balance and slumped toward the ground, skidding on one knee. Kane's head met the hard floor with a brutal impact, jarring the left side of his face beside the cut he had received from the boomerang. For a moment, dark spots raced across his vision, and he blinked them away as he got up, swinging the Sin Eater back at the woman.

Or, at least, where she had been.

Once again, she was gone, leaving just Kane and her partner's unconscious form in a room full of skeletons.

BRIGID BAPTISTE STUDIED the soldiers' patrol patterns as she waited just beyond the doorway to the colossal room that contained the Death Cry. Nine soldiers, another eight scientists and their assistants, with no easy way to just sneak in and commandeer the weapon itself.

She looked at the Fedorov rifle in her hands, wondering if a gunfight would be sustainable. She was outnumbered, and the soldiers would never trust her without an affidavit from their leader, General Serge, and they weren't about to get that. For one thing, Serge was still lying unconscious on the floor of the interrogation room, and for another he was single-minded to the point of insanity. No, she needed another way in, a distraction, an explosion, some trick or other. She looked back at her two allies, the rapidly disintegrating Dr. Djugashvili and Yuri, his handsome young assistant. Yuri looked uncomfortable as he held his own Fedorov rifle, clearly a man unused to fighting.

That's it, Brigid realized. She cupped her hand and whispered her plan to the young technician.

A minute later, Yuri strode into the vast chamber that housed the Death Cry, hefting the Fedorov and attracting the attention of the nearest sentry.

"What is it, Comrade?" the sentry asked, concerned to see the tech holding a soldier's weapon.

"It's General Serge," Yuri explained breathlessly. "He—he gave me this rifle. The prisoner…"

"What?" the soldier asked. "Slow down, man—you're not making any sense."

Yuri made a show of taking a calming breath and Brigid nodded approvingly from her hiding place by the door.

"The redheaded woman, the counterrevolutionary, escaped," Yuri explained fearfully. "The general and his men are searching every office—" he gestured back to the corridor he had just come from "—and he says that you are to check the other corridor, the whole complex."

"This is terrible," the sentry agreed. "How did she escape?"

"She…" Yuri began, shaking his head. "I do not know.

I was sent to warn you. You must move quickly while I am to check inside the Death Cry."

The soldier nodded curtly before calling the other soldiers around and instructing them to follow him into the series of corridors that Brigid had first used to enter the complex, in the opposite direction to her current hiding place with Dr. Djugashvili.

One soldier remained behind, and he spoke reassuringly to Yuri. "I will accompany you into the Death Cry."

"Thank you, Comrade," Yuri said as he watched the other sentries rush from the room. Once they had left he turned and jabbed the solid butt of the Fedorov into the man's gut.

The soldier staggered backward, but Brigid could see that the blow wasn't hard enough to fell him. She was already running across the lightning-bolt floor of the room, her legs pumping, wielding her own rifle like a club. As the soldier turned, Brigid smashed him across the jaw with the hard metal of the rifle. His head snapped back and he fell to the floor, dazed but still awake.

Brigid saw the soldier open his mouth, the start of his cry for help bursting from his throat, and she kicked him in the throat with the toe of her boot. The words stuck in his throat, and the man spit a painful gurgle as Brigid clubbed him with the Fedorov once again. The rifle slammed into his face, snapping his front teeth and knocking the soldier unconscious.

When she looked up, Brigid saw the look of horror on Yuri's face. "Keep moving," she told him, "there's no time left for subtlety."

With Dr. Djugashvili leading the way with his rolling, limping walk, the three of them made their way to the scaffolding and up to the entrance of the giant black metal cylinder that Brigid had come to retrieve.

WHEN KANE MANAGED TO get his gun pointed at her, Cloud Singer immediately slipped back into the Dreaming. She stood there now, catching her breath as the wind blew across the empty plain. She smiled as she heard the sweet song of the bull roarer, beyond sight but still audible, the promise of dreamslicing reassuring her.

This field mission was proving more of a challenge than she had expected. Though rudimentary in his strategy, the quick-thinking Cerberus man was a worthy opponent. Each time she returned to face him in the room of skeletons, he had seemingly learned more, analyzed the strategies that she and Rock Streaming were using. The very fact that he had knocked Rock Streaming unconscious was proof of that.

And I'm hiding, she told herself, sudden realization dawning. I'm no longer using the Dreaming as part of my arsenal—I'm here because I'm not confident that I can defeat my foe.

She cursed herself for being a weakling and a fool. Bad Father would brand her if he knew that she felt this way; he would certainly never let her go on a mission again.

She turned, looking around the landscape, and noticed the other one, the dark-skinned man who was built like a bear, creeping up on her, moving silently despite his size. When he saw her looking at him he smiled grimly and leaped forward, his hands reaching for her.

Why hasn't Rabbit in the Moon finished this one? Cloud Singer wondered as her automatic combat reflex took over and she thrust her pointed toes up into the man's torso. Now nowhere's safe, not even the Dreaming.

Grant's eyes bulged as Cloud Singer's toes jabbed into his gut, and he felt himself retch, the taste of bile in his mouth.

He looked up, but once again the woman was gone.

AS SHE WATCHED THE OLD MAN flip the vicious yo-yo back to his hand, Domi brought up the barrel of the Detonics pistol and sprayed a volley of bullets toward him. The old man just nodded, winking out of existence as the bullets were about to hit before reappearing in their absence.

Domi spun as she heard her bullets impacting against the far wall and the old man laughing savagely. The teenager looked as if he was throwing a punch at her, but he wasn't; he was unleashing his yo-yo at her face like a stone, trying to knock her senseless.

The Detonics kicked in Domi's hand as she fired. Suddenly the young warrior was falling back, his throat erupting in a shower of blood where the bullet had drilled through his Adam's apple and destroyed his larynx. As he fell the teenager yanked the cord of his spinning yo-yo, and the weight whizzed off into the wall before the cord went slack and it fell to the floor beside him.

Domi was still moving, firing beyond her line of sight as she turned back to face the two older men. The other warrior, the one who had used the compound bow, had reappeared from his brief hiding place in the adjacent room. He had been out of the fight for less than ten seconds, ducking in there to avoid her shots, but it seemed like an eternity.

As Domi aimed her Detonics at them, the older man,

the one with the lethal yo-yo, pushed his tongue between pursed lips and made a single whistled note, piercing despite the moaning from the spinning bull roarer. The warrior with the bow nodded in acknowledgment, turned and ran down the corridor, away from his companions and Domi. Targeting his retreating back, Domi fired three shots at the warrior and watched, incredulous, as he appeared to wink out of reality, the bullets passing through the air where he had been a fraction of a second earlier.

Whatever these people are, they're more than human, Domi thought. That is, assuming that they are human at all. They moved so fast, stepping in and out of reality, it seemed an impossible task to nail them. Still, she had managed to hit the youngster. The key was to keep moving and keep pressing her attack.

She barreled toward the old man as he flicked the yo-yo at her once again, her Detonics Combat Master spitting fire ahead of her.

STANDING IN THE WASTELAND, shale and sand at his feet, Grant shook his head to clear the feeling of nausea that had threatened to overcome him with the woman's kick. He had no clue where he was, no idea what had happened to the corridor of the facility beneath the Caucasus Mountains. Was this place the Death Cry? Was this where Brigid's consciousness had ended up when she had concentrated on the mandala?

"Brigid," he called out, raising his voice above the distant sound of the spinning thing in the old man's hand. He listened for a few moments, but there was no response.

Suddenly a person stepped onto the empty plain, close to where Grant had first appeared; it was the tattooed warrior, the one with the bow who had somehow brought him there in the first place. Automatically Grant flinched his wrist tendons as he raised his right hand, finger crooked. But the Sin Eater failed to appear.

Grant glanced at his hand incredulously; the nonappearance of his Sin Eater pistol on command was utterly unexpected. But, he concluded, he would have to worry about that later.

As the tattooed warrior dashed across the plain toward Grant, checking over his shoulder to see if anyone was following, Grant darted into action. Head down and arms pumping, Grant ran across the plain on an intercept path with his enemy.

Rabbit in the Moon looked up as he heard the approach of the ex-Mag and the grim smile on his face disappeared, replaced with an expression of irritation, annoyance. The huge man was upon him in a second, his massive right fist driving through the air as Rabbit in the Moon sidestepped out of its path. The warrior was just too slow, and the Cerberus man's fist slammed into the side of his head, knocking him off his feet and disorienting his vision.

Standing over the warrior, Grant slapped his left palm against the man's chest and drew back his fist once again. "Where the hell are we?" he snarled.

Rabbit in the Moon rolled his shoulders, shifting his weight and shaking off the pressure of Grant's hand on his chest. But as he moved, Grant's fist rocketed toward his jaw, knocking his head so hard he thought it would break his neck.

"Where am I?" Grant demanded again, his narrowed eyes brooking no argument.

Rolling on the tiny, sharp stones of the Dreaming, Rabbit in the Moon spun out of the way as the ex-Mag launched another jackhammer punch. The punch missed him by bare inches, and Grant howled as his knuckles slammed against the hard ground.

Rabbit in the Moon turned, spinning to a standing position, his vision still popping with colored lights from Grant's first punch. "You're trapped in the Dreaming, ignorant fool," he spit as the ex-Mag turned to face him, "and you'll be here forever."

"Says you," Grant snapped as he lunged at the tattooed warrior.

Rabbit in the Moon's leg muscles tightened like a coiled spring, then released, launching him high in the air. The rules were different there in the Dreaming. The Cerberus man didn't stand a chance.

Grant watched as his opponent kicked off the ground and flew—literally flew—into the sky high above. His jaw dropped as he watched the man pass through the clouds that hurtled by overhead, and then he gritted his teeth and bunched his fists in preparation. The warrior didn't move like a man at all; he moved like a force of nature.

"Great trick, you ass," Grant muttered, "but what goes up must come down." Grant stood there, watching the skies and waiting as the anger within him bubbled just below the surface.

IN THE UNDERGROUND CORRIDOR, Domi was facing just two opponents now, and both of them were old men. The one who was spinning the noisemaker didn't even seem to care about her. He was busy concentrating on his spinning task, his other hand resting on a gnarled old walking stick. But the other one, the one who had launched the weighted, razor-edged yo-yo at her, was a definite threat.

As the yo-yo lashed toward her again, Domi dropped to her knees, sliding beneath its arc and arching her back to keep herself low to the floor. The yo-yo whizzed over her head on its return journey along the string as Domi continued to slide across the floor, her momentum driving her onward.

As the old man caught the yo-yo and brought his arm back for another attack, Domi sprung up again and fired two bullets in his direction. The bullets soared through the air, but her aim was wide and they zipped past her target by just two inches.

Amazingly the old guy didn't even seem to notice, didn't so much as flinch as the bullets split the air just to the left of his head. It was weird watching him; he moved gracefully despite his age, and his movements seemed un-hurried, reminding Domi of a flowing river more than a human being.

She was still firing the Detonics as the old man unleashed the yo-yo at her. Domi shifted her weight as she saw the yo-yo's approach, but she was fractionally too late. The weight of the yo-yo slammed into her just above her right breast, and she stumbled backward as her feet continued to run forward, flipping herself in an awkward spasm of muscles.

She slapped into the floor, taking a nasty blow to the head as she tumbled over and over. Beneath the thick layer of the parka coat, she could feel a warm, damp patch and she looked down to see that the coat had been torn by one of the buzz saw–like edges of the yo-yo and blood was oozing beneath.

Domi looked up and realized, much to her own surprise, that the altercation had been a lucky one. The old man had lost control of the yo-yo when it slammed into her, and now the string was tangled. Her ruby eyes skipped over to the old warrior himself, and she saw that he was detaching the string from the simple animal-hide rig that held it to his hand. Still flat on her back, Domi raised her pistol, placing her foe dead center of her sights.

"Tough break, old man," she muttered as her finger squeezed at the trigger.

But her finger never finished the action. The other one, the man who was spinning the bull roarer, slammed the base of his walking cane savagely against her wrist, forcing her to lose her grip on the weapon as her hand slapped against the floor. Adjusting her grip where it had slipped, she turned to her new attacker just in time to see him point the walking stick in her face. The next thing she knew, a cloud of red dust burst out of the cane.

Her face burned as though with a rash or a chemical burn and she screamed, an unbearably long shriek that carried down the length of the corridor.

IN THE DREAMING, Rabbit in the Moon rocketed through the skies, descending back to the ground below. The Cerberus warrior was down there waiting for him and, as he fell, Rabbit in the Moon nocked three arrows in his bow and fired them at the man, one after the other. He laughed as he saw the Cerberus man leap out of their paths.

His instruction had been to go to the door near the end of the corridor, the one where the light originated. When the chalk-skinned girl had begun firing bullets at him he had ducked into the Dreaming as an efficient way to make the journey without getting hurt, not realizing that the Cerberus warrior he had left there might still have some fight in him despite his disorientation. Clearly his opponent was a strong warrior, strong and bullheaded.

Softly, hardly making a sound, Rabbit in the Moon's feet met the ground and he bent his knees fractionally just to dissipate the last of the flight energy.

As soon as he landed he was spinning, using the tungsten bow like a staff, thrusting the end of it at the Cerberus man's face.

Grant crouched beneath the swinging bow, instinctively raising his right hand to protect his face. The bow glided by him, but Grant's attention was suddenly distracted—the Sin Eater was gradually unsheathing from its wrist holster, like a thing moving in slow motion. It had obeyed his instruction after all, but the rules of this world were so different that it was only now starting to find its way into his palm. Maybe it was a time thing, maybe something else. Grant didn't have the luxury to think about it as the sharp curve of the compound bow swung at him again.

Grant deliberately dropped backward, falling to the ground on his buttocks and kicking out with both feet. His heels slapped against the bowman's legs, knocking the tattooed man off his feet. As his adversary fell, Grant was already driving himself back up, moving sideways in a crouch, like a crab, as he lunged at his enemy.

In his right hand, the Sin Eater was uncoiling, its parts snapping into place so that it could be used at full extension. Grant raised the weapon, his fist clamping around the butt as he drove it at his opponent's face.

With brutal finality, Grant's fist connected with Rabbit in the Moon's face, whipping his head back with a painful snap. Already wrong-footed by the kick to his legs, Rabbit in the Moon fell back, feeling the pain exploding behind his neck where a muscle strained at the impact. The Cerberus warrior's left fist swung into view an instant later, coming at him like a missile, driving into the hollow of his right eye. Rabbit in the Moon shook his head as his vision swam with blood, and he lashed out with arms and legs, struggling to connect a blow with his opponent.

Rabbit in the Moon felt it before he saw it; Grant's right hand drove a savage punch into his gut but there was a solid weight there now, the barrel of a foot-long gun. As the nose of the Sin Eater jabbed into his gut, Rabbit in the Moon made the decision to dreamslice once more, activating the implant and stepping out of the dream.

Suddenly he was in the underground corridor again, just a few steps from the open doorway to the brightly lit office. But the pressure was still pushing against his belly, and he realized that he had brought the Cerberus man back with him to Realworld. As that realization struck him, Rabbit in the Moon felt the indescribable fire above his hip bone as Grant's first 9 mm bullet drilled into him, followed by the rushing stream of its identical, steel-jacketed brothers.

DR. DJUGASHVILI LED Brigid and Yuri to a metal hatch at the back of the Death Cry. Close up, the weapon was all the more impressive, a long cylindrical construction of black metal that was at least the size of an aircraft carrier. Yet despite the scale of the construction itself, the door was small and Brigid had to duck to get inside.

Within, the Death Cry had a similar feel to that of a submarine—a perilously low ceiling, plates of metal across the floor, and a little array of controls wrapped around two seats lit from above by a dull electric bulb in a cage that cast an orange-amber light. The whole control room was perhaps twelve feet square.

"Well," Djugashvili said, "here we are, Miss Baptiste."

"I expected something more…bigger," Brigid told him with a shrug.

"The functionality of the Death Cry is a two-man operation," Djugashvili explained rationally. "One man steers the weapon into place while the other primes and fires its scream. We had no need for an expansive control room or living quarters."

Brigid nodded, smiling apologetically. "I just thought, with its being so huge…"

"That is the weapon," Djugashvili told her. "The gun you hold has enough free space to allow you to grip it and pull the trigger, nothing more. The rest is concerned with the mechanics of firing the bullet, storing and replenishing the ammunition, correct?"

She looked at the Fedorov Automat in her hands and nodded again. "So how does this baby work?"

Djugashvili gestured to the seats, and Yuri took up his post at one of them. "The Death Cry unit is pointed in the direction of the enemy flying object, a space vehicle, you understand, and bathes it in what we call its scream." He looked proud as he explained this, and Brigid recalled that a lot of this had been developed from his own work. But she also noted that Djugashvili was fading before her, flakes of his very form drifting into the air like burning paper.

"But what's the scream?" she urged.

"It is a blast of psychic matter," Djugashvili solemnly explained, "a physical manifestation of the most dangerous thoughts of the mind."

Nightmares. The Soviets had planned to fight the aliens, their so-called supraterrestrials, with nightmares.

"These thoughts will disrupt the brain of any living thing in their path," Djugashvili told her. "We experimented a little with mice, rats, chimpanzees. A prisoner once," he added, looking uncomfortable with the memory. "The man, he screamed and screamed and screamed and suddenly he was just ashes. He screamed himself to ashes, can you believe?"

Brigid nodded. "We'd better be careful where we point this thing." She smiled. "We need to get it back to Earth, Doctor. How do we do that?"

Djugashvili pointed to the free seat with a hand that no longer had distinct fingers, just wispy trails of light. "There is a pattern there, at the control panel, you see it?"

Brigid took a step closer in the small room, but as she did so there was a crash and the door behind her opened once more. General Serge stood there, his face bruised and dried blood beside his mouth and nose.

"I knew that I would find you here," he shouted as he

revealed the pistol in his hand, this one a silenced piece with a long barrel. "Insurgents! Traitors!"

Brigid swept the barrel of the Fedorov around, slamming its weight into the general's gun hand. She saw the trace of smoke as the gun went off, its noise muffled to a low stutter by the sound suppressor.

The general growled as his hand was knocked into the door frame and Brigid brought the Fedorov to bear on him.

"I'm sorry, General," she told him, "but I'm done trying to reason with you."

Serge roared as he brought his pistol around, pulling the trigger again and again as he swept it toward Brigid's face. Bullets pinged around the tiny cabin, bouncing off the walls and control panels, and Djugashvili screamed as one hit him in the shoulder.

But Serge was too late. Brigid held down the trigger of her Fedorov autorifle, spraying a stream of bullets into the general's chest. He rocked in place under the lethal impacts, and Brigid watched, revulsion welling within her, as General Serge disintegrated before her eyes. It was like watching ink dropped into water, a human body reduced to a cloud, then a mist, then, after a few more seconds, just a slightly darker stain in the air that dissipated to nothingness as Brigid ceased firing, the Fedorov out of ammunition.

As Brigid watched the stain fade away, the general's pistol dropped with a clank to one of the metal plates that made up the flooring of the control center. There were two more soldiers outside on the scaffolding, the two that Yuri had chained together in the interrogation room, and they looked bewildered as they saw their leader disintegrate before their eyes.

Brigid tossed the spent rifle aside and stepped onto the creaking scaffolding, driving the heel of her palm into the nose of the soldier on the right while he was still standing there, astonished at what had just happened. The man stumbled backward, doubling over as he reached for the bloody smear where his nose had been an instant ago, and Brigid pulled the pistol from her holster and targeted the other soldier.

"Walk away and maybe you get to live," she told him.

The soldier shook his head. "I'm sorry, but my orders—"

Brigid pulled the trigger and blew a hole in the man's chest. He stumbled for a moment, and she saw the familiar horrifying mist that was his body begin to burn away from his form. She pointed the gun at the soldier with the caved-in nose as he struggled to a standing position. "You want me to do you, too?" she asked.

The soldier shook his head, wincing at the pain in his nose. Then he turned and made his way toward the ladder that led back down to the floor as his colleague continued to evaporate at Brigid's feet.

When she was sure that he had left, Brigid returned to the control room and slammed the door closed behind her. The room had taken a few hits from the general's final attack, and one of the control panels was sparking where a bullet had ripped through a plastic-covered display. Djugashvili lay slumped on the floor, his arms and legs gone, his chest and the remnants of his face disappearing into mist.

Brigid knelt before him, her emerald eyes locking with his. "Doctor, I'm so sorry," she said, unable to think of anything better.

Djugashvili shook his head slowly, tears streaming down what was left of his disintegrating cheeks. "I thought I had longer," he told her, "but the general's shot must have..."

"It doesn't matter now," Brigid shushed him. "Thank you, Dr. Djugashvili. Thank you for your help. Thank you for maybe saving the human race with what you did here today. I'm so sorry that you never—"

"Don't be sorry," he insisted, cutting her words off. "It's not so bad, this death. I remember the feeling now, something I had forgotten for so long."

Brigid reached to touch his cheek, but her hand passed through it, the man's face turning to a cloud of dust. "Doctor?" she asked.

"It is like being born, Brigid," he told her, nodding as his head turned to nothingness and he ceased to exist.

Brigid turned away. Dr. Djugashvili was gone.

As she knelt there, willing herself to focus on the mission at hand, something caught her eye—a shining speck on her finger. Bringing her hand close, she saw a tiny trickle of water running along her index finger, where she had passed her hand through Djugashvili's cheek. A single human tear.

ALONE IN THE BUNK ROOM, Kane bent to study the still form of his defeated foe. The man was covered in tattoos, swirling tribal markings with sharp, right-angle turns like the lines on a circuit board. The man had used twin metal boomerangs, razor-sharp along their edges. Kane realized that this foe had been employing some sort of matter-transfer device, adding an inhuman swiftness to his movements, creating an almost devastating attack. And the girl had done the same. But Kane had experience with matter transfer, and he knew that what you held tended to travel with you.

Kane stood and placed his foot on the man's undershirt, pressing his weight against the man's chest and rocking his foe just a little.

As Kane watched, the man's head started to shake and Kane saw that he was about to wake up. "Let's see you jump out of this, you slimy eel," Kane muttered as he held the nose of the Sin Eater at the man's face.

The man groaned, then his eyes popped open and saw the Sin Eater pointed between them. He glanced up and his eyes met with Kane's.

"What say me and you have a little talk?" Kane suggested, holding his foot firm against the man's chest.

Rock Streaming glared contemptuously at Kane in silence, so Kane pushed a little harder on his chest.

"I'm trying to help us both out here, brother," Kane assured him.

Rock Streaming spit, still glaring at Kane with fury burning brightly in his eyes. "Then you are a fool, Cerberus man," he said, sneering.

"My name's Kane," Kane told him, his gun still trained firmly on the warrior's face. "What's yours?"

"My warrior name is Rock Streaming," the tattooed man replied, glancing away from the gun, trying to remember where exactly he was.

There was a slight rush of air then, and Kane turned as he saw the woman in the white strips appearing to his left, leaping through the air in a flying kick.

RABBIT IN THE MOON HOWLED as five bullets drilled through his torso at point-blank range. Grant's free hand was reaching up toward his neck, grabbing for the torn streamers of his tattered blue-green jacket.

Rabbit in the Moon closed his eyes as he fell backward like so much deadweight. He dropped out of reach of the grasping hand and in the same instant faded back into the Dreaming as he listened for the song of Good Father's spinning bull roarer. He was in the Dreaming as his body hit the floor.

He opened his eyes and saw the cloud of sand kicked up by his violent landing, but he had evaded the grip of the Cerberus man. He was alone once more. Lying in the dirt, Rabbit in the Moon dropped the bow and reached for the belly wound with his right hand. It burned like wildfire, and when he touched his gut he found a gore-smeared hole just above his left hip.

He closed his eyes, feeling for the bullets. There was a trick to this; Bad Father had showed it to him once when the older man had accidentally got a knife embedded in his arm during a hunt. That time, Bad Father had leaped quickly into the Dreaming before yanking the blade out. His will had stemmed the blood flow, and he had reappeared in Realworld with nothing more than dried blood to show where the knife had been, no wound beneath its smear. The whole operation had taken maybe thirty seconds, and Rabbit in the Moon had been in awe of the older man's abilities and quick thinking.

He reached into the hole in his body and felt around for the bullets, snatching three of the metal invaders out of the hole and tossing them to the ground. The others had to have passed clean through him; he couldn't feel them as he pushed thumb and forefinger into the wound in his small intestine.

His eyes still closed, his teeth clenched against the urge to scream, Rabbit in the Moon removed his fingers from inside his body and willed the wound to heal the same way he had willed the burn to heal during the multiplane practice battle with Cloud Singer. His flesh and all that was below reknitted, a process painful beyond belief, and suddenly he was whole again.

He lay in the dirt, his breath coming shallow and fast, as he felt the burning subside.

BACK IN THE UNDERGROUND bunker, Grant recovered his balance and blinked away irritation as the tattooed warrior disappeared in front of him. These tricky bastards kept pulling the same stunt on him, but there was no way they could keep it up forever. He had wounded the man armed with the bow. His fists had connected with the bone and muscle of the man's face, and bullets from the Sin Eater had definitely caught the guy.

Grant looked around, assessing his location. He was back in the Project Chernobog bunker, almost two-thirds of the way down the corridor from where he had entered. From the far end he could hear the old man's swinging pendulum making its strange, ugly song.

From a little way ahead of him he could hear the

crashing and slapping of hand-to-hand combat, swift and furious. It was coming from the bunk room opposite the canteen, and Grant raised the pistol in his hand and pointed it toward the doorway.

Grant stalked forward in the darkness, keeping his body low, and reached the open door to the Cheka-KGB office, glancing warily inside.

Brigid still sat there, cross-legged, her eyes closed. He could see where Kane had patched up the cuts on her face, antiseptic patches taped to her left cheek and the cut above her eye. There was swelling around her mouth, and he could see the shining skin where she would have a black eye before the day's end, but she looked pretty much okay.

Grant ducked into the office, swinging the Sin Eater around as he confirmed that no one was waiting for him.

Other than Brigid's static figure, the small, low-ceilinged office was empty. Grant walked across to her, looking closely, checking that she was still breathing. "Kane," he said in a hushed tone as he activated his Commtact. "I'm with Brigid in the office. You read me?"

Kane's voice came back, staggered by hard breathing, a moment later. "I'm in the bunk room, but I'm a little busy here with some warrior chick. How's Baptiste?"

"She looks fine," Grant confirmed, turning back to the doorway.

"Great," Kane grunted back, and Grant could hear the doubled report of his partner's voice coming from the corridor and the Commtact. "Think you can spare a moment?"

"I'm on my way," Grant told him as he walked to the doorway.

STRUGGLING TO FREE himself from beneath Kane's heavy foot, Rock Streaming saw Cloud Singer's blurring, swift attack. She thrust her right hand at the man called Kane's face, perfectly aimed to drive the cartilage in his nose into his brain.

But suddenly something hit her in the side of the head—the skull of one of the long-dead occupants of the room, hooked at her from the end of Kane's gun. The impact not only disrupted Cloud Singer's aim, but it also knocked her hard enough that she toppled to the floor, hitting it with a resounding crash, the life going out of her.

As she hit the floor, Rock Streaming closed his eyes and activated the implant, slipping into the Dreaming for a fraction of a second before leaping out again into Real-world.

He heard the wind playing in the trees, whispering against the grass, the cries of birds above. He was outside. His dreamslice had taken him just fifteen feet upward, back to the surface of the mountain pass.

Rock Streaming opened his eyes and saw the Cerberus warrior—Kane—still standing over him, toe just pressing lightly on his chest, a wicked smile on his face as he whipped his gun back into Rock Streaming's face.

WITHOUT WARNING, something heavy and fast smashed into Grant's back as he stepped to the doorway, knocking him to his knees. He looked over his shoulder and saw that the tattooed bowman in the shabby blue-green coat was standing over him, reappearing from nowhere.

Grant's eyes were drawn to the man's belly, and he saw the unmistakable blot of red where he'd shot the man. "I shot you," Grant snarled as he pulled himself up onto his hands and knees.

The warrior's right leg lashed out and his booted foot collided with Grant's head, knocking him back to the floor. "Yes, I wanted to talk to you about that," Rabbit in the Moon bellowed as he lunged at Grant, his fist drawn back.

Chapter 21

Brigid dropped into the seat beside Yuri as he explained the basic controls of the Death Cry.

"I have the piloting and weapons controls for the Death Cry," he said, and Brigid saw that his hands had been enveloped by twin sphincters in the console, like operating in a hazchem or radiation box, "but I require you to bring us into the corporeal world."

Brigid nodded. "No problem. What button do I press?"

"No buttons, I'm afraid." Yuri smiled. "You see the pattern on the grid in front of you?" he asked as a backlit screen came to life before Brigid's eyes. "You are now the launch mechanism, you understand?"

She looked at the backlit screen. The pattern was an intricate swirl of blues and greens, with flecks of red and green scattered within it. A mandala, Brigid realized, similar to the one that had drawn her there. "You want me to…concentrate?" she asked hesitantly.

"You are the launch mechanism, Brigid Baptiste," Yuri stated again. A red light flicked on above his head, dull in the orange lighting of the cabin. "I think you had better hurry," he added.

"Company?" Brigid asked, focusing her attention on the mandala swirl on the glass plate.

"It seems that the other soldiers have come back from their little jaunt," Yuri said.

The pattern of the mandala was intricate, but Brigid had almost memorized it already, her eidetic memory coming into play once again. "Yuri?" she asked. "What happens when we get back to the real world? I mean, it's three hundred years since you had a body to return to."

Yuri shrugged. "I would rather not think about it," he admitted. "I believe in your supraterrestrial threat, Miss Brigid. I believe in the Annunaki. And whether I am with you or not, I believe that the Death Cry will provide your ultimate salvation."

His words were sliding over her now, just distant noises as she plummeted into the deep trance triggered by the mandala.

"Besides," Yuri said as Brigid sank into the depths of her meditation, "what do I have left to live for here?"

IN THE VAST, WHITE-WALLED room of the astral factory, the remaining Russian soldiers and technicians watched in amazement as the great bulk of the Death Cry shimmered before their eyes as though viewed through a heat haze, more liquid than solid. Two of the soldiers raised their Fedorov rifles and fired at the disappearing weapon. They were expected to protect it, and now it seemed that it was being stolen. Better that it be destroyed than fall into enemy hands, they decided. Their bullets cut through the air, but the Death Cry was gone. Only the scaffolding that had been built around its enormous shell remained.

LYING IN THE SOIL AND GRASS, Rock Streaming thrust up both hands and wrestled the muzzle of Kane's Sin Eater aside as he flipped his body like a fish trapped on dry land.

Kane staggered, his toe leaving the warrior's chest for a moment, and he stamped his boot down into the man's leg lest he lose him again. Suddenly he was thrown from Rock Streaming, who had somehow used his grip on the barrel of the Sin Eater as a fulcrum.

Kane crashed into the ground on his back and his breath rushed out of him. For a fraction of a second he thought that he had blacked out but he hadn't. The blackness that encroached on his vision was a shadow, a colossal shadow of incredible magnitude, blotting out the sun in the sky above.

Rock Streaming stopped battling to look overhead in awe at the massive object that filled the sky. It was incredible, almost too large to comprehend, a giant black cylinder with irregular bumps and protrusions along its vast length. It shuddered for a moment, fifty feet above them, stretching between the mountain peaks, somehow unreal, its image doubling and tripling until it finally manifested in its full, solid glory.

The Death Cry had arrived.

BRIGID'S EYES SWAM IN AND out of focus, the lit pane of glass that showed the mandala blurring and reforming for a few moments. She looked across to Yuri in the seat beside her and saw the glazed and terrified look in his eyes.

"Did we make it?" Brigid asked, but he ignored her, staring ahead. "Yuri?" she barked. "Did we make it?"

Yuri said something, looking at her then, but she

couldn't hear the words. The whole scene—the control room of the Death Cry, Yuri, the mandala—they were fading away, indistinct as passing clouds or memories of dreams.

She was racing through the air then, weightless, like a wraith. She saw the mountains, Kane and another man looking up at her, at the looming shadow above. And she was falling, plummeting through the air. The grass came closer, the grass, the soil...

Brigid saw the room, the little gray-walled box with the brass Cheka shield on the wall, the furniture pushed to one end, the carpet hanging from the pitons that Grant had hammered into the ceiling. And there, in the middle of the room, legs crossed and eyes closed, was a woman with red-gold hair and the trim, hungry build of a racehorse. The woman was familiar, the face from the mirror but inverted.

And there were two other people in the room, close to the open door. A man that Brigid didn't recognize was standing over Grant's fallen body, swinging a vicious kick at her colleague's face. The stranger was dressed in a shabby jacket, all strands of green and blue, and he wore a cylinder across his back.

As Brigid watched, floating overhead, weightless, the man reached into the cylinder and whipped out a thin shaft of metal with a sharpened triangle at its end—an arrow. He drew back his hand in preparation to stab the helpless form of Grant through the eye, moving with savage determination.

There was the blur of incredible movement then, as Brigid's astral form dived back into her physical body, sitting cross-legged on the floor.

JUST AS RABBIT IN THE MOON brought the arrow down at the Cerberus warrior on the floor of the office, something hit him in the side and a woman's hand grasped his wrist, halting the arrow's movement.

Shocked, Rabbit in the Moon looked around as he faltered toward the wall. The woman, the redhead who had been unconscious in the center of the little office, was awake, clutching his wrist with incredible strength, cold determination in her fierce green eyes.

Her other hand swung around, connecting solidly with Rabbit in the Moon's jaw, and he tumbled back, smashing his head into the wall behind him.

He felt himself slide down the wall as the vision in his right eye turned once more red with blood. The woman had stepped away from him and he watched, unable to make his muscles move quickly enough as she swung one of her long legs at him, kicking him hard in the jaw on the exact same spot that her punch had connected.

He lay on the floor, breathing heavily, his face a patchwork of pain, and watched as the woman turned her back on him and walked away toward the far wall. She knelt on the desk that sat flush with the wall and reached up for something that was hanging there.

When she turned back, Rabbit in the Moon saw that she was holding a thick chunk of forged metal, a brass-colored plaque of some type, shaped like a shield. The way she held it made it clear that the shield was heavy.

As the woman swung the hunk of metal at his head, Rabbit in the Moon dreamsliced out of Realworld, back to the Dreaming.

BRIGID SWUNG THE CHEKA shield at the bloodied face of the tattooed man as he lay helpless on the floor of the office, but he winked out of existence the very second before the blow connected.

Brigid almost tripped as the shield whisked through thin air, and she skipped several paces before reaching out to the wall to stop herself.

A few steps across from her, Grant was wiping blood from his face as he struggled to get up off the floor. "Thanks for that, Brigid," he said. "You couldn't have timed it better."

"Oh, you could have taken him. I just thought I'd give you a hand." Immediately after the words had left her lips, Brigid sagged to the floor.

"You okay?" Grant asked as he got himself up to a kneeling position.

"I'm fine," she assured him. "My legs just…how long have I been sitting there like that?"

"Nineteen, twenty hours," Grant said, "give or take."

Once he had got himself to a standing position, Grant offered Brigid his hand and she took it gratefully.

"Any idea where tattoo boy disappeared to?" she asked him.

"Some kind of personal mat-trans," Grant explained.

"When all of this is done," Brigid said as she hurried from the room, "I'm going to have to look into that."

Grant hurried after her, his face spattered with blood. "Where are we going?" he asked.

"I came back with the weapon, the Death Cry," Brigid told him. "It's outside."

"Well," Grant said, astonished, "nice job." Then he

stopped and turned back toward the lower end of the corridor.

"What is it? Where are you going?" Brigid asked him.

"Kane's back there with…" Grant began.

"No, he's not," Brigid assured him. "I saw him outside while I was flying through the astral plane."

Grant looked quizzically at Brigid for a moment, then he shook his head and laughed. "Do I need to understand what the hell you just said?"

"No," she assured him as she placed the polymer lenses over her eyes. "Let's go."

With that, Grant and Brigid raced along the sloped corridor toward the strange ululating sound that was coming from its highest end.

EVERYONE IN THE CERBERUS ops center stopped and stared at the satellite feed that was transmitting live from the Caucasus Mountains.

"What the heck…?" Brewster Philboyd muttered as the huge black cylinder appeared from nowhere, cutting across the image like a thick vertical stripe.

In two strides, Lakesh was at his shoulder and Donald Bry, Mariah Falk, Skylar Hitch and other members of the operating crew soon joined them, staring at the incredible construction that hovered between the mountains.

"What is it?" Falk asked.

"It just appeared out of nowhere," Philboyd stated, not taking his eyes from the screen.

Lakesh was already standing at the communications terminal, adjusting the controls and slipping a headset over his ear. "This is Cerberus calling Kane and Grant. Please respond."

IN THE SHADOW OF THE Death Cry, Rock Streaming threw his third successive punch at Kane. Kane held his ground, slapping the blow aside. He had the man's measure; the warrior favored his right when he attacked, and Kane just had to time his defense while the tattooed man exhausted himself.

As Rock Streaming tried to connect another unsuccessful uppercut, Kane's Commtact came to life with Lakesh's voice: "This is Cerberus calling Kane and Grant. Please respond."

Kane launched a left hook at the warrior before him, and the blow connected solidly with the side of the man's head, forcing him to give ground. "This is Kane, Cerberus," Kane responded. "I'm mixed up in something just now, over."

Kane waited the obligatory pause as his communication was bounced across the satellite network before he heard Lakesh's voice once again. Rock Streaming dropped before him, trying for a leg sweep, and Kane leaped over it.

"Our feed is back up and running," Lakesh told Kane, "but we have a large UFO showing right above you, hovering over the mountains. Over."

"I'm outside," Kane explained as he skipped backward to the strip of blacktop, putting a little distance between himself and his attacker. "I see it…"

As he was speaking, Brigid's fragmented voice interrupted him as she patched into the communication. "Lakesh, Kane. Brigid here," she said. "What you're seeing is the Death Cry…back with me. Over."

"Good work," Lakesh responded, relief in his voice. "How are you feeling, Brigid? Over."

Rock Streaming swung a high kick at Kane's head, and

Kane weaved on the spot to avoid it before he cut in on Brigid's health report. "People, we've got more immediate problems," he explained, "namely a group of crazy tribal warrior types who seem to be able to disappear during battle. It's really hacking me off. Over."

Even as he said it, he saw Rock Streaming wink out of existence. "Damn it!" Kane growled as he grasped at thin air.

"Scans show a local field," Lakesh explained over the Commtact, "similar to a mat-trans but utilizing some different sequencing—"

Lakesh was still speaking, slipping into the scientific gobbledygook he loved so much, and Kane cut into his lecture, knowing full well that his words would take five seconds to reach the Cerberus redoubt and another five for the reply to come back. "That's great, Lakesh. How do we stop it? Any ideas? Over."

As Kane's request came across the Commtact, Lakesh flushed with embarrassment and apologized. "We'll start examining straight away, Kane," he assured the man in the field. "Stand by. Over."

Lakesh snapped his fingers, attracting Donald Bry and other Cerberus techs to examine his monitor as he brought up the scan feed information.

"One of them has just appeared," Kane said over the headset. "No, make that two...*three*. Over."

"The data's just coming through now, Kane," Lakesh said as he watched the feed split into a component analysis. Lakesh's field of expertise was the mat-trans, and the information before him revealed an interesting pattern.

GRANT AND BRIGID HAD sprinted to the far end of the corridor, where the exit to the facility was located. Through the night lenses, they could see two figures waiting at the end, but as they reached them—two old, bearded men in ragged clothes—a third man winked into existence.

Brigid recognized the tattoos on the man's coffee-colored skin—very similar in style to the man she had pounced upon in the office a few moments ago, the one who had been attacking Grant.

"Is there a whole army of these creeps?" Brigid asked as she reached for her TP-9 pistol, a reassuringly solid weight at her hip once more.

Grant was raising the Sin Eater toward the strangers, ready to unleash a deadly attack. But before he had the chance, the group of three disappeared, and the strange moaning sound that had filled the corridor went with them. "Crap!" Grant cursed with a shake of his head.

Brigid was rushing across to a room to the right, and Grant saw a pair of booted feet sticking out from the open doorway. It was Domi.

When Grant reached them, he saw Domi lying flat on her back, her legs curled in the fetal position, hands clutched to her face. Brigid was on her knees beside the chalk-skinned woman, speaking gently to her.

"What happened?" Grant asked.

"Domi's been hit," Brigid said. "Look."

Grant leaned closer. He could see that Domi was breathing, and there was no blood, no signs of a wound. But the parts of her face that were visible around her hands looked stained.

"Domi, it's Grant," he said. "What happened here?"

Domi's voice sounded bitter, her breath ragged. "Asshole had some kind of spray in his walking stick. Got me full in the face. Burns like hell."

Grant loosed a heavy sigh as he looked at his colleague lying in pain on the floor of the darkened facility. "Think you can move?" he asked. "Because, if not, we're going to have to go on without you. Kane needs us."

Domi's hands moved away from her face at last, and Grant saw what looked like a splash of paint across her eyes, nose and mouth. Beneath the dark lenses, her eyes were streaming with tears. "Go ahead and I'll catch up," she told him. "And if you see that old bastard, break both his legs to make sure he needs that walking stick for me, okay?"

Grant nodded solemnly and led the way down the corridor toward the broken vent, Brigid just behind him. A little farther along the corridor, they found the young man, thin and reedy, who had whipped Grant's Copperhead subgun from his hands. The man was lying in a pool of his own blood, his head lolled at an unhealthy angle and the majority of his throat had been destroyed by a single bullet. "Looks like she got a few hits in before they got her," Grant acknowledged as he stepped over the corpse of Neverwalk.

INSIDE THE CONTROL HUB of the Death Cry, Yuri's hands rushed across the hidden controls, watching the warning light blink on again, off again, in that slow, repetitive manner that Russian technology favored. It gave the impression that the alarm was not urgent, but he knew it was.

He glanced up at the dials above him, watching the counter trip over to zero, shouting a curse in his native tongue.

Yuri could guess what had happened. A stray bullet from General Serge's gun had to have damaged the controls of the firing mechanism. The Death Cry had been set on an irreversible countdown to unleash the scream. And Brigid, the beautiful woman from the future, had disappeared, called back to her own body as soon as she had entered the physical plane.

Yet Yuri had not. No body to go to, he realized. He was in the future. Against all expectations, he had actually achieved some kind of immortality, or at least longevity, from his time in the astral factory. Only to have it snatched away from him with the Death Cry's final shout, unless somehow he could stop it.

The Death Cry was designed as a doomsday device. The whole system could be run by two people for the simple reason that everyone on board would die in its incredible blast.

But, surely, Yuri's brain told him, there must be a way to stop it. There must.

KANE'S HEAD WHIPPED AROUND as his foe reappeared twenty feet away from him along the tarmac strip. Rock Streaming had been joined by two other men, both of them quite old, as far as Kane could judge, and Kane reported the reappearances to Lakesh over the Commtact.

The one to the left was spinning an Aborigine bull roarer over his head, and its howling pierced the air, reverberating from the high sides of the mountains around them. The sound was familiar; it was the penetrating groan that Kane had first heard in the underground burrow when the strangers had appeared.

To his side, the other man was holding what looked like a blade, but Kane knew now that it was a metal boomerang.

Kane watched for a moment as Rock Streaming pointed at the Death Cry hovering above them, and the two old men nodded. The Sin Eater hung in his hand, and he wondered what his chances were of hitting all three of them before they disappeared. As he considered this, Lakesh's voice piped up over the Commtact once more.

"Kane? We've isolated the mat-trans device that your enemies are accessing. Over."

"Can you switch it off?" Kane asked. "Over."

There was the brief silence while Kane waited for the response, and he ducked into the grass muttering, "Come on, come on," under his breath.

LAKESH'S FINGER TRACED across the analysis of the single jump that the surveillance satellite had captured.

"No can do," he told Kane. "We can't access the specific mat-trans they're utilizing from here, but maybe you can shut it down at your end. The device travels with them, generating a specific frequency that allows them to step in and out of gateways," he explained. "Do you see anything obvious that might contain this generator, a box perhaps, or maybe a radio device of some sort? Over."

KANE'S EYES NARROWED as he listened to Lakesh. "Something generating a frequency, you say?" Kane asked. "Like a loud note, something like that? Over."

Lakesh's voice came over the Commtact again a few moments later. "It may be outside of the range of human hearing, Kane," the Cerberus director said. "You might not be able to detect it by sound alone. Over."

"Oh, I've detected it," Kane growled as he kicked away from the ground and moved into a fluid sprint across the grass and onto the cracked blacktop of the little road, rushing toward the three warriors. "Sly son of a bitch had it in his hand the whole damn time!"

As Kane said it, two of the warriors winked out of existence, leaving only the old man and the bull roarer spinning through the air above his head.

WHEN HE HAD BRIEFLY materialized in the underground tunnel, Rock Streaming had said two words to his field leaders, Good Father and Bad Father: "It's here."

On hearing this, the two men had sliced into the Dreaming momentarily, metaphorically hanging on Rock Streaming's coattails as he cut a path to outside the bunker, back in Realworld. Once there, the two field leaders had seen the huge black shape that dominated the sky, and Good Father had nodded his approval as he spun the bull roarer overhead.

"We take it," Bad Father confirmed, and he stepped back into the Dreaming for a fraction of a second, Rock Streaming at his side.

The two men reappeared in Realworld atop the Death Cry, eighty feet in the air. It was glowing now, a cascade of colors rippling over its surface, and the men could feel the thrumming of its power through the soles of their feet.

Balancing with ease on the vast, curved shell of the

weapon, Bad Father crouched and placed both hands against the device. He looked up at Rock Streaming, encouraging the young man to join him.

Rock Streaming crouched beside his mentor, placing the palms of both hands against the skin of the massive weapon as colors streamed brighter and brighter across it. He looked up at Bad Father, and the old man nodded once, solemn.

"It's ours," the old man said as he and Rock Streaming activated their implants and sliced into the Dreamworld once again.

As HE SPRINTED ACROSS the cracked tarmac toward Good Father, Kane kicked off, leaping high in the air.

Still spinning the bull roarer, the old man turned in time to see the mighty figure of the Cerberus man barreling toward him from overhead.

Kane's left arm drew back, then his fist rushed forward toward the old man's face below. Kane wailed as the tough cord of the bull roarer whipped around his wrist and up his arm and its morose song came to a sudden halt. Then, as the bull roarer circled his arm, tightening around it, Kane's knuckles connected with the old man's jaw, knocking the man's head back with an audible crack.

ABOARD THE DEATH CRY, Yuri stopped struggling within the safety gloves to right the controls. The whole of its great length was shaking, ready to unleash its terrifying banshee wail.

At the control panel, Yuri cursed General Serge's foolishness, firing shots in the enclosed area like that. Sitting there, within the unit, he could feel the scream building.

Reluctantly, fearfully Yuri closed his eyes. "I'm sorry, Brigid," he muttered as the Death Cry built to a crescendo, and the scream shattered the world about him, tearing him apart.

GRANT PULLED HIMSELF over the lip of the ventilation grille and climbed out to the surface above with Brigid just two seconds behind.

As he stood there he saw the glowing object in the sky, as huge and bright as a full moon, shaking as it emitted a beam of sheer brilliance from its coned front end.

Still climbing out of the ventilation shaft, Brigid shouted an instruction to Grant: "Look away!"

But he didn't need to. The whole, incredibly proportioned cylinder, along with its devastating, bright scream, winked from existence, leaving a vacuum of imploding air in its absence.

There was a loud clap as air rushed to fill the void, and branches, leaves, rocks and birds were sucked upward, toward the space that the Death Cry had occupied a moment before.

GOOD FATHER FELL BACKWARD as Kane's left fist slammed into his jaw with pile-driver force. The spinning bull roarer in his hand was tugged away by momentum, ripped out of his hand as it whipped around Kane's arm.

The older man's body met the broken tarmac, the impact jarring every bone in his body, and he tried to focus on the implant, urging it to dreamslice once again.

As he called on the implant, he felt the drag above him and there was a loud pop from overhead, an implosion of air as the Death Cry winked out of existence.

Above Good Father, Kane roared as the cord of the bull roarer tightened around his outstretched arm, cutting through the sleeve of his jacket and cinching into the corded muscles beneath. Legs cycling through the air, he felt himself dragged upward into the vacuum that had suddenly replaced the Death Cry. Then he began to fall earthward once again, and his right foot suddenly connected with the ground.

Still moving, he trotted forward in an ungraceful, sliding turn. Kane reached out with his right arm as the ground hurtled up toward his face. With a final crunch, Kane landed in a heap on the ground. The silenced bull roarer was wrapped around the whole length of his left arm, and blood was oozing around the device's cord, seeping into the torn sleeve of his jacket. Kane's head rested on his outstretched right arm, his teeth gritted against the pain of the wrapped cord on his left, his legs a tangle behind him.

He lay there, unwilling to move, excruciating pain racking his left arm, and felt the early-morning sun beating down on his back. The shadow in the sky, the Death Cry, was gone.

HIS BODY CRYING IN PAIN, Rabbit in the Moon lay on the sandy plateau of the Dreaming, struggling to catch his breath. His face was ruined. The woman's savage blows had deadened nerves, and at least three of his teeth felt loose when he probed them with his tongue. The vision in his right eye was obscured with a red wash, and his left eye kept trying to close.

Down in his belly, Rabbit in the Moon could feel where the gunshot wound had reopened. He had moved too quickly, the recovery incomplete, undoing the miracle that had saved him.

He lay there, ignoring the aching sensations from every part of his battered frame. I'm safe here, he told himself. Nothing can touch me here. No one is coming to the Dreaming.

He opened his good eye once more, looking across the plain, as he heard the old man approach. Good Father had dreamsliced, but his neck was crooked and there was a swelling on the right side of his jaw. The old man stumbled, falling to his knees as Rabbit in the Moon watched. "Good Father?" he asked, his voice a pained whisper.

Then he saw the other thing, behind Good Father. It was incredibly large, looming in the sky, awash with colors, and Bad Father and Rabbit in the Moon's blood brother, Rock Streaming, were crouched on its shell. With all those colors running through it it looked so pretty, so pretty as it shrieked an impossible pain that wrenched apart the very fabric of the Dreaming.

I'm safe here, Rabbit in the Moon remembered as his body was ripped to shreds by the lethal, tortured scream of the Death Cry.

KANE TRIED TO LIFT HIMSELF from the ground, forcing his muscles to move, when he heard the woman's voice behind him.

"What did you do to yourself this time, Kane?" It was Brigid Baptiste.

"Can you get this thing off me?" he asked through gritted teeth as he struggled to a sitting position. "I can't feel my damn arm." He saw Brigid and Grant approaching him from the direction of the broken ventilation grille. Both of them were armed, checking the area for hostiles.

"Okay," Brigid told him. "Just sit still. You look like a bear caught in a trap."

She leaned close to him, and Kane examined the patches of antiseptic weave that he had taped to her face as she carefully unwound the bull roarer from his arm. "The weapon, the Death Cry—it was here but it's gone now," he said, confused.

"We saw it start to glow, to spit something," Grant explained, his eyes still scanning the area for movement. "Then it just disappeared."

"It went off," Brigid said solemnly. "I don't know why, but the Death Cry activated. It was about to blow when it disappeared, caught up in some kind of dimensional jump. Maybe Yuri sent it back to the factory."

Kane shook his head, wincing at the pain of movement. "It wasn't a dimension jump, Baptiste," he told her. "They were trying to hijack it, take it with them. But I cut the mat-trans they were using at the last second."

"So where are they?" Grant asked, looking around the deserted clearing that surrounded the road. The three of them were alone; even the old man who had swung the bull roarer was gone.

His left arm numb, Kane closed his eyes, feeling the

weight of exhaustion come over him. "Contact Cerberus," he said. "Maybe Lakesh can track them now that his equipment is up and running."

Chapter 22

Thirty hours had passed since the field team had returned from Georgia to the Cerberus redoubt in the Bitterroot Mountains, and a rich orange sun was resting low on the horizon as it slowly set. Lakesh found Brigid out on the plateau by the redoubt's main doors, sitting alone on the ground with her legs stretched out before her, watching the sun making its languid descent.

"Are you okay, Brigid?" he asked quietly, not wishing to shock her.

She turned and showed him her open, warm smile. There were several adhesive strips across her face, and her left eye still held a distinct bruise, but she looked healthy, all things considered. "I'm fine," she said, thanking him for his concern. "Just thinking about everything that happened back there."

"In Georgia?" he asked, sitting down beside her on the dry soil.

"Georgia and the astral factory in Krylograd," she replied. "You know, those poor people are still stuck in there, living their lives in that hidden recess in the human mind, ignorant of time's passage."

"But there's no weapon for them to work on anymore," Lakesh pointed out.

Brigid shrugged. "I didn't have time to check every room of the facility. Maybe they had the Death Cry Mark II tucked in the next room over."

"Or maybe they'll stop building arms and try to create something of their situation. Another world, a whole new society," Lakesh suggested.

"With ten soldiers and a handful of lab technicians?" she said incredulously. "You have the heart of a poet, Lakesh."

They sat there in silence, watching wisps of cloud lazily drift across the sky as the sun sank toward its inevitable meeting with the horizon. After a while, Brigid spoke again. "How's Domi?" she asked.

"I left her in bed asleep," Lakesh replied. "Reba gave her some lotion for her face, a mixture of lavender oil and chamomile. It eases the burning sensation, which Reba assures me will pass of its own accord in a few days. In the meantime, Domi is behaving like a caged lion who can't wait to get back out into the wild, of course."

"Of course." Brigid laughed.

"She was lucky," Lakesh added. The night-vision lenses that Domi had been wearing had protected her from the worst of the hot powder. According to Reba DeFore, that was the only thing that had saved her eyesight.

"Well," Lakesh said with a sigh, picking himself up off

the ground, "I should be getting back to the ops center to check on things."

Brigid nodded. "Maybe I'll pop in a little later," she told him, "help find somewhere for the new rug."

"There's no rush," Lakesh assured her as she turned back to watch the sunset. "You've earned a break. All four of you."

As Lakesh made his way back to the entrance to the redoubt, Brigid called out to him once more. "Lakesh?"

He turned, infinitely patient with the singular woman.

"Have you heard anything about Kane?" she asked.

Lakesh smiled reassuringly. "He came out of surgery a couple of hours ago. I thought you knew," he explained. "There was some nerve damage to his arm, but Reba repaired it. He'll be fine in a few days. One hundred percent."

Brigid stood, brushing soil from her backside as she jogged over to join Lakesh at the doors.

"You're really not needed in the ops center, Brigid," he assured her.

"I'm not coming with you," she replied. "I'm going to go find Kane and see if he wants to arm wrestle! Opportunities like this don't come along every day."

Lakesh laughed as the two of them entered the redoubt together.

IN A BROKEN AIR VENT, in a bunker hidden beneath the Caucasus Mountains, a woman dressed in strips of material was waking up.

Almost two days before, when she had awakened to find herself beaten and bloody on the floor of the bunk room, Cloud Singer had immediately engaged the implant at the base of her neck and tried to dreamslice. But, to her horror, nothing had happened. No jump, no transferral, nothing.

She had strained her ears, listening for a trace of the singing bull roarer, its promising salvation, but all had been silent. Then, as she listened, she had heard voices, people in the underground complex, walking along the corridor, and the beam of their flashlight danced in the open doorway.

She had moved quickly, despite the pain from all over her body, clambering into the broken vent on the wall of the bunk room, the one that Kane had shot to pieces. Inside, she had hidden herself from sight while the enemy went about their cleanup operation, sweeping the bunker for stragglers but failing to find her.

And she had tried, periodically, to dreamslice, to step out of Realworld and into the Dreaming, but nothing had happened.

Tucked there, in the absolute darkness, beside the room full of skeletons, she had slowed her breathing and willed herself into a healing coma, her heart beating at an eighth of its usual pace.

Almost two days later, conscious once more, she found herself alone.

Cloud Singer blinked, bringing her electrochemical polymer lenses to life on the nictitating membranes that slotted over her eyes, granting her night vision in the pitch-dark bunker.

On silent feet, she walked from the bunk room, checking each doorway in turn, confirming her suspicion that she was totally alone in the complex. Alone except for the corpse of Neverwalk, a bloody ruin where his neck had been.

With none of her strike team left, no access to the Dreaming, Cloud Singer was utterly alone.

Alone but alive.

Don Pendleton's Mack Bolan.

Colony of Evil

Claiming one hundred square miles inside
Colombia, Colonia Victoria is a sanctuary
for humanity's most dedicated fanatics.
Set up by one of Hitler's minions, this
Nazi Neverland is now a deadly global
threat, and it's spearheading a new wave
of terror. Mack Bolan's hunting party
includes a Mossad agent and a local guide,
and their pursuit of Hans Gunter Dietrich
becomes a violent trek deep into the jungle,
where Bolan intends to dissolve an unholy
alliance in blood.

*Available January
wherever books are sold.*

POLAR QUEST
by AleX Archer

When archaeologist Annja Creed agrees to help an old colleague on a dig in Antarctica, she wonders what he's gotten her into. Her former associate has found a necklace made of an unknown metal. He claims it's over 40,000 years old—and that it might not have earthly origins. As the pair conduct their research, Annja soon realizes she has more to worry about than being caught in snowslides. With no one to trust and someone out to kill her, Annja has nowhere to turn—and everything to lose.

**Available January
wherever books are sold.**

GOLD EAGLE®

GRA16

ROOM 59

THERE'S A FINE LINE BETWEEN DOING YOUR JOB—AND DOING THE RIGHT THING

After a snatch-and-grab mission on a quiet London street turns sour, new Room 59 operative David Southerland is branded a cowboy. While his quick thinking gained valuable intelligence, breaching procedure is a fatal mistake that can end a career—or a life. With his future on the line, he's tasked with a high-speed chase across London to locate a sexy thief with stolen global-security secrets that have more than one interested—and very dangerous—player in the game....

Look for

THE finish line

by

cliff RYDER

GOLD EAGLE®

Available January wherever books are sold.

GRM595

JAMES AXLER

DEATH LANDS

Plague Lords

In a ruined world, past and future clash with terrifying force...

The sulfur-teeming Gulf of Mexico is the poisoned end of earth, but here, Ryan and the others glean rumors of whole cities deep in South America that survived the blast intact. But as the companions contemplate a course of action, a new horror approaches on the horizon. The Lords of Death are Mexican pirates raiding stockpiles with a grim vengeance. When civilization hits rock bottom, a new stone age will emerge, with its own personal day of blood reckoning.

In the Deathlands, the future could always be worse. Now it is...

Available December wherever you buy books.